VENDETTA

THE MERMAID CHRONICLES BOOK FIVE

MARISA NOELLE

Cover art by Fay Lane - https://faylane.com/

FIRST EDITION

THE MERMAID CHRONICLES SERIES

Secrets of the Deep
Quest for Atlantis
Fight for Freedom
Ghost Pirates
Vendetta
The Mermaid Chronicles Companion Guide

REVIEWS FOR VENDETTA

"If I could give this 10 stars, I would!" — Goodreads Reader

"Romeo & Juliet for today." — Amazon reader

"Romance, mermaids vs sharks - what more do you need? This is a thrilling read with great characters that you won't want to put down!" – SJ Willis, best-selling author of *Bite Risk*

"Packed with twists, could not stop reading!" — Louie Stowell, best-selling author of *Loki: A Bad God's Guide to Doing Good*

"Marisa Noelle does it again with her charming and gripping story of Cordelia and Wade as they navigate the tricky waters of love in a time of change and challenge." — Lynn Lipinski, author of *God of Internet* & *Bloodlines*

"A refreshing take on an emerging genre. I found this book so hard to put down. Lots of drama mixed with a dollop of romance and just a touch of the supernatural." — Melissa Welliver, author of *My Love Life and the Apocalypse*

"The premise is laced with conflict, and you'll cheer for Cordelia all the way through as she battle to overcome inherent differences and conflicts." — Author Stuart White, CEO of WriteMentor

"This is a brilliant series! I love it! It's like a mixture of Sirens the TV series and *Aquaman* and a *Romeo & Juliet* forbidden love story." — ARC reader

"*Vendetta* weaves a spellbinding tapestry of revenge, love, and magical realms—an unputdownable fantasy romance that will linger in your heart long after the final page." — Amazon Reader

"Marisa Noelle's *Vendetta* is a fantasy romance masterpiece— a breathtaking blend of revenge, friendship, and the intoxicating magic of a love that defies the tides. An absolute gem for fans of the genre!" — Goodreads reviewer

"Enchanting! Mesmerizing! Captivating! Heart-breaking!" — Book Blogger

"Deliciously romantic!" — Goodreads reader

"This series is so good, it got me out of my slump!" — ARC reader

"Gripping, emotional, and utterly enchanting!" — ARC reader

CONTENT WARNINGS

This book contains themes and references that some readers may find distressing, including, but not limited to:

- Violence
- Minor sexual content
- Death or dying
- Blood, gore, graphic injuries
- Mental illness, depression, alcoholism, anxiety
- Swears or curses
- Murder
- Monsters

VENDETTA PLAYLIST

Mermaid – Train
Round Here - Counting Crows
Walk alone - Rudimentral
More than words- extreme
Livin' On A Prayer - Bon Jovi
I Don't Want to Miss a Thing - Aerosmith
Water Runs Dry - Boyz II Men
Walk Alone - Tom Walker
Rewrite the Stars - Zac Effron, Zendaya
What A Man Gotta Do - Jonas Brothers
Don't Look Back In Anger - Oasis
I'm So Tired - Lauv, Troye Sivan
Another Song About Love - McFly
Montero (Call ME By Your Name) - Lil Nas X
Happier - Marshmello, Bastille
Should I Stay Or Should I Go - The Clash
Beggin' - Maneskin

Found What I've Been Looking For - Tom Grennan
Someone To You - Banners
Thousand Miles - The Kid Laroi
Bubbly - Colbie Caillat
Outnumbered - Dermot Kennedy

For Sasha

RECAP OF BOOK 1 – SECRETS OF
THE DEEP

On the approach Cordelia Blue's eighteenth birthday, she decided it was time to break free from the shadows of her tragic past. The loss of her mother and twin brother in a devastating shark attack had haunted her for five long years, forcing her to abandon her once-promising swimming career. She even shied away from taking a simple bath.

With unwavering support from her best friends, Maya and Trent, Cordelia embarked on a journey to conquer her deepest fears head-on. Little did she know, this leap of faith would reveal a world of enchanting secrets lurking beneath the surface. As she dipped her toes into water for the first time since the attack, Cordelia unearthed her astonishing destiny—she was a mermaid, and her long-lost twin, Dylan, was alive too. Trapped in an aquatic realm, he was unable to shift into human form. Dylan entrusted Cordelia with a mystical pearl, a key to locating the elusive High Council— the sole authority capable of granting mermaids their precious legs once more. However, the mermaids weren't the only ones hunting for this gem. The selachii, shark shapeshifters cursed to the depths, yearned to regain their legs too. And would stop at nothing to find it.

Old flame, Wade Waters, swam back into Cordelia's life. Sparks flew, but lurking in the shadows were Wade's shady cousins, and Cordelia couldn't shake the feeling that he was harboring a deep, dark secret. And keeping her own secret concerning her mermaid lineage under wraps took a toll on their relationship.

When the pearl mysteriously vanished from Cordelia's grasp, she discovered Wade's secret—he was one of the selachii and had betrayed her. Worse yet, Trent, her loyal friend, fell victim to a brutal shark attack and was transformed into one of them.

With trust shattered and alliances uncertain, Cordelia turned to Maya and the ancient tome, *The Mermaid Chronicles*, which held the key to unraveling their intertwined destinies. Maya insisted that mermaids and selachii must unite to reclaim their lost glory. Cordelia delved into the book's secrets, uncovering a forgotten era of harmony between mermaids and selachii on the fabled island of Atlantis.

As Cordelia unmasked Zale, the leader of the selachii, as the thief behind the pearl's theft, she and Wade joined forces to retrieve the precious jewel, but almost cost them Wade's life. When Cordelia and Wade reunited, the pearl's secrets unraveled, whisking them away to another dimension to confront the enigmatic High Council.

The High Council, comprised of representatives from mermaids, selachii, dragon kings, and eelusionists, agreed to grant them legs once more. Yet, it came at a price—Cordelia and Wade were tasked with the monumental quest to unearth their lost homeland, the mythical Atlantis. The epic adventure had only just begun, and the fate of two worlds hung in the balance.

RECAP OF BOOK 2 – QUEST FOR ATLANTIS

When mermaids began mysteriously disappearing, stolen away by humans for display or sinister experiments, the hidden realm of mermaids and selachii was unveiled. Cordelia, Wade, and their friends fought valiantly, rescuing one of their own from a science lab. Yet, the global onslaught continued, casting an ever-growing shadow over their existence.

Their mission was clear: unveil the enigma of the lost island of Atlantis—an aquatic sanctuary where all ocean shifters could find refuge. To unlock its secrets, the team embarked on a quest for the fabled, scattered jewels that held the key to Atlantis' portal. But their journey was fraught with peril.

Beneath the icy depths of Mount Rainier and the treacherous Puget Sound, Cordelia and Wade faced near-death encounters with ice demons. Gal, a formidable dragon king and council member, defied convention to save them. The

Power of the Sea surged through them, healing their wounds and bestowing incredible gifts—a Herculean strength for Wade and the untamed power of fire for Cordelia.

Tensions flared as Wade's ex, Stephanie, intruded on the mission, determined to win him back, fueled by his mother's approval. Cordelia grappled with doubt, their bond tested by misunderstandings and painful infidelities, fracturing their once-unbreakable unity.

Maya's life hung by a thread after a harrowing accident, compelling Dylan to transform her into a mermaid. But the toll of their perilous journey didn't end there—Cordelia's father faced certain death in the unfathomable Mariana Trench, only to be transformed into a selachii through a desperate ritual led by Wade.

Amidst near-tragedies and heartaches, Cordelia and Wade rekindled their love, poised to confront those who sought to tear them apart. Armed with the keys to Atlantis, they crossed dimensions into a magical realm. But a harrowing sight awaited them—an island in ruins, guarded by legions of dragon kings. A savage battle ensued, with Cordelia mastering her fiery abilities to vanquish the malevolent force, at the cost of her dear mentor, Gal.

As the Power of the Sea was plunged into the Fountain of Youth, the island blossomed anew. Amidst the rejuvenation, Cordelia made an astonishing discovery—a long-lost captive, her mother, believed dead for over five years, was alive and well.

In a joyous reunion, Cordelia found her family and a newfound sanctuary where all could walk on land, hidden from prying human eyes. Amidst the serenity, Wade proposed to Cordelia, promising a blissful future, until the pages of *The Mermaid Chronicles* started turning once again.

RECAP OF BOOK 3 – FIGHT FOR FREEDOM

A year after the discovery of the long-lost Atlantis and their showdown with the fierce dragon kings, Cordelia and Wade tied the knot, ascending to their rightful thrones as the rulers of the mystical island. Hidden away from the prying eyes and judgmental gazes of ordinary humans, Atlantis basked in tranquility, shielded by an enchanting veil that isolated it from the rest of the world.

As the brave folks of Atlantis cautiously reconnected with their mainland families, a shockwave of devastating news rocked their world. A cataclysmic nuclear war had erupted, and fingers were pointed squarely at none other than the merfolk and selachii.

This apocalyptic nightmare was set in motion when a wealthy baron's wife met a watery demise. With no ocean shifters around to perform the life-saving resuscitation ritual, the baron pointed the finger of blame at the mysterious Atlantis, threatening to unleash nuclear annihilation unless the world revealed the whereabouts of the elusive merfolk. But nobody had a clue where the merfolk had vanished to, and humanity paid the price with widespread devastation.

Venturing back to the mainland, Cordelia, Wade, and their loyal friends stumbled upon two distinct groups of surviving humans. There were those desperate for survival after the nuclear apocalypse and a faction hell-bent on extracting vengeance from the ocean shifters.

Wade and Trent fell into the clutches of a former mercenary turned captor, the enigmatic Sean Wilson. Meanwhile, Cordelia found herself face-to-face with her high-school rival, the determined Babette, who pledged to aid her in freeing Atlanteans from the clutches of hostile humans, and giving them hope surrounding the latest prophecy in *The Mermaid Chronicles*. While distracted, Wade's ex-girlfriend, the ever-jealous Stephanie, resurfaced as a formidable sea witch, swearing vengeance on Wade and Atlantis.

While Cordelia and her fearless squad embarked on a daring rescue mission to free Wade from the clutches of mercenaries, they crossed paths with Blaze, the last surviving dragon king and Gal's only son, Cordelia's late mentor. With Blaze's remarkable abilities and Cordelia's fiery powers, they launched a mission to free the ocean shifters from captivity. Their journey back to Atlantis, however, took a treacherous turn when Stephanie and Aquaria unleashed the dreaded Hound of the Ocean, a venomous sea monster with a lethal breath.

Simultaneously, Sean Wilson invaded Atlantis, leaving a trail of death and destruction in his wake, including the loss of crucial High Council members. As the situation spiraled out of control and their people faced annihilation, Cordelia's powers went haywire, forcing an uneasy alliance with Babette, her father, and their human army, and fulfilling the prophecy.

Just when all hope seemed lost, Cordelia's wedding ring revealed astonishing powers, creating an impenetrable force-field around the ocean shifters and saving them from the deadly breath of the Hound. But humans were still dying. After vanquishing Aquaria, Cordelia confronted the monstrous sea beast with her fire abilities. Entrusting the ring to Babette, it extended its protection to the humans too, truly uniting all three species. With Wade by her side and a glimmer of the Power of the Sea from Edward, a High Council member, they finally achieved victory, though Stephanie managed to slip away.

Back on Atlantis, Cordelia and Wade threw open their island's gates to the surviving humans, offering refuge from the radiation and nuclear chaos ravaging the mainland. Babette was entrusted with the guardianship of the Power of the Sea by the last surviving High Council member as he breathed his last, ensuring that humans would forever feel a part of Atlantis.

In a poignant ceremony honoring those lost in the attack and the venerable High Council, Stephanie unleashed her venomous snakes, poisoning Atlanteans. Jordan, Wade's devoted cousin, who had once been enamored with Stephanie, delivered the fatal blow, stabbing her through the heart and ending her reign of terror.

Only then did tranquility return to the island, with Cordelia dropping the bombshell that she was pregnant. But the pages of *The Mermaid Chronicles* never remain still for long.

RECAP OF BOOK 4 – GHOST PIRATES

During the seven years that passed since Cordelia and Wade's son, Gal, came into the world, Atlantis enjoyed a period of relative tranquility under their rule. However, Cordelia's inner turmoil festered as she battled the shadows of her past, haunted by the ever-present fear that something might befall her beloved son. As the Fountain of Youth didn't work for Gal, Cordelia rarely let him out of her sight, believing she was the only one who could protect him from harm. Despite concerns from friends and family about her mental well-being, Cordelia remained fixated on Gal's safety, pushing him to train in martial arts for self-defense.

When the pages of *The Mermaid Chronicles* began to turn, indicating a new prophecy was on the way, Cordelia's anxiety heightened, and she suspected one of her oldest enemies would return. The arrival of a reclusive shifting clan, the orcana, brought an unusual winter to the ordinarily temperate island, and the kids discovered a new sense of joy along with a fresh blanket of snow. That was until one of them went missing. Searching for the young girl in the tunnels beneath the island led to devastating land collapses. Cordelia and Gal were trapped in a cave-in and accidentally discovered a powerful elemental orb, which enhanced Cordelia's affinity with fire. While Gal recovered from a concussion in the hospital, more children went missing, leading the Atlanteans to believe there were nefarious motives behind their disappearances.

All became clear when the leader of the orcana admitted to placing a cursed stone in the Fountain of Youth, ultimately blinding Maya, the oracle of Atlantis, and stunting the prophecies within *The Mermaid Chronicles*. Ghost pirates were behind the children's disappearances, and they returned each night to steal more, lashing with their poisonous whips and scattering their venomous spiders on the island. Cordelia discovered they were not merely undead, but immortal. Only by combing all six elemental orbs could they be turned to flesh and therefore become mortal. With two orbs in their possession, a hunt for the remaining orbs ensued. When Gal was taken, Cordelia risked everything, including her own life, in her desperate search for the elemental orbs, shunning those close to her and turning the residents against her with her rash actions.

When Caol, an evil selachii from her past, appeared on the island, it confirmed Cordelia's suspicions that her oldest enemy, Zale, was after her. Caol claimed he had the last remaining orb in his possession and she killed him without remorse. The island was thrown into a deep depression as they realized the last orb was lost to them, and therefore all the children.

Cordelia vowed to make it up to her people, and with the help of her friends and family, discovered the last orb and turned the pirates to flesh once more. The Atlanteans accepted her apology, and it took uniting all the ocean shifters as well as the humans to defeat the ghost pirates in a deadly battle. Reunited with her son once more, Cordelia's joy was short-lived as Zale finally launched his attack. Protecting her son, she threw herself at Zale's mercy, only to discover he had none. With her powers depleted and unable to defeat his new megalodon size, Zale got the better of Cordelia and put an end to her life, leaving her son and husband distraught.

The entire island mourned the loss of their queen, but the story was far from over...

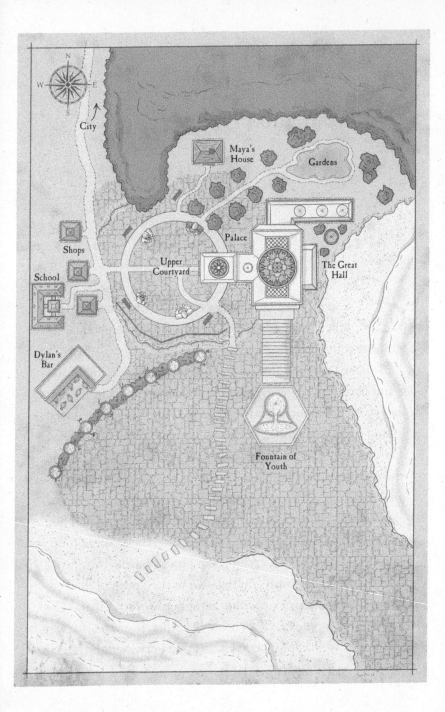

CHAPTER ONE

*E*nough was enough. I was sick of the book. It had killed my mother, and I refused to be trapped by its ominous prophecies any longer.

I moved through the palace, my footsteps echoing in the grand corridors, my eyes fixed on the ornate doors leading to the great hall. Preoccupied with what lay beyond those doors, I flung them open, the heavy wood slamming shut behind me. The Power of the Sea, a magical blue orb that fueled Atlantis and granted the Fountain of Youth its healing properties, hovered atop a marble column, surrounded by five other elemental orbs, each marginally larger than a marble. They had remained unchanged for twelve years, their potent properties combined to defeat the ghost pirates when I was just a boy. But my focus wasn't on the orbs or the Power of the Sea; it was on the ancient tome that rested on its own pillar—*The Mermaid Chronicles*. The book held the history of ocean shifters, as well as prophetic visions that entwined the fate of

Atlantis with my family. And I hated it with every fiber of my being.

Last night I'd heard Maya mention the pages were turning once more, which meant a new prophecy was forming. The book had remained still for years, ever since my mother's death, but now something was coming. As the Prince of Atlantis, there was no doubt it would involve me or a member of my family. I'd grown used to the ignorant bliss over the past few years, training with Ford, helping Uncle Dylan in his bar, spending time in my room with my books, ignoring my father. It wasn't really a state of bliss, to be fair, but at least I was left alone without a treacherous threat looming on the horizon, the abilities Ford had trained me in unused, untested. And I had no intention of allowing that to change.

I stared at the book, its pages glowing ominously. Nope. I would not allow that book to change my life again. I walked around the glass case, flipped it open, and touched the ancient cover. Two mermaids swimming around a depiction of the orbs.

My heart raced as I flicked through the glowing pages, half-expecting an alarm to sound and summon the palace guards. But there was silence, broken only by the rustle of ancient parchment beneath my fingertips.

Although Maya, Atlantis' oracle and main interpreter of the ancient language used within the pages of *The Mermaid Chronicles*, had translated most of the book and loaded it onto the island's Wi-Fi, my knowledge of our world's history was limited to what I'd learned in school. Which I had left three years ago, jobless, directionless, but forced to fulfill my princely duties.

Only the four members of the High Council could read the ancient language within the book. Yet now, an inexplicable force enabled me to read the cryptic markings, the words transforming into English in my mind. I glanced over my shoulder, suddenly fearful there was an elaborate trick or joke at play, but there was nothing unusual in the room. A chill swept through my veins. There was no doubt my sudden ability to read the book had something to do with the new prophecy still forming within its pages.

I slammed the book closed, tugged it out of its case, and strode toward the cold hearth. After making sure the doors were closed, I built a fire, even though the weather had not yet turned. I watched the flames dance, wondering what it felt like for my mother to wield fire. I would never know. Being the guardian of the orb of Snow and Ice, fire had always been an enigma to me. And considering we only had two weeks of cold weather per year on Atlantis, I never had the opportunity to explore my connection with the colder climate. Nor did I particularly care. The orbs were tiny, practically useless, their power leached from them several years ago. Some speculated it would take a lifetime for them to regain their power. Whatever.

I flipped the book open once more, couldn't ignore the words floating off the page and seeping into my brain.

Celestial Abyss...

Vorago's Trident...

Parting the sea...

Disregarding the provocative words, I tore the page

from the book, crumpled it into a ball, and threw it into the fire. It didn't immediately take, as if magically protected. I foolishly hadn't considered that. Gritting my teeth and muttering several curse words under my breath, I tore out five more, ripped them to shreds, and threw them into the fire too.

The fire hissed and spat, as if angry with my actions. A cold wind swept through the open windows, toying with my collar, slipping down the back of my shirt, and the book glowed a little brighter.

Abandoning the cover to a couch, I tore more pages, huge chunks. The cover dimmed, its golden glow fading, as I ripped and shredded and crumpled and burned. Not all the pages took. Some of them stubbornly remained, so I pushed them deeper into the flames until they acquiesced to my will.

Celestial Abyss...

Vorago's Trident...

Parting the sea...

I blocked out the words, refusing to let them penetrate my thoughts, guarding my heart against the potential for future trials. I would not entertain anything that infernal book had to say.

As I held the last chunk of pages in my hand, the door swung open and Maya entered the room, Una trailing a few paces behind her.

"It's a little warm for a fire, isn't it?" She smiled, not yet aware of my actions, of what I had done to her precious book.

Her eyes moved from the fire to my hands, to the dimming cover I'd tossed on the couches. She gaped at me, a fury I'd never associated with her burning in her eyes. Her skin leached color as she marched across the room and ripped the remaining pages from my hands.

"What have you done?" she demanded. Una stood by her shoulder, her face as shocked as her mother's.

I turned to face my mother's best friend. "What I should have done a long time ago."

Maya's face turned from bone white to beet red. "How. Dare. You."

Una retreated a few paces, her expression torn, her gaze wavering between us.

"That book has brought nothing but trouble," I said, jabbing my finger in the air. "Nothing but death and destruction and war."

Clutching the remaining pages against her chest, Maya shook her head, took a deep breath. "The book didn't cause any of those things. It *warned* us of those things."

"That book killed my mother."

Maya's face softened. I looked away.

"It didn't kill your mother. Zale killed your mother."

"Do not speak his name to me," I snarled. Maya had taken a breath to calm herself, but no amount of air would still my anger. "And you didn't interpret the prophecy well enough to prevent her death."

Maya flinched as if I'd slapped her. "That's not fair."

"Isn't it?" I took a step forward, attempting to intimidate her. "You were busy having your fourth child, your eye wasn't on the ball—"

"I was blinded by the blinding rock."

Una raised her hand. "Gal—"

I silenced her with a look, then turned back to Maya. "Is that your excuse?"

Maya pushed her shoulders down. "You're right. I did let the island down. Your mother. You."

"Mom—"

"It's okay, Una," Maya said, then looked at me. "I ask myself everyday if there's something more I could have done. Your mother was my best friend and I miss her constantly. I mourn her every day. And I will mourn her tomorrow even more during the remembrance ceremony. But I also must live my life. She wouldn't want me or you or your father to wallow in grief. She would want us to live our lives."

"She would want revenge."

Maya tilted her head, relaxed her grip on the pages in her hands. "Perhaps she would. And if the opportunity presents itself, perhaps we can seek justice for her murder. But without *The Mermaid Chronicles*, we're fighting in the dark."

"We were fighting in the dark anyway."

Maya sighed. "Actually, we weren't fighting at all."

"You said there was a new prophecy coming."

"Prophecies aren't always bad."

"I guess we'll never know."

"No, I guess not."

We stared at each other in a silent stalemate. The fire crackled in the hearth, burning through the last of the pages. All but the few Maya had ripped out of my hands; a selection of paragraphs about the creation of Atlantis. Nothing useful.

"I'll have to inform the senate, the High Council, and your father, of course."

"Of course," I said.

"They're going to be furious."

"Like you."

"Una was next in line to be the oracle." Maya glanced at her daughter. "And you've taken that away from her."

My hands fisted at my sides. Like being the prophet of doom was anything to aspire to. "I'm sure the two of you will figure it out."

"I see." Maya's lips pressed into a thin line. She said nothing more, but turned and walked out of the room, the last few pages tucked under her arm.

Una stared at me, her short blonde hair reminding me of an angry hedgehog, her bright blue eyes filled with...I don't know what, but it was nothing I wanted to look at.

"Don't you start," I told her.

"I wasn't going to say anything." She walked toward me, laid a hand on my shoulder, which I immediately shrugged off.

"I don't need your sympathy."

"I'm only trying to be a friend. I know how hard this is on you. Tomorrow...twelve years—"

"I don't need your friendship either."

She took a step back, her eyes filling. Why did girls always have to cry?

"We grew up together."

"So?"

"You don't have to be alone."

"I'm not."

She sighed. "You can't live the rest of your life like this."

"Like what?" I didn't know why I was still there, still listening to her spout words I wasn't interested in. Maybe there was an ounce of good manners still left in me. Or perhaps an iota of guilt for taking away her future career. And let's face it, it was more than a career, it was a calling, passed through the females in her family for generations.

"I wish I could help you."

I laughed. "I don't need help."

"No, you've made that patently obvious." She gave me a sad smile. "And I do understand why you did what you did, but know this: your actions have consequences for the entire island."

She left, her footsteps echoing her retreat, sealing my fate in the wake of my defiance. The room was left in silence, the remnants of *The Mermaid Chronicles* consumed by flames, a bitter taste of rebellion on my tongue.

CHAPTER TWO

$\mathcal{F}$earing the impending wrath of the High Council, I loitered in the great hall for another half hour, watching *The Mermaid Chronicles* burn to oblivion. Despite the fury waiting for me, I didn't regret my decision to burn the book. Perhaps without the portentous prophecies, we could learn to live without Fate's shadow hovering over us. At least, that is what I wanted. I also wanted my mother back, but I knew that was a foolish, childish dream. Death was death, even in our world, even with the miracle of the fountain.

I summoned my courage and slipped out of the room, the grand doors sealing my actions with a soft yet ominous thud. Ford, my father's most loyal bodyguard, caught me as I emerged. Of all the people on the island, he was the person I respected most. During the hours we spent in the palace turret gym, he taught me valuable lessons, not just in fighting skills, but in life as well. I wasn't too blinded by rage to recognize that. Perhaps he felt it was his duty to provide me with a paternal figure, seeing as my father rarely left his suite. But then I remembered he had always imparted his pearls of wisdom, even when my mother was alive. But they were pearls of wisdom I no longer cared for. I had developed my own.

"Going somewhere?" he asked, halting in front of me. His eyes skimmed my face, but his expression gave nothing away.

I shrugged, feigning nonchalance. "Thought I'd take a walk by the beach."

He gave me the briefest of nods, as if the suggestion was ridiculous. "I thought I might help you compose a speech. I think you'll need your Aunt Raina too."

I rolled my eyes. "What is it this time? Can't my father deliver it?"

Ford raised both brows. "The apology should come from the source. Destroying *The Mermaid Chronicles* is no small matter. And to be frank, I didn't know such a thing was possible."

My entire body tensed. Word had spread already, quicker than I'd feared. Ford was one of the four members of the High Council, and it was his responsibility to read and help interpret the prophecies, on top of his duties as head of the royal guard. Perhaps he'd be thankful I'd created more leisure time for him. "I have no intention of apologizing."

Ford looked me up and down, the only person on the island capable of it, the only one taller than me. "What *are* your intentions?"

I didn't have an answer, not one which would satisfy him or the population of Atlantis. In truth, I hadn't thought much beyond destroying the book. I knew people would be angry, but I didn't plan to stick around to see it. Atlantis wasn't the right place for me. Not now. Not without my mother. Not when her murderer was still out there. It would be twelve years tomorrow since her death, and what better day to leave to seek justice?

The thought of facing Zale—the most enormous shark shapeshifter in existence—sent electricity racing through my veins. I remembered the day he killed my mother. I remembered diving into the water to save her...and failing. For twelve years, I had lived with the gnawing fear he might return. A fear so strong it woke me in a cold sweat in the dead of night and prevented me from entering the water. I hadn't shifted into my merman form for over ten years. But now it was time to seek justice, to put an end to Zale's reign of terror, to exorcise my demons. That was why I had destroyed the book. I didn't want to know if I was going to fail.

Celestial Abyss...

Vorago's Trident...

Parting the sea...

"None that concern you," I finally answered his question, my tone sharper than I had intended.

The last complete prophecy, whispered by the book, lingered in my mind like a chilling refrain. *Old enemies die hard.* Zale was that ancient foe, and his time had come. His death, when it arrived, would be slow and agonizing, a poetic justice for my mother's untimely end.

"I'm worried about you," Ford said, as if he was still responsible for me even though I was nineteen years old.

I made to leave, but Ford blocked my path. "There's a crowd gathering outside."

I glanced through the marble archway at the courtyard below. There was the fountain, the vines circling the marble pillars, the yellow stretch of sand in the distance. And Uncle Dylan's bar. The one place which didn't make my skin crawl. But between the bar and the palace was a growing mob of people. It was only now I heard their building conversations, whispers loud enough to reach my ears, but none of the words were distinct enough to make out.

"They know about the book?" I asked.

"Bad news spreads quick," Ford said.

I nodded, contemplated using the tunnels to go to my uncle's bar, but I'd have to face the wrath at some point. Might as well be now.

I turned to go, but Ford caught my arm. "You can't avoid it forever."

"I don't intend to." I broke free from his grasp and approached the palace steps.

Jogging down the laborious stone steps, some in the crowd noticed me. One or two threw a wave or a pleasant greeting, but most wore frowns on their faces accompanied by angry, compressed lips.

"What did you do?" The accusation hung heavy in the air.

Someone grabbed my arm. I was getting sick of people touching me today. "How could you?"

"You've doomed us all."

"Why? Why did you destroy the book?"

I took in the accusing faces, a sea of furious people forming a singular, judgmental entity.

Celestial Abyss...

Vorago's Trident...

Parting the sea...

"You don't know what it's like," I protested, my voice drowned by the rising tide of their outrage. I paused by the fountain. "Living with constant dread."

But they weren't interested in my words. Weren't interested in my motivations. Not really. They just wanted their damn book back. Well, fuck 'em.

I hurried past the fountain, ignoring their calls and demands, ducking under the low-hanging vines until I was hidden by the surrounding columns. They didn't follow me, and I took a moment to catch my breath. The guilt caught up with me, a physical ball that lodged in my throat. A new prophecy was about to appear. Had I condemned my people to death? I was their prince. I was supposed to guide and protect them, as I had been raised. But if my father had shirked his duties, why did I have to be the one to carry the burden? Kings and queens were relics of the past on the mainland, figureheads at best. Atlantis didn't require a royal line to survive. They had the senate, the High Council. They didn't need me.

"What's got them all riled up?" A voice, familiar yet unexpected, pulled me from my thoughts. "I haven't seen this many angry faces since the last time someone suggested putting tentacles on pizza."

I turned to find Ember leaning against a pillar, sucking hard on a spliff. He grew his own weed in a distant meadow north of the mountain. One only he could reach with his dragon king wings.

Facing my cousin and only friend, I searched his face for an accusation. Did he really not know?

"What?" he asked, looking at me through a curtain of wild, dark hair.

"I destroyed the book."

"What book?" He puffed a perfect smoke ring into the air.

"*The Mermaid Chronicles.*"

"Holy shit." Both eyebrows rose over his head, and smoke poured from his nostrils. Not the weed, his own smoke. He'd only ever been capable of smoke and a few sparks, never producing the fiery breath dragon kings were famous for. "I always thought stirring up trouble was your hidden talent, but I didn't expect you to turn it into a full-blown spectacle."

"Yeah. I might need to lie low for a while."

"I'd offer you a spot at ours," he said. "But with Dad being on the High Council..."

"I know. Thanks."

"What are you going to do?" He took another drag, sucking the smoke deep, his eyes wide and dilated.

The crowd drifted into the path between the columns, a few eyes spotting my inadequate hiding place. I pushed off the column and headed toward Uncle Dylan's bar, throwing the words over my shoulder. "Kill Zale."

"Wait...*what?*" Ember dropped his spliff on the ground, didn't bother grounding it out before he hurried after me. "Are you *insane?* He's a megalodon. Which is basically a sea monster on steroids. Or a hydra on testosterone injections. I mean, why not tame a pack of wild unicorns while you're at it? Or invite a kraken for a game of checkers. Or—"

"I get it. He's big. He's powerful." I strangled the images threatening to consume me. "But I'm going to find a way."

"That's a suicide mission, buddy."

"Maybe."

"Definitely."

"Thanks for the vote of confidence."

Ember raised both hands. "Not going to deny your strength...but you're not your dad, and you're not a megalodon. You've only got a merman tail, and you haven't been in the water in years."

I decided not to respond to his astute, but unwelcome, observations.

He kept pace beside me, one of his wings digging into my shoulder. "Do you have a plan?"

"Working on it."

"You should talk to your dad."

I snorted. "When was the last time he was interested in anything I did?"

Ember ran a hand through his long hair, plucking green leaves and God knew what else from the tangled strands. "Still, man, this is dangerous, even for us."

"Us?"

"You can't go alone."

"I didn't invite you."

"I didn't ask you to."

"Oh, fuck off, Ember, I don't need you. This is my issue, not yours."

"Come on, dude, don't be like that."

I spun around on my heel. "How should I be? How

would you be if your mother were murdered? If twelve years had passed and justice still hadn't been served?"

Ember backed off a step, sighed, planted his arms across his chest. "I'm sorry."

"Yeah, you and me both." I stormed away, yanked open the door to the bar, and slammed it behind me.

I stood in the entrance, anger prickling my scalp, fists clenched, with no idea what to do with the vying emotions coursing through me. My eyes fell on the sea wolf rug in front of the cold hearth, its menacing face daring me to challenge it. But it was just a rug, an old skin, a dead animal with more bark than bite.

"Rough day?"

I glanced across the room. There were a few people gathered around the various tables, but none looked my way. I assumed the news hadn't yet reached the bar.

I walked across the room to meet my uncle, slid onto a stool at the bar. "Yeah. Hit me, will you?"

He poured an amber liquid into a glass, the sharp scent of alcohol filling the air. I didn't care to know its name; I just needed the burn, something to drown the chaos inside. I cradled the glass, feeling its weight, then downed the fiery liquid, letting it scorch my throat.

Dylan refilled the glass. "How bad is it?"

"I don't want to talk about it."

"Isn't that why you're here?"

I downed another glass, feeling the heat spread through me, numbing the sharp edges of my pain, diluting my shame, burning away my guilt.

"Well, if you're not going to talk, the least you can do is help me restock the bar."

I nodded and slipped off the stool, followed my uncle to the back door and the dimly lit alleyway behind the tavern. A few boxes of wine and a couple of kegs of beer leaned haphazardly against the stone wall, standing sentry like the island's most ineffective guards.

Uncle Dylan pointed to the kegs. "You're stronger than me."

I glanced at my biceps; toned, muscular, maybe even oversized. All the hours I spent with Ford in the gym. Training was the only thing that got me out of my head. So, I spent hours there, whenever I could. It was also a great way to escape royal duties. No one wanted to climb the six flights of stairs that led to the turret to find me, so they largely left me alone.

I hefted a keg over my shoulder and made my way back inside the bar. Uncle Dylan had shown me years ago how to attach the hoses, and turned a blind eye when I stole the odd sip. I ducked behind the counter and got to work, went back for the second keg, then the boxes of wine, sliding them into their shelves with practiced ease.

"Why has no one gone after Zale?" I asked him after I took the two empty kegs outside.

Uncle Dylan blanched, set his jaw, blew hair off his face. "A lot of reasons."

"Such as?"

He refilled our glasses, his hands steady despite the turmoil in his hazel eyes. "Your mother was the most powerful person on this island...and she couldn't take him down."

"There must be a way."

Dylan shrugged. "Maybe."

"But?"

"He's a megalodon." He held my eyes. I noted the pain in his. He looked as haunted as I felt.

"Everything living can be killed."

"That's true enough." He ran a cloth over the counter, wiping messes that weren't really there. "I still have nightmares," he said quietly. "So I drink. And I stay in my bar. Because I'm not brave enough to seek him out."

"You're plenty brave," I said. Dylan wasn't as muscular or as tall as my father, but he possessed his own inner strength. And his orb of Air and Flight had lent him extraordinary abilities during battle. "I remember the ghost pirates."

"Not anymore." He shook his head. "Not when it comes to him."

"I have nightmares too," I said, clinking his glass like it was something to celebrate.

"Maybe you should talk to someone about that."

"I talk to you."

"Besides me."

"What, like you talk to people about your problems?"

Uncle Dylan sighed, stilled his hand on the counter. "Babette left. She was the only one who really understood me."

"What about Grams and Pops?"

"It's been a long time since I've confided in them," Uncle Dylan said. "After Zale, I learned to depend on myself to get through...I don't know...don't listen to me, I don't know anything."

"You know more than me."

Uncle Dylan slammed his glass on the counter, startling me. "Find someone to share your life with, to make the pain tolerable, to endure the bad times and share the good. Make it count for something. Don't bottle it up. Don't do what I did. Don't be me."

I slid my glass toward him for a refill. "No fucking way. Have you not noticed what my mother's death did to my dad? You think I'm going to fall in love with someone? To let someone fall in love with me, just to watch them die? Or leave them alone? Not a fucking chance."

"It doesn't have to be that way."

"You need to follow your own advice. "

"It's too late for me."

"It's too late for me too."

Uncle Dylan sighed, fidgeted with his cloth. "I really hope not."

I drained my glass; the alcohol fueling my defiance, blurring my senses and my speech. "I am the *Prince* of fucking *Atlantis*. The only one. Did you know my mom was pregnant when she was killed?" Uncle Dylan paled, shook his head. "I'm not supposed to know, but I do. I am marked for death. Along with anyone who gets close to me. So no thank you very fucking much, you can take *The Mermaid Chronicles* and shove it up your ass."

"There could be something about how to defeat Zale in there."

I laughed, a great belly-aching laugh which almost made

me lose control of my bladder. "Too late."

"What do you mean?"

"I destroyed the book."

Dylan raised an eyebrow, laughed along with me, but there was no joy in it. "Fuck me, you're either exceptionally brave or incredibly stupid."

"Both."

We clinked our glasses, nearly shattering them, and downed another round.

After Uncle Dylan served a few waiting customers, many of whom gave me meaningful side-eyes, he leaned over the counter once more. "Don't do anything stupid."

"Define stupid."

"Do I need to remind you that the fountain doesn't heal you? So whatever you're going to do, be careful. I cannot tolerate losing my favorite nephew. And don't tell Ember I said that." He ducked under the counter, rummaged around in the cupboards, and returned with something wrapped in old towels. After laying it on the counter and checking no one was watching, Uncle Dylan removed an edge of the covering to reveal a rifle. "Rob taught you how to shoot, right?"

I nodded. "You got bullets?"

Uncle Dylan placed a battered box of bullets next to the rifle. "I don't know if bullets can kill Zale, how powerful he might have become in the last twelve years, but at least it's something."

"At least it's something," I echoed, feeling a stirring of resolve vying with the alcohol in my stomach. This was it. The moment I had been waiting for. The chance to avenge my mother's death.

CHAPTER THREE

*W*ith the rifle gripped tightly in my hands and the box of bullets weighing down my pocket, I staggered out the back door of Dylan's bar and headed along the narrow path toward the marina. It was only half a mile, but it took me twenty minutes. Once I had to stop for a leak, another time I fell in a bush and laughed so hard it took me five minutes to pull myself out. At least the gun wasn't loaded.

When I finally reached the marina, a strong wind swept in from the ocean, cutting through my drunken haze. I tilted my face toward the cool air, relishing the sting that snapped me back to reality. I navigated the floating docks, almost falling in once, chuckling at my distorted reflection as I stood there swaying in the moonlight. If I weren't so drunk, I might have considered setting sail tonight, but you don't hunt down a megalodon with eight whiskies inside you. Even I knew that was stupid.

I weaved an unstable path to my boat, a thirty-five foot

beauty of chrome and fiberglass, its mast nearly touching the moon. *The Cordelia*. It was my father's, but he hadn't used it in years, so I had adopted it, often spending hours, days, even weeks aboard when I wanted to avoid the island.

Now I unlocked the cabin and went inside, stashing the rifle and bullets under the seat bench in the galley. The remnants of my previous visit lay scattered around—rumpled sheets, empty tankards, a used spliff in an ashtray. Ember. The Navy cap. Once it belonged to my grandfather, then my mom, and now to me. A battered, faded thing which was more holes than material. I picked it up and ran a thumb over the softened fabric, then put it on my head as I set to scrubbing the counters and decks, restocking water jugs, and loading the boat with dry provisions. I raided the marina's supply shed for food, stuffing my arms with as much as I could carry, planning to plunder the palace larder later. I didn't know how long this journey was going to take, so I'd rather have too much than too little.

I would leave tomorrow. I'd pay my respects to my mother, endure the memorial service, suffer through the elaborate palace dinner, and then I'd set off to seek justice for her death.

By the time I was ready to return to the palace, it was after one o'clock in the morning and I'd started to sober up. Despite a few groups of people savoring the last warm evening for a couple of weeks, nobody approached me as I weaved through the courtyard. Perhaps I was emitting a vibe. Good. Let them know the Prince of Atlantis was no one to be fucked with.

I gave the fountain a cursory look as I staggered by, imagining what it would be like to be healed by it, then offered it the finger and stormed up the steps.

Approaching the palace's ornate archway, I noticed the door to the great hall was ajar. Curiosity piqued, I pressed my eye to the crack and glimpsed the senate and High Council gathered near the dead fire. The pages of *The Mermaid Chronicles* were nothing but ash, apart from the few Maya still had clenched in her hand. Couldn't she ever let anything go? The cover of the book remained on the couch where I'd tossed it, the once faded image of two swimming mermaids and the elemental symbols gone, turned an opaque black.

I backed away, almost colliding with a guard, and hurried up the staircase to the royal suite. As I tiptoed into the room, I attempted to avoid the central living area where my father sat in an overstuffed armchair, his eyes fixed on a roaring fire. He lit it every night, a ritualistic homage to my mother, as if he expected her to emerge from the flames. I think he slept in his chair.

"You missed dinner."

"I ate." In truth, I hadn't eaten anything substantial, surviving on a liquid diet of whiskey and regret.

Silence settled between us, broken only by the crackling of the flames and the chilly wind sweeping through the open windows.

I almost left him alone and then thought better of it. Walking to his chair, I said, "I destroyed *The Mermaid Chronicles*."

"I know."

Tomorrow marked not only the anniversary of my mother's death but also the beginning of the two weeks of snow which enveloped Atlantis every winter, a phenomenon triggered by the arrival of the orcana twelve years previously. When the orca shapeshifters left, they took the weather with them, but ever since, for two weeks a year, Atlantis experienced snow and cold weather. It was a time of mixed emotions for me. I hated the memorial service which was publicized to the entire population, but I relished the feel of the cold, the sting on my skin the icy wind brought, the frigid starkness of our transformed island.

"Don't you have anything to say?" I asked.

Dad turned his head to look at me. Although he wasn't yet forty, what I saw was an aged and crumpled man. Lines on his face, despite his daily drink from the fountain. Hunched shoulders, hands with a permanent tremor, eyes that never focused on anything but the fire.

"Did it make you feel better?"

No one had asked me that, and I hadn't thought to consider how I would feel after committing the act. There was the obvious guilt, knowing I would have let people down, but I was willing to shrug that off. But did destroying the book change anything? Initially, I'd felt a deep satisfaction in never having to hear another prophecy from the book again. But prophecies were still prophies. Our fate would occur whether the book existed or not.

"Don't know yet."

I didn't wait for his response and marched into my bedroom. Fully clothed, I collapsed onto my bed, on top of the covers. I was asleep in seconds.

THE COLD WOKE ME. With all my windows thrown open, a few flurries of snow had crept into my room during the night, dusting the windowsill and coating my floor. I pushed myself out of bed, relishing the symbolism of my departure. Today, the guardian of the Snow and Ice orb was leaving Atlantis, just as the first snowflakes graced the land.

The years I'd spent on Atlantis since my mother's death had been perfunctory, duties fulfilled with resentment, directionless goals sought with no meaning or purpose. But now I knew what I wanted.

During the palace buffet breakfast, where my entire extended family ate, and often those who lived in the cottages in the gardens, I filled my plate high with eggs and bacon, toast and hash browns, needing to absorb the alcohol from last night.

Aunt Raina gave me a curious look. Pops touched my shoulder and whispered some inane platitude in my ear, and Grams enveloped me in a suffocating embrace, her eyes already welling up.

"I'm worried about you," Grams said, her eyes lingering on my mountain of food.

"I'm fine." At least I was going to be. As soon as I killed Zale.

"What you did..." she sighed. "I can understand it, but it can't go...unquestioned." She wanted to say "unpunished," but she was trying to be more delicate about it considering it was the anniversary of my mother's death. "After the services, tomorrow..."

"I'll give the speech, apologize, do whatever's expected." Of course, I had no intention of doing any of that. I'd be long gone by then.

"Oh good, I'm pleased to hear you say that." Grams gave me another hug and swept away.

"Congratulations, my friend," Ember said at my ear. "You've successfully turned our family reunion into a high-stakes drama. Even the fire-breathing aunties are upset!"

"What fire breathing aunties?"

"Exactly." He rolled his eyes. "I think my mom has already written a speech for you."

"Figures."

"There was a meeting last night," Ember said, steeling a rasher of bacon from my plate. "Went on *all* night. They're worried because a new prophecy is coming."

"Don't you start."

Ember raised both hands and his wings. "Just giving you the info."

I sighed, stared at my plate of food, which I no longer had an appetite for. "Thanks, cuz."

"Want me to fly you out of here to my meadow? Get you stoned on the good stuff to help you get through it?"

I chuckled. "That actually doesn't sound like a bad idea. Later."

He nodded, turning away as his father beckoned him over.

I gulped down my food, not tasting, merely for the primitive reason of gaining calories, then went back upstairs to change into my ceremonial clothing. A ridiculous tradition of silk trousers and shirts and long waistcoats which trailed to the knee. And the crown. Couldn't forget the crowd that weighed a ton. It wasn't badly designed, as far as crowns go, a whole lot of gold with aquamarine stones and carved seashells, but I wasn't a crown kind of person.

Emerging from my room, I found my father stepping out of his own, dressed in matching white and blue, a crown more elaborate than mine perched atop his head, our eyes locking for a brief moment, before his shifted away.

"Shall we get this over with?" he asked.

Together, we stood by the suite's door, shoulders squared, chins raised, reluctance rolling off us both.

Ford opened the door, and we descended the grand staircase. "A speech has been drafted. You'll need to practice with your aunt after the services today."

"Today? Really?" I grumbled.

"I guess you were too young to remember when unrest swept through our island before," Ford said as we crossed the vast foyer, his boots echoing on the pristine marble. "They were furious with your mother. Because of her reckless actions...until she united them once more. You will have to do the same."

My stomach churned. I pulled at my cuffs. "Sure. Whatever. Right after the services."

Ford gave me a sidelong glance. "I know it's hard for you."

"You don't know shit."

"Gal—"

We reached the palace steps and there was no more time

for conversation. It seemed the entire population of Atlantis filled the frozen courtyard. People were packed so tightly around the fountain, pressed up the steps, concealed behind the pillars, and trailed to the surrounding streets, that I couldn't make out a hint of snow. Crowds even appeared on the frosted beach and people hung out of windows to see the memorial procession.

My father delivered a solemn speech on the palace steps, the same one he delivered every year, his breath puffing in the frosty air. I mouthed the words alongside them, having committed them to memory years ago, and refused to catch the eye of a single person in the crowd. Perhaps I was terrified of their anger. Why subject myself to that when I'd be out of their hair in a matter of hours?

When the speech concluded, everyone sang "*Atlantis' Lament*" as we circled the fountain, taking ceremonial sips from the healing waters. Obviously, it did nothing to help me, and it was shit at curing emotional wounds.

"*In the depths of the deep blue sea,*
Where the coral blooms and the waves run free,
Lived our queen, Cordelia, so fair,
A mermaid's grace, beyond compare.
With her flowing tail and her crimson hair,
She ruled Atlantis, just and fair,
Her heart was pure, her spirit strong,
In her presence, we all belonged."

As the song paid homage to my mother, we stood by her statue. Gal, the former High Council member I was named after, shielded her. She had a fireball in her hand, wild hair caught in a moment of battle, snow dusting her head. I'm not sure that was how she'd choose to be remembered, but she wasn't here to complain about it. Looking at the statue was the one thing which almost made my knees buckle. It brought back the memories of the battle with the ghost pirates, how hard she fought to rescue me, and then Zale. I couldn't not think about Zale when I looked at that statue. But this year, I would avenge her death.

When the song came to its sorrowful conclusion, Dad and I walked the slushy streets, shaking hands and accepting condolences. So much love expressed. To my father. No one said much to me. Since I'd reached adulthood, they no longer saw the grieving little boy in need of reassurance. I'd buried that kid long ago, when Pops told me how they'd thrown rocks and stones through my mother's windows. Traitors. Would they do the same to me if they had half a chance, if it wasn't such an auspicious day? But I smiled and nodded and shook hands like I was supposed to.

The procession ended at the beach where a pyre had been built and decorated with ocean grasses and seashells. There was no body resting on the driftwood, of course, but it was lit by Uncle Blaze and pushed out to sea all the same. Over the years, an unspoken tradition had been established that no one would leave until the fire could no longer be seen. So I stood there with my father, my family, my people, for over an hour, and watched the reenactment of my mother's death for the twelfth time.

During the subsequent palace dinner, my father sat at the head of the table, relieved of his fancy clothes and crown, absently sipping wine. I stuck to water, and ate as much as I could, lining my stomach for the long night ahead. Pops made a speech about the time he and my mom had lived without Dylan and Grams. Dylan rolled his eyes at me, like we hadn't heard this story every year. Then Pops recounted his first meeting with my father, which wasn't particularly favorable, and elicited a ghost of a smile from my dad. Normally, Una and Ember would flank my side, tell me jokes to keep my spirits up, but they were nowhere to be seen and I was mildly annoyed they'd not bothered to turn up. Maybe they were pissed at me for treating them like shit yesterday. I didn't blame them. But I had kind of wanted to say goodbye.

When I could escape without causing offense, I left, evading Maya's pointed looks, giving my grandparents a hug, and even telling Aunt Raina I'd be at her service early the following morning to practice the speech.

To avoid mingling with the public during the celebrations, I used the palace tunnels to access the alley behind Uncle Dylan's bar. The entire system had been secured and lit, the dangerous areas closed off, like the ones which led to the lava lake. I thought about saying goodbye to Uncle Dylan, but he knew where I was going, and neither of us wanted to discuss the possibility of me not coming back.

I emerged into the dim alley, leaped over the low wall separating town from beach, and made my way to the marina under a starlit sky. Pausing by the beach, I scooped a handful of snow, shaped it into a dense ball and launched it into the sky. Maybe it would reach the stars. Nope. It plopped into the ocean a few yards ahead, instantly melting.

When I arrived at my boat, I spent twenty minutes

double-checking my supplies, ticking things off my mental list, before releasing the ropes and gunning the outboard motor. With my mother's cap perched on my head, I inched past the other boats, creeping out of the harbor.

I had no idea where Zale was, but I knew where to start.

Once the harbor was nothing more than a speck of light at my back, I raised the sails and turned off the motor. Atlantis was situated a few miles off the coast of San Diego, so all I had to do was plot a southern setting and let the boat steer itself, wind dependent, obviously. Thankfully, the cold front shrouding the island brought powerful gusts and with my boat taking off in a bream reach position, I was accumulating miles quicker than a whale collected barnacles. I had calculated it would take me around sixty hours to reach the southernmost tip of South America, then another two days to arrive at Machu Picchu Base. I doubted there would be anyone there, but the island marked the beginning of the massive ice continent where I would begin my search for Angelica, the leader of the orcana.

I spent a couple of hours reviewing my plotted route, checking the sails, fussing with the halyards and the radio. I didn't know who I'd call if I ran into trouble, but the weight of the small radio in my hand gave me a measure of reassurance. I'd been sailing on the water alone more times than I could count, disappearing for weeks at a time, but embarking on this journey, where I could be gone for months with nothing more than my own company and relying on nothing but my own resources...it felt different. No safety nets in the great big blue.

After a couple more hours of sailing on autopilot and

nothing to do but watch the stars race by, I went below deck to make coffee. Stepping off the ladder, I rubbed the chill out of my hands and swept my frosted hair off my face. My movements were automatic, this environment more familiar to me than my bedroom; filling the kettle, switching the burners on, spooning the coffee granules into a chipped mug. As I waited for the kettle to whistle, I walked to the seating area to check on the rifle. I might need it soon. But as I turned to open the seat bench, a foreign item of clothing caught my eyes. A hooded sweatshirt, brown, a small crest on the chest. Not one of mine.

I backed across the small galley until I butted up against a cupboard, knocking a few things off the counter. Eyeing the crowded room, I looked for anything else out of place. I glanced at the ladder I'd climbed down; there had been no one on deck with me. Then I shifted my gaze to the door leading to the six berths. I hadn't checked in there since the night before. That was the only place someone could be hiding.

The kettle whistled, startling me, and I let out an involuntary yelp. After removing the kettle from the burner, I strained to hear any unusual sounds, but all I could hear was the thundering of my pulse in my ears.

What if Zale was already here? What if he knew I planned to kill him? What if he'd been spying on me all these years and now that I was on the ocean alone, saw his opportunity to finish me off once and for all?

Get a grip, Gal.

I moved to the seating area, whipped open the bench, and put my hand on the rifle. Yanking it out of its hiding place, I grabbed the box of bullets with my other hand. I flicked the safety off. After sliding the bolt, I pushed in the six cartridges the gun could hold, the sixth going into the chamber. I kept my eyes on the closed door as I moved the bolt back into place. "I know you're in there," I called.

I left the safety off and aimed the gun at the door. "Better come out before I start shooting."

A thud sounded on the other side of the door. My heart rate ratcheted up a notch. Despite the training I'd had with a gun, I've never shot at a living person before.

"Don't shoot," a muffled voice said through the door. "We're coming out."

I lowered the rifle, but didn't turn the safety on. The door creaked open, and Ember and Una emerged.

CHAPTER FOUR

*E*mber and Una stood in the cramped galley, their hands raised in surrender, Ember's expansive wings nearly brushing the walls. Both wore sheepish looks. My thumb hovered over the rifle's safety, a moment suspended in time before I finally flicked it on.

After placing the rifle on the table, I faced them, my eyes flaring with anger, my hands planted firmly on my hips. Is this what my mom had felt like before she'd released her fireballs?

"What the fuck are you two doing here?" The words sliced through the charged atmosphere. They exchanged uncertain glances. "You can't be here."

"Too late," Una shot back.

"You have to go back."

Ember lowered his hands, then his wings. "Dude, we're not letting you hunt Zale alone."

"How did you know?"

"I do have ears." Ember pointed to them.

"I didn't ask you to come," I said, tossing a hand at them.

Una squared her shoulders. "We decided not to give you a choice."

"That was stupid." I shook my head. "You're going to get yourself killed."

A heavy silence hung in the air, suffocating the room.

"Wait, you don't want my legendary rubber ducky to help tame the megalodon?" Ember said.

I glared at him. "This is not the time for jokes."

"There's always time for jokes," he replied. "You need to lighten up."

"I'll lighten up when Zale is dead."

"Come on, man, we only want to help," Ember said.

"This can't happen." I sighed. "I can't be responsible for you both."

Una arched an eyebrow. "You may be two years older than us, Gal, but we are capable of making our own decisions."

"Stupid ones," I muttered.

"And you think yours was smart?" Ember asked.

"Says the guy who smokes weed all day."

Ember placed both hands over his chest. "Ouch. That actually hurt."

Apologies hovered on the tip of my tongue, but I didn't voice them. I had come here to escape the chaos, to be alone and avoid dealing with everyone else.

Una stepped forward, her nostrils flaring. "There is a prophecy—"

"I burned the book."

"Not before it had started to form," she said. *"Vorago's trident—"*

"Stop it." I lunged at her, intending to cover her mouth with my hand, but she twirled out of the way. "I don't want to know. That's why I burned the book. Leave it alone, Una. I don't want to second guess every decision I make. *I don't want to know.*"

But the words I glimpsed before burning the book resurfaced in my mind.

Celestial Abyss...

Vorago's Trident...

Parting the sea...

They taunted me, but I pushed them away, refusing to delve deeper.

"I'll drop you off at Cabo San Lucas," I said. "It's only a couple of hours away."

Both their mouths dropped open.

"And then what?" Ember's wings shook, angry or indignant, I couldn't tell, and I didn't care.

"Not my problem," I said.

Una slid a pointed look at Ember. "Remind me why we're friends with him?"

Ember shrugged. "Blood's thicker than water?"

"He's not *my* cousin," she countered, then faced me. "You're not shaking us off that easily. The mainland is a nuclear wasteland. And we're not going to swim all the way back to Atlantis. Not with Zale in the water somewhere. So, you're stuck with us, whether you like it or not."

I glared at her, hoping she'd back down, but she only stood taller as she challenged me. Her fiery presence loomed, despite her being over a head shorter than me. "Then I'm taking you back."

"No," she said. "If you go back, you'll have to face the music. No one will let you leave."

"I'll sneak away, just like I did this time."

"Gal, get serious," she said. "They'll see your sail approaching miles away and they won't let you escape so easily."

"Then I'll drop you off a few miles away and you can swim back."

"I won't get off the boat."

"I'll push you off."

"I'll climb back on."

"Guys!" Ember cut through the argument. "I've seen more harmony in a herd of warring walruses. Can we take a chill?"

"No!" Both Una and I shouted.

The three of us stood in the cramped galley, breathing heavily, eyes anywhere but on each other. There was no way they could come on this journey, and there was no way I was going back to Atlantis. I'd already started this voyage, and going back now, even if it was just to unload unwanted cargo, involved more wasted hours than I was willing to commit to. Besides, if I went back, I was worried I'd lose my nerve.

"I brought antibiotics, a first aid kit." Una indicated the berths at her back where I could make out a large waterproof backpack.

"I brought a flask of fountain water," Ember offered, as if he should receive five gold stars.

"Fountain water doesn't work outside Atlantis," Una said,

patting his hand. "But points for effort."

It took all my restraint not to pound my fist into the table. I turned on my heel and mounted the ladder. "Stay out of my way."

Back on deck, I slammed the hatch closed and went to the helm to check our course. My course. It was *my* fucking course, not *ours*, not *theirs*. Autopilot had done its job and corrected our direction according to the wind speed. The relentless wind whipped at my hair, lashing my cheeks with a biting fury, which mirrored the storm inside me. Unable to suppress my bubbling anger, I kicked at the neat coils of sheets, slammed my fist into the boom, the sharp pain momentarily eclipsing my frustration.

Why, oh why had they come? Zale was a megalodon. He'd eat them both alive in one gulp. I had envisioned a solitary battle, on my own beneath the moon and sun. Me and Zale going head-to-head. I didn't care if he killed me. No one would miss me much. The island was furious with me anyway. And at least if I took him down at the same time, I'd rest easy in the afterlife, if there was one. But now an insurmountable pressure built between my shoulders, gripped the back of my neck, and triggered a throbbing migraine. My cousin and the daughter of my mother's best friend. I had to keep them alive. *Idiots.*

I slumped into the cockpit chair and watched the night unfold. As we sailed southward, the wind tangled my hair and stung my cheeks, yet it tethered me to the present, grounding me in reality.

An hour later, the hatch creaked opened and Una's head emerged, her presence accompanied by the aroma of coffee and Ember's distinctive weed. She balanced two cups in one hand as she clambered onto the deck and shut the hatch behind her.

Wordlessly, she pressed a warm mug into my hands, then slipped into the chair next to me, her eyes fixed on the endless expanse of the ocean. Although the water was calm, the wind whisked waves into little peaks, occasionally throwing the boat into shallow valleys. I took a sip of the coffee, relishing the way the warmth slipped down my throat and settled in my stomach, its comforting heat seeping through my chilled fingers.

"I know you're hurting," Una said, her gaze still fixed ahead.

You don't know the half of it.

Silence stretched between us, pregnant with unspoken words, as if she expected me to fill the gaps. Nope. Not falling for that one. I stole a glance at her profile, the unruly spikes of blonde hair, the mere suggestion of a button nose, an elfin chin, the dimples which dented her cheeks when she smiled. She wasn't smiling now.

"You may not want us here," she said, cradling her mug in her lap. "But you can't do this on your own."

"Yes, I can."

"No, you can't."

"Thanks for the faith."

"It's got nothing to do with my faith in you."

"Oh, so you do have some?" I asked, tucking my chin into the collar of my jacket.

"Of course I do."

"You've got a funny way of showing it."

"Stop being such a dick," she snapped, her words sharp as a blade.

I ignored the dull stab of pain in my chest. "Thanks a lot."

"You're welcome." She stretched out her legs on a crate, crossing them at the ankles. Great. She was settling in.

I clenched my hands around my half empty mug. "If I'm on my own, then I'm the only one who can get hurt."

"Is that what you think?" she asked, her gaze piercing through my defenses.

"It's what I know."

"What about all the people you hurt by leaving them behind?"

I scoffed at the ridiculous suggestion.

"People care about you, Gal," she said, her tone gentler, laced with an undercurrent of concern.

"I don't know why."

"Stop it."

"Stop what?"

"Stop being such a selfish asshole. Stop pushing people away. Just...*stop*."

"I am who I am," I muttered into my mug.

"You're nineteen years old. You've got plenty of time to work on yourself."

"What are you working on?" I shot back.

"This isn't about me."

"Why not?"

"Because I'm not the one who left my friends and family behind to go on a suicide mission."

"Again, thanks for the vote of confidence."

"Again, not about your ability."

"Besides, you're here too. You left family and friends behind," I pointed out, seeking a shred of justification.

"I said goodbye first."

I groaned. "They know you're here?"

"Yep."

Now I wasn't going to be skinned alive just for destroying *The Mermaid Chronicles*, but for putting my best friends in danger too. "Are they coming after us?"

"No."

No. Hmm. "Why not?"

"Because they understand this is something you need to do. Something the three of us need to do. Together. The prophecy—"

I raised a hand. "Already said I don't want to know."

A fragile smile ghosted her face and her blue eyes glimmered with sympathy. Sympathy I didn't want or need. "There isn't a single prophecy in the book that has been fulfilled by someone going it alone."

I didn't know what to say to that, so I remained silent.

"Every prophecy which involved your mother involved your father too. And my parents, and your grandparents, and all their friends. United. That's always been the key."

I wanted to deny her words, I wanted to find evidence to the contrary, I wanted to throw her smart arguments back in her face, but I had never read the book, I had never spent time dwelling over the prophecies and now that she spelled it out, I found myself nodding, begrudgingly acknowledging the logic in her argument.

"Not everyone survived those events," I said.

She lowered her feet to the deck and swiveled to face me.

"No, they didn't. But that's got nothing to do with you. And we've got a hell of a better chance if we put our talents together."

I barked out a laugh, hunching further into my jacket. "Ember is a dragon king who can't produce fire. You're a selachii, a shy lemon shark when transformed, and I'm...practically human. What are our talents, exactly?"

"You underestimate us." She poked my thigh. "You're the guardian of Snow and Ice. I'm the guardian of Spirit and Soul. Ember might not breathe fire, but he does offer light relief. And he can fly. Besides, I brought a portion of the Power of the Sea with us."

I sat up straight. "You did *what?*"

"It saved your parents' lives before. I thought it might come in useful."

Why hadn't I thought of that? "Smart."

"You see, it isn't all bad." She settled back into her chair, recrossed her legs. "And you should probably apologize to Ember. I know you're angry. I know you're hurting, but that doesn't excuse bad behavior."

Before I could retort, Ember's head popped through the hatch, a spliff dangling from his mouth and down to the dregs. I reached out and took it, inhaling deeply. If I was going to endure the next few days with them on board, I was going to need all the help I could get.

"I'll get more," Ember said, turning to go back inside.

"I think you've had enough," Una called after him. "Don't want you falling overboard."

Ember grinned mischievously. "Good thing we're all ocean shapeshifters then."

Una laughed, and I couldn't help but let a small smile grace my lips. "If you fell in the water, I think you'd stone all the creatures for miles around with your breath."

Ember grinned. "I kinda want to try that."

Una nudged me and gestured to Ember.

My ears burned. The last thing I felt like doing was apologizing when they'd trespassed on my boat, but I sucked it up. Ember was family after all. "I'm sorry I was rude to you. To both of you."

"No problem, buddy," Ember said. "I've seen angrier sea cucumbers. You're practically a Zen master compared to them."

Una patted my thigh. "See? That wasn't so bad, was it?"

"Are you going to apologize for trespassing on my boat?" I stood to tack, altering our course to compensate for the strong wind.

"Nope." She winked at me.

"Typical," I muttered.

"We're in this together, like barnacles on a ship's hull—impossible to shake off," Ember said. "So where are we going, anyway?"

"Antarctica," I replied.

Una shivered as if we'd already arrived at the frozen continent. "You think Zale is there?"

I pulled the mainsheet and the boom swung across the boat. "Not sure. But Angelica will be, and she might know where he is."

The air buzzed with anticipation, and as the ship sailed into the unknown, a sense of foreboding settled over us like a thick mist on a ghost ship.

CHAPTER FIVE

For two days straight, I commanded the ship; the wind chafing my skin raw, and my so-called friends offering unsolicited advice. Una finally shoved me aside, urging me to eat and rest.

"I've got this," she said, her voice confident, eyes squinting against the sun's glare.

I couldn't deny the exhaustion clawing at my limbs, and the moment I descended below deck, the relief was palpable. After shoveling a few mouthfuls of a stew Ember had cooked into my mouth—surprisingly delicious, and without any traces of weed—I shoved open the door to the cabin and rolled into a bunk, falling asleep as soon as my head hit the pillow, the scent of smoldering weed lingering in the air. I stayed there for twelve hours straight, and when I woke again, we were halfway to Antarctica.

I took my time before joining Una and Ember, savoring the rhythmic sway of the boat and the symphony of waves against the hull. After slathering some of Una's moisturizer onto my wind-burned cheeks and ensuring I didn't smell like rotten seaweed, I climbed the ladder with three steaming mugs of tea. Una and Ember were deep in a card game, the wind challenging every move as they stuck cards into any crevice they could find and weighed down the deck with a rock.

I handed them the mugs of tea while they dealt me in. At least playing cards I didn't have to talk, and I allowed their easy conversation to flow over me. Una caught my eye a couple times, as if checking to see if I was okay, that I wasn't going to throw myself overboard or plot a course to take them back to Atlantis after all. It was hard to avoid her blue eyes. So bright and so sincere that they managed to strip away a few layers of the walls I'd cemented around me.

Begrudgingly, I had to admit having the two of them aboard made things a little less lonely, made thinking about the future a little less scary. But it did nothing to loosen the tightness in my chest when I contemplated their safety.

"Do you have any idea how to find Angelica?" Una asked, as she dealt a new hand.

"Nope." I shook my head, a humorless smile playing on my lips. "Thought I'd sail around a bit until I caught sight of an orca dorsal."

Ember chuckled.

"You do know how big Antarctica is, right?" Una asked, but there was amusement in her eyes.

"Feel free to leave at any time," I said.

Ember slapped my chest. "Don't even think about it."

Then he patted his pocket. "I stole the keys to the cockpit. You can't go anywhere without us."

I punched his shoulder. "I got that message loud and clear."

"Do you at least know where her clan hangs out?" Una asked.

"Vaguely," I said. "I remember something about Machu Picchu Base. Thought I'd start there."

"*We'd* start there," Una said.

"What?"

"*We'd* start there. All of us."

"Yeah. Right. Whatever," I mumbled.

"I thought we'd moved past the *whatever* stage." Una kicked my foot.

I mustered a smile. It wasn't that hard. It was easy to wind her up. "Yeah. Sure. Whatever."

We all burst out laughing. Una tossed her cards at me, the wind snatching half of them away.

"Hey!" Ember protested, shaking a fist at the wind. "We need those! What else are we going to do?"

"Get stoned?" I suggested.

On cue, he tugged a pre-rolled joint from his pocket and lit it with his sparky breath. I nudged his shoulder as he passed it to me, taking a solitary drag before passing it to Una. Delicately, she inhaled, then erupted into a fit of coughs.

Ember and I collapsed in giggles. "Haven't you tried that before?" I asked.

Una shook her head. "Watching you numbnuts get stoned was always enough to warn me off."

"Fair enough," I said, taking the spliff back. "I can show you a way without making you cough, if you want to try it?"

Una tilted her head, eyeing me. "Okay, I'm game. Can't play cards anymore anyway."

I crooked my finger and gestured for her to lean closer. She inched forward, hands resting on her knees.

"Open your mouth," I instructed, placing a finger gently under her chin.

She gave me a quizzical look.

"Just do it," Ember said.

As she complied, I took a deep inhale, the smoke swirling in my mouth. I leaned forward, closing the gap between us, noting how her eyes slid closed. I hovered less than an inch away from her lips and released the smoke into her mouth. She startled, but managed to keep it down.

"Well done," Ember said.

"You want more?" I asked.

"I'm good," Una laughed, her cheeks flushing, looking anywhere but at me. "Thanks though."

"More tea?" I asked as I collected our mugs.

Una nodded and Ember slapped my ass.

I made my way to the hatch, aware of a lingering gaze on me as I covered the short distance. When I flung the hatch open and descended the ladder, I caught Una's eyes, her gaze roaming my face. Not *just* my face. Heat flooded my cheeks and I ducked below. It wasn't the first time I'd caught her looking at me like that over the years. And every time I noticed it, I avoided her for at least a week. But there was no avoiding her on a thirty-five-foot boat with only three souls on board. She was just going to have to take her googly eyes and stick 'em.

THE FOLLOWING DAY, the weather took a sharp turn for the worse, a bitter gust of wind sweeping up from the south. The three of us, clad in thick coats, beanie hats pulled low over our ears, woolen gloves, and heavy boots, braced ourselves against the elements as icy rain lashed the deck. Each raindrop felt like a needle pricking my skin, a reminder of the harsh reality we were sailing through.

The day after that, we navigated around the southern-most tip of South America, the coastline a mere smudge on the distant horizon. It was tempting to stop, to restock the few supplies we'd made a dent in, but no one knew what might await us. The aftermath of the nuclear war before I was born had left the mainland a wasteland, pockets of survivors scattered and undocumented, their existence known only to a select few like Babette or my grandfather from his previous visits. The blame for the war had fallen on the ocean shifters, and docking anywhere risked encountering hostility, or worse —utter silence, a land devoid of life. So we clung to the boat, eyes fixed on the hint of land passing by in the distance.

"I've never left Atlantis before," Una said, her shoulders hunched against the cold.

I hadn't either. I'd spent weeks at sea before, but I'd never set foot on a different land.

"I've flown over the Californian desert with my dad,"

Ember chimed in, his words muffled by the scarf wound around his face. "It was weird. Different. Desolate. You're not missing anything. Although it's prime for planting a new weed farm."

"I'd like to see where my mom grew up," I confessed. "One day."

Una stuck her gloved hand in mine, squeezed. I didn't shake her off. It wasn't worth the stern look she'd give me.

"Maybe after we've found Zale, we can all visit the mainland and take a trip down memory lane," Una said.

Images of the three of us filled my mind—Ember soaring through the sky, performing daring loop-de-loops, Una and I in an open-top Jeep, wind whipping through our hair. I longed for the experience, even though I had never seen a Jeep before, let alone knew how to drive one. Mom used to talk about her red Jeep, the freedom she felt as she cruised along the ocean roads. I wanted to feel that freedom too.

"Yeah," I said, feeling a burst of sentimentality. "I'd like that."

"Dad showed me the army camp where he met all your parents, where he helped rescue Uncle Wade," Ember said. "There's still a small community there. I can show you around, if you want."

Una nodded.

"Thanks, buddy." I patted Ember's shoulder. "Sounds like a plan."

We rounded the tip of South America, the land disappearing as we headed south. Ice clung to the sails and slickened the deck.

"Can't you melt the ice, or something?" Ember asked me as he rubbed ice out of his thick eyebrows. "The cold is playing havoc with my fire."

"*What* fire?" Una teased.

I shrugged. "I've never known what being the guardian of the orb of Snow and Ice really meant. I like the cold, the snow, but I don't have any magical powers or anything. Not like my mom did."

"The orbs' power was drained in the battle with the ghost pirates," Una said.

The memory of our abduction by the pirates surfaced. The three of us had been held against our will for two weeks. I didn't remember many of the details, only that Una was tethered next to me. We were both terrified. The pirates used a contraption which sucked something out of our mouths. Dad told me it was our innocence, which they used to power their ship. It happened to both of us twice. And both times, it left me exhausted, like my limbs could sink through the deck. There were a few kids who were worse off, a couple who didn't make it.

I remembered the sound of creaking wood, even though the boat wasn't made of wood, but cobwebs and dust. And the cackle of the pirates' laughter. Evil laughter that set my teeth on edge and made my skin prickle. And those spiders. Those horrible white venomous spiders. They didn't bite us, but they crawled all over us.

Ember shuddered. "I don't want to think about them."

"Me neither." Although I understood trauma could cause avoidant behavior, I'd never been afraid to board a boat since.

I was thankful for that, thankful that I could find solace on my vessel, still feel that it was an escape from everything.

"I still have nightmares," Una admitted, her dimples flaring.

I turned toward her. "You do?"

She nodded, color rising in her cheeks. "I don't know what I would have done if you two hadn't been there."

"I have nightmares too." I recalled the medley of grisly images which often interrupted my sleep. "But not about the pirates. About my mom. Zale."

"That's understandable," Una said.

"You too," I said.

"I have nightmares too." Grimacing, Ember toyed with the end of his scarf, puffed out a smoky breath which caused my eyes to tear. "That someone sets my meadow on fire and all my weed is destroyed."

That made us all laugh.

As we sailed further south, the first icebergs appeared on the horizon, massive frozen behemoths floating in the frigid waters. I kept my eyes trained on the water, looking for the form of an ocean shifter. "Last chance to bail. Zale could be hanging around Angelica still."

"Nope," Ember said, although his face portrayed the very image of uncertainty.

"Not leaving." Una gripped the guardrail and scanned the icebergs in the distance. "Despite the fact that I'm freezing my boobs off."

"I'd offer to warm them, but that might not be appropriate," Ember said with a mischievous grin.

Una laughed and chucked him on the tip of his wing.

"I'm so cold, I'm seriously tempted to take you up on that offer."

My cheeks heated and I looked anywhere but at Una's chest. I wasn't blind to her curves. I knew she had a killer body under all her winter gear, but hearing the two of them talk so cavalierly about body parts...*female* body parts... brought a flush to my cheeks. Not that I was completely inexperienced. I knew my way around the female form, but this was Una. The girl I'd grown up with. She was practically family. I busied myself with the boat and prepared to tack while the two of them continued a sexually suggestive exchange.

As I maneuvered around the floating icebergs, the ice loomed above us, casting long shadows on the choppy water. Sea spray clung to my cheeks and hair, dampened my thick jacket, slickened the ice on the deck.

"No way could I live here, dudes," Ember said. "It's emptier than a gorgon's salon after a bad hair day."

"I think it was like this even before the war," Una said, suppressing a smile.

Our journey led us between islands, the wind dropping until we reached a tiny township named Villa Las Estrellas. Slowing to take in the shoreline, the small homes looked deserted, the yards a mixture of snow, ice, slush, and dirt.

"Anyone want to stretch their legs?" I asked.

Una hovered under the awning of the cockpit, as if afraid to reveal herself to the frozen world. "No thanks."

Ember, however, stood on top of the awning, his wings frozen in place. Although he could appear one hundred percent human, he preferred to air his wings more often than not. "Who do you think lived here?"

"Probably a stop for explorers or scientists on their way to the main ice sheet," I replied, as I examined the abandoned buildings. The rifle lay on the seats within easy reach.

After Ember leaped down to the deck, he and Una helped me adjust the sails, ducking under the boom as it swung to the port side. We sailed away from the deserted township, past Nelson's island, and entered the Bransfield Strait. It was so quiet. So still. Part of me was disappointed. The other half mourned the death of a world I'd never known. The stories I'd heard, of people and cities and businesses and skydiving and stock market crashes and terrorist acts and theme parks and...the list when on. Of course, Atlantis had its own marvels, including the miracle of the Fountain of Youth, but I yearned to understand the world my mother was born into. The one where she went to a restaurant for brunch every weekend with my pops and ate waffles drowned in maple syrup. As I stood in the middle of my boat, looking for signs of life, I could almost taste those waffles. We sailed on until there was nothing but blue surrounding us once more.

After a few minutes of drifting across the water, with the sun dipping toward the horizon, Una tapped my arm and pointed off our starboard side. I glanced in the direction in time to see a large dorsal fin duck under the water. Not a shark. An orca.

My heart boomed in my chest. Although I had prepared to sail up and down the coast of the massive continent until I made contact with the orcana, I dreaded having to spend weeks in the lonely climate, unsure if my supplies would last. Spotting an orca now filled me with hope. I was one step closer to securing my goal.

"Another one there." Ember pointed to the port side. "And there." This time he faced the stern.

A frown flickered across Una's face. "We're surrounded."

CHAPTER SIX

The waves crashed against the boat, a cacophony of splashes and roars, as if the ocean itself were trying to drown out the tension gripping our vessel. I scanned the choppy water, counting the four-foot dorsal fins circling the boat. Fifteen.

"Still glad you came?" I asked, my voice tight with tension.

Ember, standing beside me, hesitated before replying, "I'm having some reservations."

"The orcana are kind," Una said. "We have nothing to worry about."

I nudged her with my elbow. "Then why do you look so stressed?"

"I'm not." She crossed her arms.

"Uh-huh."

A splash of water on the port side caught my attention. An eruption of foam followed, causing the boat to rock precariously. A massive shape emerged from the water. An orca, its black and white markings glistening in the overcast sky, soared through the air, higher than I'd ever thought possible. The beast was headed straight for our boat.

Una clutched my arm. "Holy shit!"

Ember ducked, as if that small action could save him from impact.

As the orca flew through the air, it transformed. Its dorsal fins disappeared, and its snout contorted into a human face. It was a man, perhaps in his early twenties, who landed on the deck with surprising grace. Water dripped off his body as he steadied himself on the swaying boat.

He stood tall, his icy white eyes darting between us. Una handed him a towel to cover his modesty, but he didn't seem concerned. They probably rarely left their full or half orca forms and thought little of exposing themselves when human. The other orcas continued to circle the boat, causing waves to constantly pummel the hull.

"Coffee? Tea?" Una blurted. "Warm soup?"

"Una," I said, giving her a pointed look.

"What? I'm just trying to be welcoming."

The man turned to us, a small smile playing on his lips. "You must be Gal, Una, Ember."

"You know us?" I asked.

The man nodded. "We've met before. When you were younger. After the ghost pirates. Besides, the red hair is a giveaway. Just like your mother."

I winced.

"Sorry, that was careless," the man said.

"Frost?" I questioned.

"Last time I checked." He made a show of glancing at the

length of his body, taking in his swirling skin markings. All orcana had them, a patchwork of different skin colors when in human form which reflected their ocean shifter shape. The markings often pulsed when they were injured or emotional. Frost's were black against white skin, strong and vital. "What are you doing in these parts?"

"Looking for Angelica."

He studied me, then turned to face the water, stuck his fingers between his lips, and released a whistle that followed a complicated tune. An orca dorsal fin made a circle around an iceberg, then headed toward the boat. As the shifter neared, the dorsal fin disappeared, and a human form took shape. Long dark hair. The same icy eyes as Frost and the same mottled skin markings. Angelica. I recognized her instantly.

"She's beautiful," Una whispered.

Ember couldn't take his eyes off her.

She raised a hand over the port side. "A little help?"

We all rushed to help her at the same time, tugging her lithe body upward until she'd made it over the guardrails and stood on the deck. She grabbed the towel Frost had ignored and wrapped it around her naked form.

"It's nice to see you three again." She smiled. "All grown up, no less. And I'll take you up on that coffee."

"Coming right up." Ember threw her a salute and disappeared below deck.

"Can't remember the last time I had coffee," she said as she wrung water from her dripping hair. Her markings pulsed, ebbing and flowing, a beautiful display which matched the emotion in her white eyes. "How are things on Atlantis?"

"Fine," I said.

Una raised an eyebrow at me, but this wasn't the time to go into my indiscretions and the chaos I'd left behind.

Angelica lowered herself to a chair. "I'm assuming you're not here for a friendly sail around the world?"

Ember reappeared, pushed mugs into both Angelica's and Frost's hands. Angelica leaned over the mug, the steam warming her face and softening her features. "That smells better than I remember."

"It's the caffeine," Una said. "I need at least five cups a day."

"Coffee makes me more wired than a lightning bolt in a thunderstorm," Ember said. "Weed is so much better."

Angelica laughed, the sound more delicate than falling snow. She took a sip of coffee, swallowed slowly, as if savoring the taste, then trained her eyes on me. "Gal?"

Her clan continued to circle the boat, their edgy movements filling me with nerves. I had come all this way to ask Angelica one question, and now the time was here, I couldn't bring myself to voice it. Whatever her response was would define my future, and suddenly I was terrified of where that future might lead. "Do the rest of your clan want to come aboard?"

"There's plenty of room," Una said.

Angelica glanced at the sky, at the rolling gray clouds obliterating the sun, casting the frigid ocean in a gloomy darkness. "Storm's coming. There's no time for pleasantries, I'm afraid. You'll need to be on your way before it hits."

I opened my mouth to speak, but the words stuck in my throat.

Una poked me. Ember fluttered a wing in my direction, tapping the back of my head.

"If I'm not mistaken," Angelica said. "The anniversary of your mother's death has recently passed." She glanced at the deck, as if pushing away sorrow, then straightened her shoulders and met my eyes. "Are you here to kill me?"

I blanched. "Kill you?"

Frost stepped between us, raised his fist, guarding the orcana leader.

"Why would I want to kill you?"

"Stand aside, Frost." Angelica's skin markings pulsed with an unsteady rhythm. Frost did as he was told, but didn't stray far. "My actions brought about your mother's death. If I were you, I'd want revenge too."

I shook my head. "You didn't kill my mother. Zale did."

"While that's true, she might be alive if I'd never come to Atlantis."

"I destroyed the book," I told her. "So that we never have to feel threatened by the prophecies again."

She took a measured sip of her coffee. "I can understand that."

"The whole island is furious with him," Una offered.

"They need more weed," Ember said, causing a smile to curl Angelica's lips.

"I like you," Angelica said to Ember. "You seem fun."

Ember grinned, puffed out his chest, released his wings so they floated high above his head.

A deafening crack of thunder echoed in the distance,

startling us. It jolted us all to attention. The thunder was followed by a flash of lightning, then the sudden onslaught of rain. The boat rocked, the water churned. The surrounding dorsal fins ducked beneath the surface.

I clenched my hands into fists as the rain drilled the top of my head, soaking my beanie. "I want to know where Zale is."

Angelica's voice cut through the brewing storm, tinged with unease. "You want to kill him."

I nodded.

"I can't say I'm not relieved that you're not here for me," Angelica said, walking close. She laid a gentle hand on my clenched fist. "But you've come a long way for nothing, I'm afraid. I haven't seen Zale since we left Atlantis."

"You must know *something*," I insisted. "You knew him well. You know his movements, where he hangs out. You *know* him, Angelica."

"I used to know him," she said quietly, as if afraid of upsetting me. "It's been twelve years. He made a pact with the Denizens of the Deep, became a megalodon. I have no idea what his motivations are, or where he hangs out. But I can tell you he hasn't been around here. The last I heard, he was in the arctic. But that was a few years ago."

Ember let out a frustrated groan.

Una slumped into a seat. "That's miles away."

"The arctic is a big place," I snapped. "Can you narrow it down?"

"You found us, didn't you?"

"You weren't hiding. You had nothing to fear from us."

"I didn't know that, until now," Angelica said. "Zale

won't fear you. If he knows you're looking for him, he'll make himself available to finish..."

"What he started," Una whispered.

"He can't get to you or your father on Atlantis," Angelica said. "But out here, he can."

I clenched my jaw. "Not if I get to him first."

"I admire your courage," Angelica said. "But do not underestimate him."

Another rumble of thunder underscored the urgency of our situation. Rain lashed down, and lightning painted the horizon with menacing strokes of light. The waves whisked high, curling over the side of the boat.

"You need to leave before it's too late." Angelica's voice held a note of finality.

There were so many questions I wanted to ask her. About my mother. About their time together. But there was no time.

"You're welcome on Atlantis any time," I said.

Angelica bowed her head. "I appreciate that. But we're a reclusive bunch. And we love the cold."

"So do I." I offered my hand, and she shook it warmly.

"Good luck," she said, before turning her attention to Frost. She handed Ember their used mugs, Una the towel, and the two of them leaped overboard, transitioning before they hit the water. I watched them swim away, their dorsal fins towering above the waves, wondering what their lives were like.

"Come on, we need to get going." Ember said, already pulling at the mainsheet. "I guess this is karma for the time I laughed at that mermaid who couldn't find her land legs."

"We go due north, round the other side of Antarctica."

Una busied herself with the computer system, her fingers dancing over the controls and throwing her soaked beanie to the deck. "I can't believe we're sailing around the entire world."

"We're not going due north." I pulled the collar of my jacket up to protect my chapped chin. "We're going back to Atlantis."

They both stopped what they were doing and stared at me. The wind slapped at our cheeks, the thunder roared its protests, and the rain pooled on the deck. We didn't have time to argue about this. I had to make them see I was right.

"Angelica is right," I said, my voice firm. "Zale is a megalodon. I may not survive a confrontation with him. And if you come along, you may not survive either. So we're going back to Atlantis, and I'm going to drop you both off."

"Like hell!" Una yelled, her eyes burning.

"Turn back? Pfft. I've been in more danger at Dylan's bar during karaoke night..." Ember trailed off when he caught my determined look, tucked his soaked wings into his back. "Not cool, man."

The boat rocked, throwing us all into each other. We stumbled against each other, throwing out hands to stop us all going down on the slick deck. Ember's thick stubble scraped against my cheek, adding to the burn from the wind and sun. Una landed with her head in my chest. She clutched my arms as she found her footing, her hands digging into me even through my thick jacket. There was desperation in her touch, and fear, making me more resolute in my decision.

When we'd found secure footing again, I said, "I am not going to put your lives at risk. Everyone on Atlantis is already furious with me. Can you imagine what will happen if I get the two of you killed? Nope. No thanks. That's not a burden I want to live with."

Thunder roared above our heads, sending shock waves of sound from sky to water. The wind stole our words and we had to scream at each other to be heard.

Una glared at me. "I'm so sorry we're such a burden for you."

"I didn't mean it like that—"

"Like hell you didn't."

"You've got a better chance of beating Zale with us," Ember said, his face unforgiving.

"We're not completely incompetent, you know," Una said. "We are actually capable of helping. And maybe keeping you from being Zale's snack while we're at it."

"This is not open for discussion."

Una slammed a button on the console. It beeped at her, then flashed a red light. "Too late. Course is set."

"You're being childish," I said. "I can easily reset the course—"

"*I'm* being childish?" she shouted. "Have you looked in a mirror lately?"

"Una—"

"No, fuck that shit. It's time you got over yourself. It's time you accepted a little help. It's time you realized the world isn't just about you."

"I do appreciate you being here," I said. "Really, I do. It means a lot. But I can't risk your lives."

"Why don't we sail north for a bit?" Ember said, his wings over his head to keep the lashing rain off us. "Then we can decide. But we need to get out of this storm. Can we at least agree on that?"

Una and I nodded at the same time, then the three of us set to work. The tempest raged around us as we tacked through the tumultuous waves, desperately trying to navigate our way out of the storm. Water spilled over the deck, icy rain drenched our clothing, and lightning flashed perilously close. As the sails filled with wind, we shot out of the Bransfield Strait, leaving the icy expanse behind. But the storm held us in its unrelenting grasp, surrounding us completely, only offering danger no matter which direction we attempted to sail. The sea rose in a vicious fury, waves like mountains threatening to swallow us whole. I clung to the control console, my fingers white with the strain, while Una and Ember fought the sails.

"I can't believe we're sailing through this madness," Una yelled, her voice barely audible over the storm. "We're like ants battling a hurricane!"

"We don't have a choice!" I shouted back.

Those were the last words spoken. It took all our energy to battle the storm, and the howl of the wind made speaking impossible anyway. Drenched, miserable, and furious with each other, we sailed into the storm. Or rather, the storm sucked us into its violent grasp. We no longer had a choice in our direction, could only cling to the guardrails and allow the elements to have their way with us.

I caught Ember's eyes as he wrestled with the mainsheet. I'd never seen a dragon king look so pale, so frightened, so ill at ease on the ocean. A quick glance at Una confirmed she was equally terrified. She clung to the guardrails. Water ran down her face. I couldn't tell if it was rain or tears.

I should never have let them come aboard. I should have turned back the moment I discovered them. We might not survive this storm. Even ocean shifters could drown in tempestuous water.

This was all my fault.

CHAPTER SEVEN

The storm surrounded us, violent and vengeful, as if trying to prevent us from reaching our goal. Rain pelted down like shards of glass, stinging my skin. Was Zale behind it? Was he able to wield such terrible power like the gods of the old? Had he already heard I was hunting him and sent this storm to kill us?

Drenched all the way to my untransitioned fins, I threw off my thick coat and clung to the wheel. The wind attacked the sails, tore at my hair, slapped at my skin, and made speaking impossible. I couldn't hear anything above it, not even Ember and Una shouting. Waves surged over the side of the deck, coating us all in salt and seaweed. The boat spun, even as I clung to the helm, dipping into the valley of an enormous wave. The water crested over us, certain to drown us. We'd been battling the storm for five hours straight. Exhaustion overwhelmed my limbs, making them tremble, making my fingers ache from where I'd gripped so tightly to the wheel.

"I need to get the sails down!" My voice was nearly lost in the howling wind as I shouted over the chaos, desperately trying to make myself heard.

Both Una and Ember clung to the guardrails, the fear in their eyes too real to process. The boat groaned under the immense pressure of the waves, threatening to succumb to the depths below, the sails skimming the surface of the violent water. I yanked on the wheel, using every ounce of strength I had left.

With a mighty crash, a colossal wave engulfed us, swallowing Una and threatening to drag her deeper into the abyss. She clung to the guardrails on the wrong side of the boat, her big blue eyes wide with fear. Abandoning the helm, I lunged toward Una, my heart in my throat. Time slowed as I reached out, fingers grasping desperately for her hand. I would not let her drown. No way I would carry her death on my conscience.

We locked eyes. She shook her head, glanced at the tumultuous water. She wouldn't let go of the rigging.

"No!" My shout was drowned out by the roar of the storm. "Trust me! Please, Una!"

The faintest of nods. I grabbed her hand, yanked it high, taking her with me as the boat slammed back onto its hull. We landed on top of each other on the deck, panting for breath, but there was no time to rest. Another monstrous wave loomed on the horizon; its frothy jaws ready to devour us whole. I propelled Una toward the helm, urging her to secure herself. Ember mirrored her actions, both of them fighting against the relentless onslaught of the sea.

I scrambled toward the sails, fingers numb and unresponsive in the biting cold. The mainsail flapped wildly. I seized the halyard, muscles straining against the resistance. On the third attempt, the sail surrendered, billowing down the mast like a defeated beast.

"Turn the engine on!" I yelled at Ember as I allowed the motion of the waves to hurl me to the other side of the boat. There, I anchored myself against the guardrail and grabbed hold of the jib sheet. This time, my frozen fingers cooperated. With a triumphant shout, I released the sail.

Rain lashed at my face, mingling with the saltwater streaming down my cheeks. Seaweed coiled around my ankles as waves washed over the deck. I stole the briefest of breaths and sent up a prayer. I didn't know if anyone was listening, but it was all I had left.

Planting each foot with measured care, I made my way back to Ember and Una. I found them struggling to control the ship. Without warning, the wheel spun uselessly, the connection to the rudder severed. Panic flooded my veins, turning adrenaline into something hard and useless. Without the ability to steer, we were at the mercy of the storm's cruel whims.

I lunged for the console, fingers fumbling as I pressed the engine button. Lights flickered to life, a glimmer of hope. As Ember and Una got to their feet, weaving their arms into the rigging, I grabbed the radio.

"Mayday! Mayday! This is *The Cordelia!* We're going down! Any vessels in the vicinity, please help!" In that moment, I felt more human than ocean shifter. The sky was so vast, the storm so relentless, and my actions so reckless. What had I done?

I glanced at my friends. They wore matching terrified looks. I bet they were regretting coming on this journey. But we were past the "I told you so's."

I repeated the message several times. The engine churned, then cut out. Our boat was at the mercy of the storm. We no longer had control.

"Mayday! Mayday!" I hated the panic in my voice. I hated that we'd only been gone a week and already our journey was going to end in disaster.

"Mayday! Mayday!"

"...position...?"

A voice. Someone had heard us. I screamed our coordinates into the radio. Over and over.

"What's...position...static...?"

"Grandpa?" Although I'd only heard a few words, the voice was unmistakably that of my grandfather. "Please, help us!"

Relief washed over me, but it was short-lived. The wind tore the radio from my hand, disconnecting it from the console, killing the handset completely. I watched it twirl in the air, get swallowed by the next wave.

I clung to the rigging to prevent myself from getting swept overboard and made my way to my friends. "We're going to have to transition and swim." I yelled over the wind.

They both nodded.

Una glanced at the hatch. "Wait! I need my bag!"

"You don't need your bag!" I shouted. "We need to go!"

But Una had already untangled herself from the rigging, was sliding across the deck. She grabbed hold of the hatch handle, yanked it open. The wind slammed it closed. She yanked it open once more. Water poured into the opening. She caught my eyes as she stepped onto the ladder. "Don't wait for me."

"Whatever's in that bag, it's not important!" I yelled. I thought of the rifle where it was stowed under the galley seating. My mother's Navy hat sitting on the galley table. There was no time to retrieve them.

"It's the Power of the Sea." She ducked below, the hatch slamming after her.

"Fuck!"

"We have to wait for her!" Ember yelled.

Time ticked away, each second stretching into an eternity as we waited for Una to resurface. The ship groaned and shuddered under the storm's assault, a fragile vessel combating the ocean's fury. But Una did not reappear, and with each passing second, my hope dwindled like a fading ember in the dark.

I glanced at the swirling water, the towering waves, the gloomy sky. Lightning flashed, streaking toward us, and struck the mast, snapping it in half like it was no more than a toothpick. The mast fell into the water and was stolen by a forming whirlpool.

The hatch door burst open with a violence matching the wrath of the storm above. It flung wide, the wind howling like a banshee, a force that threatened to tear the ship apart. Una, her eyes fierce, emerged from the chaos, clutching a waterproof backpack to her chest as if it held the key to our survival. Maybe it did. My mother's Navy cap was on her head. My heart broke. Una knew how much it meant to me and the fact that she'd taken the extra seconds to retrieve it filled me with a sentiment I couldn't put into words.

Ember and I rushed to help her. With all our might, we held the hatch open, a futile attempt to defy the raging elements. As she stepped onto the deck, the wind ripped the hatch out of my hands, stole it from its hinges, and tossed it into the sky. It sailed through the air and collided with Una's head. She crumpled, her body hitting the deck with a sickening thud, the sound of bone meeting wood echoing over the roar of the storm.

Unconscious, Una slid across the deck, a lifeless ragdoll in the grip of the gale. Ember and I ran after her. A colossal wave rose above the broken mast, its shadow eclipsing everything in its path. The ship teetered on the edge of oblivion, and Una, still unconscious, slipped overboard, vanishing into the churning water below.

Instinct took over. Blindly, I hurled myself after her, the world becoming a blur of wind and water. My fingers closed around the handle of the waterproof backpack. Perhaps it would float. Behind me, I sensed Ember transforming, his majestic dragon king form coming to life. My merman tail flicked into existence, propelling me into the depths. As I dove, I pushed my arms through straps of the backpack and followed the glint of Una's blonde hair as she sank. My mother's cap was nowhere to be seen.

Una was defenseless in her unconscious state, unable to shift into her shark form. Ember and I dove together. He was in full dragon king form, wings grown to a twenty-foot wingspan, four massive paws paddling through the water, tail acting as a rudder. Ember and I reached her simultaneously, our hands wrapping around her arms, hauling her back to the surface.

When we emerged above the waves, there was no sign of the boat.

I treaded water, my body aching from the battle against the elements. I checked Una's pulse. Weak but present. But she wasn't breathing.

"I need your help to keep us afloat," I pushed the telepathic thought to Ember.

He used his paws to tread water and his wings to keep us above the churning surface. Anchoring myself against Ember's wing, I held Una close to my chest, supporting her head with my arm. Pinching her nose, I breathed life into her. Once. Twice. Three times. My heart pounded in my chest, almost drowning out the noise of the storm, and then finally her eyes fluttered open and she sucked in a huge breath, as well as a mouthful of seawater.

"You need to transition," I shouted the thought at her.

She nodded briefly, then her tail morphed into that of a lemon shark, gills flaring open to breathe.

"Dive!" Ember called, his telepathic command cutting through the storm.

The three of us ducked under the next punishing wave and dove for the depths, seeking calmer currents. Fearful Una was still injured, that she would be unable to swim, I clutched her hand, refusing to let go. She remained in her half shark and half human form as we swam for the depths.

After several harrowing minutes of battling the torturous currents, we found calmer waters deep beneath the surface. Ember called at us to use his wings, and Una and I rested against them as he swam us out of the danger zone.

Una's eyes drooped closed once more. I swept an arm around her waist and anchored her to Ember's wing. I contemplated digging for the Power of the Sea in her backpack, but I wasn't sure what would happen to the magical orb if I released it in the ocean. Would it know what to do? Would it know how to heal her? So I left the straps firmly tied to my back and prayed her head injury wasn't too serious.

Blood leaked from a gash on her forehead. Curious sharks swam close. Darker shapes moved at the edges of my vision, ominous shadows hinting at unseen terrors. My limbs trembled, the effort of clinging to Ember and securing Una's safety taking its toll. They should never have come. I couldn't be held responsible for the events we might face. I wouldn't survive another round of grief.

"I don't think I can hold on much longer," I pushed the thought at Ember.

"The storm is still raging! Raging harder than the rave in the tunnels last month!" Ember replied. "Just hold on a little longer."

But I didn't have a little longer. My grip on Una slipped, first one hand and then the other, until I was adrift in the ocean's expanse, my strength spent, unable to muster the energy to use my tail.

The void of the abyss beckoned, its depths promising both refuge and danger. As the storm's fury erupted above and the unknown loomed below, I closed my eyes, bracing for whatever fate had in store.

CHAPTER EIGHT

*T*he world exploded into sharp focus as I jerked awake. Pain shot through my spine, but my eyes flew open, catching the sight of a dismal sky painted in shades of stormy gray. The air crackled, and a biting wind clawed at my skin, urging me to move. I shifted, and that's when I felt it —something digging into my tail fin, something else pressing into my back.

A rough jolt sent my senses reeling. I twisted my head, ignoring the searing pain in my neck, to find myself suspended above the deck of a massive fishing vessel. Ember, surrounded by a cluster of rugged men, stood nearby. My grandfather stared up at me, his hands resting on his hips, his expression unreadable. I was cocooned in netting until I was unceremoniously lowered to the deck, the abrasive rope falling away as I landed, my mother's cap miraculously landing on the ground with me. Grandpa seized my hand, pulling me upright as my tail transformed to legs, while

Ember tossed me a towel, which I hastily wrapped around my waist.

"I'm relieved to see you unharmed," Grandpa said, his voice carrying the weight of the storm we had just weathered.

After grabbing the cap, I searched the deck, but there was no sign of Una's familiar blonde hair. "Where's Una? Is she okay?"

"They took her to medical," Ember replied.

I headed to the nearest door. "I have to see her."

Grandpa's firm grip closed around my arm. "Slow down there, son. You young people, always in such a hurry."

I shook him off. "I need to make sure she's okay."

"You're the one everyone was worried about." Grandpa jabbed a grimy finger into my bare chest. "Had to trawl through the storm for three hours until we found you."

"I'm fine!" I lunged for the door, yanked it open, and plunged inside the massive vessel. My father had told me stories about this boat. *The Albacore.* From when he and my mother searched for the jewels which opened the portal to Atlantis. It held mixed feelings for him. To me, it was a barrier separating me from Una.

I raced along the narrow passageways, clutching the towel to my waist, my feet slipping on the slick floor. Spotting signs for the sickbay, I skidded to a halt, threw open another door, and clambered down a metal staircase. The small porthole window of the medical bay came into view and I pushed my way through the door, ignoring my grandfather's shouts from behind.

Una lay on a bed, her hair wild, wires connecting her to

blinking monitors. I glanced at the screen. Everything looked okay. Steady.

I walked to her side. Her eyes fluttered open. The smile on her face grew so wide it warmed my heart, maybe the rest of my body too.

"You found the cap."

"Thank you for going back for it." I sank to my knees beside her, leaning my head against the bed. "I'm so glad you're okay."

Her fingers brushed my shoulder. "I was worried sick. You were in the water for hours."

"You shouldn't have come," I said, ignoring the fact that I, too, had almost drowned. "It's too dangerous. Your parents are going to kill me."

She pulled my salt-crusted hair, forcing me to look at her. "Shut up."

I snapped my mouth closed.

"Now you listen to me, Gal Waters, this is the last time I'm going to lay it all out for you." Something on the monitor beeped, which she ignored.

I fixated on the rhythm of her heart. "Don't exhaust yourself."

She held my chin, turned my face back toward her. "You may be too caught up in your own drama to give a shit about anyone right now, but I know, deep down, you have a ginormous heart, and that it's capable of actually caring. It's not stone. It hasn't been turned to granite by a sea witch. And you, Gal Waters, have yet to realize that. So I'm going to forgive this bullshit about you wanting to be alone, you saying you don't need Ember and me. You do. And we're here. So start dealing with it."

"I don't know what to say to that."

"Say, *thank you, Una. You are right.*"

"Thank you, Una, but I'm not sure you're right."

She rolled her eyes. I couldn't suppress a smile. I'd always admired her spunk, her feisty nature, her never-say-die attitude. Even if it did get in my way.

Grandpa burst into the room. "Everything okay in here?"

"Everything is fine," Una replied. "I was about to tell Gal that while I love a view of a mostly naked male with only a towel wrapped around his waist, he's freezing. He needs clothes and food."

Grandpa chuckled. I blushed furiously, unable to form a coherent sentence.

"A cabin has been prepared for you and Ember to share. There are clothes on the bed. And there's a hot meal waiting for you in the canteen," Grandpa said. "Let me show you."

I glanced at Una, my concern lingering. "You going to be okay?"

"I have a concussion, which is being treated. They've given me some awesome painkillers. So yeah, I think I'm going to manage without you hovering by my side like an overprotective sibling." Twin dots of color formed on her cheeks.

"Right. Yeah. Sure. Okay. I'll get dressed. Maybe grab a bite. Then I'll be right back. Okay? Yeah. Good."

Una threw her head back and laughed, then winced and pressed a hand to her temple. "Don't make me laugh, it hurts."

"Sorry."

I followed my grandfather out of the room, along a passageway, up a steep, metal staircase, along another passageway until we came to a cabin. The two beds inside were made with military precision. Soft sheets, thick duvets. My entire body sagged with the idea of diving between the covers. I eyed the clothes folded neatly on top of the bed. Sweatpants, a T-shirt, a sweatshirt, thick socks, and heavy boots. I laid the cap on the bed to dry.

"If you plan to go out again, there's a jacket hanging here." Grandpa said, pointing to a waterproof jacket hanging on a hook.

"Thanks," I said. "For everything. If it weren't for you—"

"You don't need to say it." Grandpa opened the door. "Have a shower, get dressed, get some food in you, then we'll talk."

He closed the door behind him and left me alone in the room. I eyed the arch leading to the bathroom, a cramped wet room which offered little comfort, but I wasn't fussy. Shivering, I dropped the towel and stepped into the bathroom, set the shower at a scalding temperature, pleased to note the pressure was decent.

While I waited for the water to heat, I leaned back against the tiled wall and caught a glimpse of my reflection in a small, cracked mirror. My fiery red hair was a tangled mess, knotted with remnants of saltwater. Thick stubble clung to my jaw, and my eyes... I didn't recognize the lost soul staring back at me. Maybe I'd be found once I killed Zale.

I stayed in the shower until the heat ran out, shampooing my hair three times and scrubbing my body raw. When I emerged, I finally felt clean. I teased the knots out of my hair with my fingers, got dressed in the clothes provided, and made my way to the canteen.

Grandpa was there. He poured me a cup of coffee when I entered.

"I'm not going back to Atlantis," I said, before I accepted the mug.

Grandpa pulled out a chair with his foot. "Have a seat, son." His eyes, though aged, held a wisdom which cut through my defenses.

"Why do I feel like I'm in trouble?"

He stroked his bearded jaw. "Should you be in trouble?"

"I guess that depends on your perspective."

I caught a smile through his thick mustache and beard. "What happens at sea stays at sea. That's always been my philosophy."

"I like that philosophy." I took a seat. Another fisherman planted a bowl of warm stew in front of me. Fish. Naturally. But it was delicious. I devoured it, the taste of the sea filling my senses as I ate.

Grandpa sat opposite me, refilling my mug before placing the coffeepot on the scratched Formica table. "Why don't you tell me what you're doing out here."

After placing my spoon back in my bowl, I leaned back in my chair, searching his face for some kind of judgement, but I found none. "I'm looking for Zale."

Grandpa's expression didn't change. He took a sip of his coffee. "I see."

"You think I'm stupid, don't you?"

"I said nothing of the kind."

"You didn't have to."

"Why don't you stop making assumptions and we'll have ourselves a real talk?"

My ears burned, but I swallowed my pride and nodded. "I can't let my mother's death go unpunished. I can't be on that island and listen to all those prophecies...prophecies which ended her life..." I looked away, unsure why the onslaught of emotion was bursting out of me.

"Your mother was a very special person."

I blanched, scanned Grandpa's face for a hint of a lie. "You hated my mother."

"Is that what you think?" He shook his head. "I admired your mother. I admired her courage. The way my son loved her...loves her still...well, Christina and I never had that type of love."

I frowned. "But you didn't want her to be with my dad. You tried to separate them...didn't you?"

He tilted his head, drummed blunt fingernails on the table. "I did try to separate them, but not for the reasons you think."

"Then what?" I refilled both our cups. Finally, I was feeling warm.

"The reason Atlantis was lost wasn't just because the dragon kings invaded. The island was ripe for the taking." As Grandpa spoke, I settled in, hoping somewhere within his story would be information I could use. "Merfolk and selachii had lived on Atlantis for centuries. It was paradise, but they grew complacent, stuck in their ways. Divisions grew, and the dragon kings seized their opportunity while they were bickering. They blamed each other for the loss of the island, and the rift between merfolk and selachii widened, forcing them to scatter across the ocean—"

"What's this got to do with my mother?"

"Patience, son," Grandpa said, his eyes holding mine. "Because of the estrangement between the merfolk and selachii, I was wary of a relationship between your mother and my son. I didn't believe their love could bridge the gap between two races that had been at odds for centuries. I feared there would be problems, threats which they might not survive."

I eyed my grandfather carefully, reassessing everything I'd been told about him and all I'd discovered for myself. He was the rightful king of Atlantis, but he'd abdicated the throne to my father. I had thought he'd turned his back on his people, that he didn't want the headache of dealing with sovereignty. Maybe part of that was true, but it was now obvious his reasons for remaining on the water away from the island were more complicated. "You were right."

"Yes and no," Grandpa replied, his gaze never wavering. "Your parents' love did transcend all odds, but not everyone embraced the unity of merfolk and selachii. And when humans entered the picture, it only complicated matters."

"But that's all changed," I said, clinging to the hope that our island had progressed beyond ancient prejudices.

"Has it?" Grandpa's question hung in the air. "If all three races are equal, why doesn't the fountain work for the humans?"

"Why doesn't it work for me?" I challenged.

"I don't have the answers, only my suspicions. Things aren't as they should be. It can still go either way."

"So there's a way to make the fountain work for humans?"

"Maybe. I don't know for sure." Grandpa shrugged. "But I suspect so. But you're not here for that. You're here for Zale."

"Do you know where he is?" I asked. This was my last chance for a lead.

"I don't." Grandpa sighed, crushing my hopes. "I'm not...I don't...I'm not interested in a confrontation with him."

"But he held your wife hostage for three years! Don't you want revenge?" I cried, my anger surfacing like a rogue wave.

Grandpa's lips pressed together. He turned his mug in his hands. "I'm a simple man, Gal. I don't need much in life. Just me, the boat, my crew, and the water. I'm not a vengeful person."

I stood abruptly, causing my chair to topple over. "Not like your grandson, you mean."

Grandpa raised a liver-spotted hand. "There's nothing wrong with wanting justice. But it's not something I can put myself through. Not again. In previous battles..." he looked at his hands, shook his head. "It didn't always go the way I planned."

I narrowed my eyes. "You're a coward," I said, my disappointment in him as bitter as the sea.

"Aye." Grandpa stood to face me. "I can admit to that."

We stared at each other; two generations locked in a battle of ideals. My grandfather, unexpected in his complexity, stood before me, revealing a side I had never anticipated. He was not a heartless villain, but a tired, scared old man haunted by his past mistakes.

"Do you at least know how to kill him?" I asked.

"He's a megalodon now."

"I'm aware."

"I'm taking you to England," Grandpa said. "To see the Lady of the Lake. You're going to need Vorago's trident to kill him and she's the only one who knows where it is."

CHAPTER NINE

The Lady of the Lake had always been a mythical story to me, a tale my mother read to me before she died. King Arthur, Lancelot, Guinevere—characters from a distant world of magic, honor, love, and betrayal—had filled my dreams with wonder. The round table, a symbol of unity, the sword Excalibur, a beacon of hope. It was a tale of heroes and villains, of destiny and magic. But in my heart, it was just that—a tale. A fantasy woven into the fabric of my imagination. To hear the Lady of the Lake was a real live being and resided in the Lake District in England...well, I didn't know what to do with the information.

"She was responsible for putting Excalibur in the hands of King Arthur," Ember said as we sat in the canteen picking at bowls of pasta. Three days had passed since Grandpa had rescued us from the storm. Una was out of sickbay, though she remained under strict orders to conserve her energy and rest as much as possible until we reached our destination. "At least, that's how the legend goes."

"That's what I remember too." I tried to recall the words from the storybook my mother and I had shared, but the memories felt distant, buried beneath layers of grief.

"I wonder if the trident *is* Excalibur," Una said, her hands wrapped around a steaming mug of black tea.

A laugh burst out of me, then quickly deflated as I contemplated her words. "But I'm not called Arthur. I'm not a King. And I don't have magic."

Una gave me a knowing look. "You might not bear the name, but you carry the legacy. You are a prince, the guardian of Snow and Ice. That, my friend, is magic in itself."

"No," I said automatically.

"Maybe the story of King Arthur is a prophecy of its own," Ember said, then shoved an oversized forkful of spaghetti in his mouth.

I shook my head, clenched my fists. "It's just a story."

Una reached across the table, her touch gentle as she uncurled my fingers. "We'll ask the Lady of the Lake when we see her."

"Eudora." Grandpa pulled out a chair and sat at the table with us, his own bowl of pasta set before him, his eyes clouded with memories. "Her name is Eudora."

"Do you know her well?" I asked.

Grandpa shook his head. "I met her once in passing. She told me..." he dropped his gaze, took a sip of water. "She told me to get my act together. And she didn't mince her words."

"Did you?" I asked. "Get your act together?"

Grandpa tilted his head. "I did my best."

"How long until we reach England?" Una asked.

"A couple weeks," Grandpa replied.

"*Weeks*?" I half stood. "We don't have a couple of weeks."

Grandpa leaned back in his chair, looked up at me. "In a hurry to dance with death?"

"No, but..." I wanted to get it over with. I'd spent my entire life hating Zale, wishing someone would kill him. And now that I'd decided to do it, I wanted to get it done. I needed this over. Before I lost my nerve.

"Your friend needs to rest." Grandpa nodded at Una. "And so do you. You were nearly dead when we pulled you out of the water. So, take a minute. Build up your strength. You do not rush into a confrontation with Zale half-cocked."

I slammed my palms on the table. "I'm not half-cocked."

"Gal, sit down." Una grabbed my arm and yanked me back to my seat.

I raked a hand through my hair, tearing through tangles, ripping out strands at the roots. "*Two weeks*."

"Plenty of time to get a nice buzz on." Plate polished off, Ember sat back, his feet propped on another chair, and rolled a spliff.

"Can't you take anything seriously?" I snapped at him.

Una slammed a palm on the table. "We're in it together, remember?"

With a heavy sigh, I pushed away from the table and stalked out of the canteen. I marched to my cabin. I stayed there for two days. Sulking. Ember offered me a spliff. He'd protected his weed in Una's waterproof bag and rolled up whenever he finished whatever chore my grandfather had assigned him, saying he had to get his last fixes in if he was going to die fighting Zale. Like I needed that guilty thought on my conscience. I'd already come close to killing them. More than once.

Una knocked on the door a few times, but I ignored her. Ember finally gave up telling jokes and blowing smoke in my face and left me alone. The hours stretched into days, my body healing, but my mind still cluttered.

A few days later, I finally mustered the courage to venture out of my cabin. The equator lay ahead, and the fishermen had embraced the sun's warmth, their rugged bodies glistening with sweat as they shed layers of clothing, donning T-shirts and shorts. On the upper deck, amidst the glow of the tropical sun, I found Una and Ember.

Ember, his bronzed physique only covered by a pair of shorts, acknowledged me with a nod before applying sunblock. Una reclined on a sun lounger, her eyes closed, lost in the music's rhythm blasting from an old-fashioned stereo nearby. Her bikini, a vibrant electric blue, covered little of her sun-kissed skin and accentuated the alluring curves of her body. I had no idea where she'd sequestered it from until I noted her waterproof backpack on the floor, contents spilling across the deck. Had she always had it with her? Had she planned for some chill time all along?

I couldn't take my eyes off her, the curve of her neck which led to the delicate hollow of her throat. The sinewy strength of her arms, the line of her breasts that led to the dip in her stomach. Her hips, her thighs...ankles, toes. *Yep. You can name body parts, well done, Gal.*

Una's eyes, the same piercing shade as her bikini, flicked open and locked onto mine. Her lips curved into a warm smile. "Hey stranger. Feeling better?"

I managed a weak nod and settled onto the edge of Ember's lounger. The salty scent of the ocean surrounded us. No matter which direction I looked, I saw only blue. But this time the water was calm, not like during the storm which had tried to kill us. "I needed...time."

"I get it. Everyone needs a little me time now and then." She propped herself up on elbows, giving me a better view of her breasts. I quickly averted my gaze, annoyed at the physical reactions taking place in my body. But Una was the only female for miles around, and I was only human, or merman, so it wasn't unusual that I was having a perfectly healthy male reaction. "But people also need people time too. Especially you, King Arthur." She flicked my nose.

Ember chuckled.

"Do not call me that," I said. "I am not a *king*. Certainly not *King Arthur*."

Una winked. "But I could be your Lady Guinevere."

"Who had an affair with Lancelot. Thanks a lot."

"Oops," Una said. "I forgot about that. I promise I'd be faithful."

"I'm not falling in love," I said. "People get hurt. Get killed. No way am I going through that."

Una stared at me. Ember raised his eyebrows.

"You can't avoid love just because you're afraid." Una rolled onto her side.

"Yes, I can."

Ember slapped my shoulder. "Dude, you need therapy."

"I had years of therapy. Didn't work."

"Because you don't open up to people," Una said, her words cutting deep.

"I don't want to get hurt."

Ember stuck a spliff between my lips. "Smoke weed. Chill out. It numbs all your emotions. You'll never feel hurt again."

I passed the joint back to him. "Thanks. But I'm good."

"And that's how you're going to live your life?" Una pushed herself into a sitting position, swung her feet to the deck. I couldn't avoid the way her body moved, all creamy skin and curvy contours, even when she was pissed at me. "Alone. Lonely. Never getting over the death of your mother? Never allowing anyone else in? Are you hearing yourself right now?"

"It's got nothing to do with you," I said.

"Like hell it doesn't!" She smacked my thigh. "Do you know how often I have to listen to my parents worry about your welfare? Dissect every decision you make? Everyone is worried about you. So yes, I do care. And you're not alone, whether you like it or not. Too many people on that island won't let you be alone."

"I didn't ask anyone to do that," I said. "And I'm not on Atlantis now. People can quit worrying about me."

She stood, wrung her hands at me, roared at the sky, and stalked off.

"What did I say?" I asked Ember.

He leaned back on his lounger, arms tucked under his head. "You know what she's like. Guardian of Spirit and Soul? She's an empath. She cares."

"I don't *want* anyone to care."

Ember chuckled. "Yeah...good luck with that, dude."

The music blared a happy love song. I jabbed the off

button. Silence descended. The purr of the engines provided a steady rhythm, a stark contrast to the chaotic cadence of my racing heart.

The next few days passed in a silent war of stubbornness, Una and I equally matched. The air between us hung heavy with unsaid thoughts, but our lips remained sealed, our gazes sharp as knives. When the three of us weren't helping with the fish, which wasn't often as we had no idea what we were doing and often got in the way, we retreated to the upper deck and laid on loungers facing the sun. To prevent Una pestering me with questions, trying to psychoanalyze me, or give me extra therapy sessions I didn't want, I kept the stereo blaring at full volume, a wall of sound which made conversation futile. Some days I felt the penetration of her glare so severely that I took Ember up on his offer of weed and smoked until I was blissfully numb.

The only comfort I found was in witnessing the slow healing of the gash on Una's forehead. The skin changed from an angry red to a neat, thin line. It would scar. But the fountain water would heal her when she returned to Atlantis. She caught me looking once, her hand immediately flying to the wound, pulling her hair over her face to cover it.

"Don't do that," I said, easing her hand away. "It's a sign of life. Of the battles you've fought. It's beautiful."

"Thank you, Gal." After that, she left it exposed. "And you know I'm here when you're ready to talk?"

"The weather is pretty fine today."

She raised an eyebrow.

"The ocean is sparkling like it's encrusted in diamonds."

The other eyebrow shot up.

"Don't you love the way Chef seasons the fish, a pinch of spice and slathered in butter? Perfection." I threw a chef's kiss into the air.

"Gal!" She threw her hands in the air. "When are you going to say something meaningful?"

"You don't like my chat?" No way was I going to let her badger me into unlocking my feelings. She went back to sulking for the next two days.

Dinner times were a collective affair in the canteen where my grandfather and the crew regaled us with stories of their maritime exploits. They recounted tales of ferocious storms, harrowing periods of dwindling fish stocks, and the comrades they had lost to the sea. I clung to their words, yearning for stories which weren't bound to my past or my uncertain future. But the reprieve was fleeting. As soon as my head met the pillow, ominous visions seeped into my mind, dominated by one figure—Zale. I recalled his ferocious attack, his emergence from the water channel, and the gaping jaw that had ensnared my mother. They say time erases memories of trauma, but for me, every second remained etched in my mind.

Christmas came. It wasn't a holiday I'd paid much attention to before and none of us had brought gifts. Ember rolled spliffs, tied them with string, and handed them out to the crew. Grandpa gave everyone the day off, partly because they were stoned out of their minds, and partly because it was Christmas. We sat on the deck and listened to the crew tell stories of what Christmas was like on the mainland before the war. Santa and elves and snow and flying reindeer. It sounded so magical. So pure. So innocent. But innocence was something which had been stolen from me a long time ago.

I caught Una with her eyes on me. She didn't look away. She didn't blush. Just held my gaze, imparting silent messages. Messages I didn't care to interpret or understand, but I felt a shift in our relationship. We may not have presents and a tree, but I could quit being mad at her, quit snapping at her, quit being irritated by her presence. Maybe.

That evening, Chef made a meal with fish and mashed potatoes and green beans from cans. Christmas puddings soaked in brandy for dessert. And Grandpa found some old Christmas crackers in a dusty storage container. While we sang carols, we crossed arms and pulled the crackers, the bangs going off like fireworks. After telling the jokes that had fallen out of the crackers, we played charades, even the toughest of crew members cracking a smile. It was the first Christmas without my father. My first Christmas away from Atlantis. A surprising stab of homesickness shot through me as I thought about what everyone back home would be doing. How Una and Ember weren't celebrating with their families...because of me, although their presence made the homesickness more bearable. I swallowed it down with another few shots of the whiskey Grandpa was passing around.

"Shame we don't have any mistletoe," Una said as we wound our way to our cabins that night.

I blushed, fought to walk in a straight line. "You planning on kissing all the crew?"

"Not all of them."

I raised both brows, gestured for her to return along the passage. "Don't let me stop you."

Her dimples vanished. Then she turned on her heel and disappeared into her cabin.

"Whatever," I muttered as I tripped over the threshold to my cabin and fell face first onto my bunk.

That night, I didn't dream of Zale, I dreamed of Una, and it took me the best part of the day to get the image of her feisty blue eyes and spiky blonde hair out of my head. And the freaking mistletoe. Pinned to her blue bikini. I didn't have time for intrusive thoughts. I only had time to focus on Zale.

With each passing nautical mile toward the English shores, fear tightened its grip on me. Though I couldn't understand the full extent of the trident's power, I knew I couldn't confront Zale without it. The thought of him finding me before I'd got my hands on it filled me with dread. And the idea of bringing Una and Ember down with me didn't bear thinking about. The guilt weighed on me, sometimes making it difficult to breathe, so I would sit up and watch the moon through the porthole and the gentle rise and fall of Ember's chest as he slept.

What was my father doing now? Was he worried about me? Had he sent a search team to find me and return me to Atlantis? And what about my mother? Was she watching from the heavens above? Would she approve of my actions? All I ever wanted was to make her proud. I didn't know if she'd want this for me, but I couldn't let her death go unavenged.

Once I'd killed Zale, *if* I killed Zale, then I would return to Atlantis and fulfill my royal duties. Or perhaps I wouldn't. Perhaps I'd stay on the sea and be a reclusive sailor like my grandfather. Maybe he had the right idea all along.

CHAPTER TEN

The jagged cliffs of the English shore appeared on the horizon. The view didn't just stir anticipation, it triggered a pulse of anxiety. The next leg of our journey was about to begin.

At the bow of the ship, Una and Ember joined me, their eyes fixed on the coastline as we navigated around England's southwestern edge and into St. George's Channel.

"Your grandfather says we'll reach Whitehaven Marina by dawn," Ember said, his voice cutting through the salty wind.

"I don't know how I'm supposed to sleep tonight," I said.

"We better," Una said. "We've got a twenty-hour hike ahead of us to the nearest lake, and if that doesn't work, a shit ton more miles."

I removed a crumpled piece of paper from my pocket and looked over the instructions Grandpa had given me. Eudora demanded offerings representing elements—fire, water, earth, air, spirit, and ice. Una represented soul and spirit, I was snow and ice, and if only Ember could conjure flames, we'd have fire too. But I was pretty sure it wouldn't be too hard to find a matchbox somewhere. That left water, earth, and air, elements which surrounded us, yet remained elusive in their manifestation. I wasn't sure what to present to the mysterious figure. There had to be an offering too. I wondered if she'd accept a virgin sacrifice, or the blood of a lamb, and chuckled at my thoughts.

As the ship sailed through St. George's Channel, I watched the desolate coastline passing by—beaches, cliffs, villages, repeating in a monotonous loop. But never a sign of movement. England had been one of the worst countries hit during the nuclear war, and I wondered if there were any survivors here at all. Una brought me a mug of coffee, Ember a bowl of soup. And still I didn't budge. While we'd been on my grandfather's trawler, I'd felt...safe. It had been a reprieve from the danger of my adventure. A place for Una to heal and for all of us to catch our breath. But now, after three weeks of comfort and safety, I was about to launch myself into the unknown once more.

But that was why I was here, I told myself, searching deep for my well of courage. This was merely a pitstop on my journey, a steppingstone toward my ultimate goal—the confrontation with Zale. My resolve hadn't wavered; if anything, it had strengthened. But the fear, the gnawing terror, persisted beneath the surface.

Exhausted, I fell asleep on a sun lounger, only to wake damp with dew, my throat sore. As I stretched out the kinks from sleeping in a plastic chair, Grandpa appeared beside me and handed me a mug of coffee and a plate of bacon.

Together, we moved to the prow, watching as the marina grew closer, boats of all kinds gleaming in the morning sun, their hulls swaying on the gentle currents. Sailboats, yachts, dinghies, catamarans, and the powerful rib of the coastguard perched on the access ramp.

Rolling green hills backdropped the marina. A small village was nestled among all the greenery. A picturesque scene, marred only by the absence of movement.

"There's a camping store near the marina," Grandpa said, eyes on the beckoning shore. "You'll be able to find everything you need. Tent, sleeping bags, clothes, packaged food too. It should still be edible."

"You told me already."

"You've got the incantation?"

I patted my pocket. "Right here." That was the other thing Eudora needed to be summoned, a magical incantation. It had to be written by the people summoning her, and it had to be respectful. And it had to rhyme. Ridiculous. I was beginning to wonder what kind of woman this lady was. One who liked to make people jump through hoops.

"I know you lost your rifle in the storm," Grandpa said. "I have another one for you before you go."

I glanced at his profile, at his serious features set into an unreadable mask. "You think there's going to be trouble?"

"It's been twelve years," Grandpa said. "There are more survivors than you'd think. And they've grown accustomed to doing things the hard way. Doesn't pay to be too careful."

"I don't want to hurt anyone."

"Aye." That was all he said. I couldn't tell if it was in agreement or sympathy.

Side by side, we watched the sun play on the marina, my eyes searching for any sign of life among the boats. Nothing but the natural sway of the waves.

Grandpa drained the last of his coffee. "Won't be able to go all the way in, boat's too big. We'll have an access ramp dropped at the outer rim of the dock." He turned to go.

"Grandpa?"

He turned back, gave me a faint smile. "You'll be okay, son."

"Why do I feel like this is goodbye? Won't you come with us? You've met Eudora before, you could—"

"Let me stop you right there." Grandpa held his mug in both hands. "I'm an old man, Gal. Arthritis in my back. My time for adventure is over. I've radioed Babette to come and pick you up in a few nights' time. She'll take you on to your next destination."

"You're really going to leave us here?"

"You're a man now, Gal. A brave one. Braver than I ever was. And you've got some good friends risking their necks for you too. The three of you will do just fine."

A wave of doubt threatened to drown me on the deck. "What if we don't?"

"That's the fear talking," Grandpa said. "Don't let it beat you."

"Don't let it beat me," I echoed, then opened my mouth to say something else, but Grandpa was already halfway through the door leading below deck. That was the last time I saw him.

THE HARSH CLATTER of the access ramp hitting the concrete dock reverberated through my bones. A rifle was thrust into my hands, its weight eerily familiar, a grim reminder of the day I had left Atlantis. Meaningless words of encouragement followed, as well as a box of bullets.

Ember flew to the strip of concrete. Una clambered down the ramp carrying her waterproof backpack. Wearing my mother's Navy cap as a token of luck, I followed. As soon as my feet touched the dock, the metallic clank of the ramp being retracted echoed behind us, severing the connection to *The Albacore*. I turned to scan the faces on the trawler, hoping for a glimpse of my grandfather, but he was nowhere to be seen. Perhaps goodbyes were too hard for him. They were hard for me too, but if this didn't go well, it could be the last time I saw him. I tried not to let that thought weaken my courage as I marched along the concrete dock and stepped foot onto land for the first time in weeks.

We crept through the marina, my legs unsteady after so many days at sea. The once-vibrant boats, now corroded and decaying, bobbed lifelessly in the stagnant water. Sea gulls swarmed the air above us, a wintry breeze swept around the corners of buildings and rushed down the back of my neck. Trash cans overflowed; their decade-old contents unrecognizable from what they once were. The air was thick with a palpable sense of dread, a heavy blanket which clung to the skeletal remains of the surrounding buildings. Every step was accompanied by the crunch of debris underfoot, a reminder of the world that once was. Amidst the wreckage, there was an underlying tension, a feeling that danger lurked around every corner. This was a ghost town.

As we curved around the far side of the village, we came across the camping store. The door hung from its hinges and the windows were shattered. Broken glass and torn goods lay strewn across the threshold and clung to disused lampposts and rusted bike racks.

Eyes fixed on the shadowy depths of the store, Una hunched her shoulders. "I was hoping for at least a jacket."

"We need the other elemental objects for Eudora too," I said.

Ember picked his way over the broken glass toward the damaged door. "Might as well check it out."

Judging by the outside landscape, Whitehaven Marina hadn't been in the initial blast zone, but had become more an object of looting as people tried to escape. The three of us ventured into the gloomy store. Shelves, once adorned with gleaming camping gear, were now stripped bare, their contents plundered by desperate hands long ago. The atmosphere inside was stifling, a suffocating blend of mold and stale urine.

As we moved deeper into the darkness, my footsteps echoed in the empty space. The silence was broken by the occasional creaking of sagging shelves and the distant howl of the wind outside. Among the debris, glimmers of forgotten treasures lay strewn about—a rusted camping stove, a cracked headtorch, a torn map. My hand brushed against a frayed tent fabric, and for a moment, I could almost hear the laughter of children and the crackle of a campfire.

"Let's check the back." Ember pointed to a closed door; paint peeled, wood warped into its frame.

It took the three of us to shove it open, and when we stepped inside the large storeroom, I heaved a sigh of relief. Boxes. Everywhere. Clothes, food, tents, and a plethora of other camping supplies.

"Thank God!" Una said, tearing open the first box and spilling the contents on the floor. Fleeces. A medley of muted colors. Una tore off the plastic wrap of one and threaded her arms through its sleeves. It draped over her petite frame, but it was warm, and finally she stopped shivering. It was navy blue and emphasized the color of her eyes. What was it with her and the color blue? I watched her as color bloomed in her cheeks. My gaze must have caught her attention, for she looked at me, smiled, and threw me a fleece in my size.

We found sleeping bags, roll mats, kerosene, matches, a hurricane lantern Ember thought we could use as our fire element for Eudora, as well as a stack of packaged food. Well past their expiration date, but we had little choice. Could package food laden with salt and sugar and preservatives ever really go off? All we had to do was add cold water and we'd have succulent pasta with red pesto sauce or even a steak risotto. My mouth watered at the thought.

Una stuffed a few packets in her bag. "Dad used to tell me about Twinkies on the mainland."

"That cream cake thing?" Ember asked. "Perfect munchy food."

"Yeah," Una replied. "Apparently they have a seventy-year shelf life because they're only one molecule away from Styrofoam."

"Yuck," I muttered. "And people used to eat that shit?"

"Lots of people," Una said.

Ember found a couple of backpacks and we loaded them with supplies. We wore thick jackets over our fleeces and discovered a few boxes of what looked like expensive hiking boots. Everything was covered in dust, or mouse droppings, but with a wipe of an old rag, they came up as good as new.

"We should get going if we want to reach the lake before nightfall," Una said, tying her shoelaces in double knots. "Your grandfather said it was twenty miles."

Shouldering my stuffed backpack, I groaned against the weight. But I'd rather have too much than too little. I carried my grandfather's rifle in one hand, fully loaded but the safety turned on, and used a hiking stick to guide my path with the other.

Outside the entrance, Ember grabbed a torn map from where it lay anchored under a pile of broken glass, shook it off, and traced a route with his finger. Then the three of us set off, leaving the destroyed village behind us.

It was only five minutes later, when the houses began to blur into the background, that we encountered the first casualty of the war. A woman, her features frozen in a gruesome mask of death, lay before us. She wore jeans and a sweatshirt, and her hair was clumped to a decaying skull. Most of her features were still intact.

While I retched into the bushes, Ember kneeled and inspected the corpse. "This person was near a blast zone. Radiation effects slow decomposition."

"How the hell do you know that?" Una asked, glugging water with her back turned to the dismal scene.

"Came across it in California with Dad. He explained it," Ember replied. "Depending on the conditions, you can get mummification, or saponification too."

"I don't know what that means, but I don't like the sound of it," I said. "Can we put a bag over her head, or something?"

We searched for something to cover her with, but the best I could find was the branch of a fallen pine tree, the needles turned a miserable brown.

"I don't think we can stop and do this every time," Una said, her eyes scanning the path ahead. I followed her gaze. What I'd initially thought were burrows or small mounds of dirt or even haystacks, turned out to be more bodies. My stomach lurched. The smell of death seeped into the air.

Ember lit a spliff. We all took drags. It wouldn't erase the haunting sight of the lifeless bodies around us, but it offered a momentary reprieve from the stench. There was no time to give them a proper farewell, no opportunity to cover them or offer prayers for their souls. They would remain where they fell.

Climbing a small hill, the enormity of the death toll weighed on my mind, causing a creeping sense of hopelessness to seep into my bones. Was this the fate that would befall the three of us at the end of our journey? Would we too be lost, not to the land, but swallowed by the merciless sea?

As we walked, signs of the war became more apparent. The remnants of humanity's once bustling world were reduced to crumbling ruins and rusted skeletons of cars. Using my hiking stick to hack through overgrown foliage, my fingers brushed against the scorched leaves of mutated plants that dared to survive. Trees, gnarled and twisted, stood tall like ancient guardians, their leaves rustling with an eerie melody.

We didn't stop for a break. We didn't stop for food, but ate as we hiked, all of us eager to reach our destination. Occasionally, I glimpsed movement in my peripheral vision, but whenever I turned to look, there was nothing there. Irrational fears of victims of radiation poisoning—now turned zombie—haunted my thoughts. These grotesque creatures, barely resembling humans, intruded on my imagination, marching across the meadows in search of brains to devour; a ridiculous idea that clung to me. The sooner we reached the lake, the better I'd feel.

Wild Ennerdale came into view, a welcoming expanse of water. Although I had recently left the ocean behind, I sensed the familiar pull which all ocean shifters feel near water—a magnetic force nearly impossible to resist.

Una dropped her bag on the ground. "We're here."

The lake shimmered under the soft light of the moon, its surface rippling with untold secrets.

CHAPTER ELEVEN

The three of us stood on the shores of the lake and watched reflected moonlight drift across the water.

"We should wait until morning," Una said, checking her watch.

"I'm not sure." I scanned the surroundings, squinting to decipher shapes in the shadows. "I think something was following us."

Ember nodded. "If I had a fiery breath for every time I glanced over my shoulder, this entire country would be in flames...there's definitely something out there."

"Like what?" Una took a step closer. "There's no sign of life anywhere."

"Zombies." I forced a laugh. "Ferral dogs, sick people, survivalists."

"A hallucinogenic nightmare," Ember muttered.

"But I'm so tired." Una gestured to the three backpacks heaped on the ground. "We've been hiking for over twenty hours. We'll need to rest before we can hike back, and we might as well do it now while it's still night."

"You sleep," I said. "I'll keep watch. I'll light a fire to keep the zombies away." I attempted to inject humor into my tone, but it fell flat.

"You might attract something." Ember turned a slow circle, his eyes sweeping the towering trees. Some were dead, ready to fall with the slightest breeze. It reminded me of the philosophical question Ford had once asked me during one of our training sessions. If a tree fell in the woods and there wasn't anyone around to hear it, would it still make a noise? We had debated it endlessly, never reaching a satisfying conclusion. "Something we don't want to attract."

If animals turned into zombies without someone witnessing the transformation, would they still lust for blood? I swallowed. "Okay. No fire."

By the light of the moon, we unpacked the tent and set it up, securing it with pegs dug into the soft earth. Una unrolled the sleeping bags while Ember prepared food for us all. We ate a silent meal, all three of us watching the lake as though Eudora might appear without us having to summon her. Movement at my periphery continued to distract me. I kept one hand on my rifle, the other on my box of bullets.

"You two get some sleep," I said, zipping my coat high to protect my chin. "I'll take the first watch."

Una and Ember crept into the tent, exchanged a hushed 'good night' with me, and sealed the flaps shut. While they settled in, I unpacked a few plastic containers. One was filled with soil, another remained empty, containing nothing but air. I then filled the hurricane lantern with kerosene and positioned the box of matches beside it. Only water was left. I dipped a container into the lake to collect some. All preparations were complete; all I had to do was wait for morning.

A haunting howl pierced the stillness. It sounded like a wolf, but wolves had vanished from England decades ago. The aftermath of a nuclear holocaust was unpredictable; who knew what monstrosities had arisen from the ashes? Maybe wolves were back? Mutated wolves? Starving wolves? Starving zombie wolves? Which was worse? Zale or a pack of ravenous, undead predators? I couldn't make up my mind.

I sat, rifle cradled on my lap, eyes fixed on the shifting shadows, ears attuned to the faintest sounds of the night. Every snap of a twig sent shivers down my spine, as if the forest itself was alive, watching, waiting. The night stretched on, and the darkness seemed endless, filled with unseen threats.

"WAKE UP, SLEEPYHEAD." Una's voice sliced through my dreams, pulling me back to reality.

I jolted upright, squinting against the assault of daylight. Still half-immersed in the remnants of my dream world, I clung to the rifle.

"Some night guard you made." Una laughed.

I rubbed sleep from my eyes and struggled to my feet. The campsite looked different in the unforgiving light of day. Our tent clung to the side of a gentle slope, the world beyond obscured by a thick curtain of trees and a heavy layer of mist. The lake stretched out, a boundless span of water which disappeared into the thickening fog. Docks protruded like skeletal fingers, and small sailboats bobbed lazily in the morning breeze, their tattered sails billowing like ghosts against the horizon.

"I'm so sorry I fell asleep..." My words trailed off, my mind conjuring horrifying possibilities of what could have happened while I selfishly slept. "It won't happen again."

"Relax, dude," Ember said. "I'm pretty sure your snoring scared away any potential threats."

"I don't snore—"

"You needed sleep," Una added.

"Still," I said, my grip tightening on the rifle. "If anything had happened..."

Una stood on tiptoes and placed a hand on my shoulder. "Do you need a morning spliff?"

I chuckled. "Are you trying to turn me into an addict?"

Una smiled, shook her head. "It's good to see you laugh."

"Feels good too," I admitted.

"What's with all the containers?" Ember nudged the one filled with earth with the tip of his boot.

"They contain the elements needed for Eudora."

"We have them all?" Una asked.

"As long as she accepts you and me as a representative of soul and ice," I replied.

Una crossed fingers on both hands. "Let's hope."

After a quick breakfast, we packed the tent and approached the lake, the jars representing the elements in our arms. I carried the rifle on a strap across my shoulder. I wasn't taking any chances.

Placing the jars on the sandy beach, Ember kindled the

hurricane lantern, using its glow to symbolize fire. I retrieved a crumpled piece of paper from my pocket and passed it to Una and Ember. Together, we read the incantation, Ember's voice gusting with tiny sparks, Una's tone melodious and tuneful.

The incantation floated across the lake, carrying our intentions to the depths where Eudora slumbered. Would she heed our call, or would our words be lost in the vast expanse of the supernatural?

"Oh, Lady of the waters clear,
With grace and wisdom, draw near,
From depths unknown, your presence wake,
A gentle request, we humbly make.
With reverence true and heart sincere,
We ask you, Lady, now appear,
To share your wisdom, ancient, grand,
And guide us with your steady hand."

I shoved the paper back in my pocket and waited. And waited. The fog closed in around us, its icy fingers clutching the back of my neck and permeating my skin. The seconds turned to minutes. Time stretched on. The weak winter sun was a blur of light in the gray sky.

"Maybe we should read it again," Una said.

We read the incantation once more. My nerves pulsed, and I clenched my fists, trying to keep my composure. How long would we have to wait?

"What if she's been summoned to a lake on the other side of the world?" Una asked.

"England is her home," I replied. "That's why we came here."

"Something's happening." Ember pointed to the middle of the lake where a small whirlpool formed.

My heart raced as the whirlpool grew, its powerful presence creeping closer to the shore, to us. And then, with an otherworldly light, a figure emerged from the water, casting a saintly glow over us and the churning waters.

A golden-haired head rose above the surface, adorned with an elaborate do, skin glowing with ethereal luminance, and lips the color of a rose. Depthless blue eyes locked onto each of us, scrutinizing our every detail. The figure, draped in an elegant dress of icy whites and ocean blues, sent shivers down my spine.

"She's beautiful," Una whispered.

Ember's mouth hung open. A twist of nerves tightened my stomach.

Eudora floated above the water a few feet away, her presence both enchanting and unnerving. She spent a full minute scanning each of us, during which I had to clench my jaw to prevent my nerves from showing.

"Eudora—"

She raised her hand, silencing me, her scrutiny unwavering as she examined the plastic containers by our feet. Finally, she lowered her hand and inquired, "What brings you to the shores of my lake?"

Feeling it was the only appropriate response, I kneeled, and Una and Ember immediately followed suit. "I seek your guidance and your wisdom."

A small smile graced Eudora's painted lips. "I see you

have brought the elements. Fire. Air. Earth. Water from my own lake." She turned her gaze to Una. "Spirit and soul." Then, her eyes shifted to me. "Snow and Ice. You have done well. But what of your gift?"

The offering my grandfather had spoken of. I'd forgotten all about it. "Are the elements not enough?"

"Knowledge is not free," Eudora replied, her tone as cool as the waters surrounding us.

"Please," Una said. "It's taken us so long to travel here. We've been through so much. We can't turn back now."

A memory surfaced. I glanced at Una's bag, recalling something she'd said when I'd first found her hiding on my boat.

"We do have a gift." I stood, went to retrieve Una's bag, and thew it on the sand at my feet. "The Power of the Sea."

"No!" Una leaped on the bag. "We can't give away the Power of the Sea. We might need it. To defeat Zale. Or if one of us is mortally wounded."

I pulled Una to her feet and cupped her face in my hands. "We only need the trident to defeat Zale. And we have all been near death. We can face it again, if need be."

She chewed on her lip, her eyes searching my face. Then finally, she nodded.

"The Power of the Sea," Eudora said. "A generous offer."

Una removed a box from her backpack, then opened the lid. A small sphere of the Power of the Sea floated out of the box, its mesmerizing striations of blues whirring with magical properties.

Eudora's eyes brightened, and she extended her palm. The orb began to drift in her direction.

"Wait!" Ember called, halting the orb in its flow. "You haven't given us what we want yet."

"Very well," Eudora said, the orb hovering between us. "What is it you wish to know?"

I stepped forward. "I'd like to know how to find Vorago's trident."

Eudora fixed her blue-eyed gaze on me.

"In Galapagos' depths where waters gleam,
Beneath the ocean's vast, cerulean dream,
A cave lies hidden, where Vorago's trident rests,
Guarded by seawolves, fierce, in ocean's crests.

To tame these beasts of the wild sea,
An ice flute you must seek, with urgency,
From Iceland's glacier, where frosty breezes sing,
Crafted by the Guardian of Snow and Ice, the winter king.

Once in your hands, the flute of icy breath,
Play the tune, weave the spell, and challenge death,
The seawolves, entranced, by melodies so deep,
Shall slumber soundly in their watery keep.

Then to the merman, trident in hand,
Gift from the ocean, a noble strand.
Vorago's power, now yours to wield,
In this enchanted, watery field."

"Why does everything have to be a riddle?" Una said, both hands raking through her blonde hair.

"We'll figure it out," I whispered, as Eudora repeated the directions twice more. Her words echoed in my ears. I struggled to jot down her cryptic instructions, my pencil racing to keep up with her rapid speech.

"And if there are no other questions." Eudora flicked her wrist at the Power of the Sea and it sailed into her palm.

"Wait!" Ember said. "If you don't mind, Lady Eudora, I do have a question."

"Yes? What is it?" she said, with a trace of impatience.

Ember stepped forward, feet resting in the water, hand over his chest. "I'd like to know why I can't breathe fire."

A faint smile flickered over Eudora's lips. "You have all the necessary elements to succeed in your endeavor." Without another word, she sank beneath the surface.

Ember kicked the ground, causing sand and dust to drift into the air. "What the hell does that mean?"

Una patted his shoulder. "I think it means you're capable of it, so you need to figure out why it's not working."

"It's psychological," I said. "Or too much weed."

Ember glared at me, his nostrils flaring.

"What?" I splayed both hands. "Just saying."

"Maybe we both need therapy," Ember muttered.

"Not a bad idea," Una said. "And where the hell are the Galapagos anyway?"

Ember snorted, a few fiery sparks escaping his nostrils. "Far, far away."

"Great." It was my turn to kick the ground. "How far, *exactly*?"

CHAPTER TWELVE

The rain pounded on our hoods as we picked a path through the decaying remnants of the English countryside. With every step, I couldn't shake the feeling of unseen eyes boring into the back of my skull. I clenched my hands around the rifle, the metal cold and unforgiving in my grip.

Thunder echoed in the distance, a low, menacing growl which shook the earth under our feet. Lightning streaked across the sky, illuminating the desolation in stark, fleeting flashes. We retraced our steps through the minefield of dead bodies, keeping our gazes averted. I kept mine trained on the horizon, glancing back every few seconds to see if whatever was following us had materialized.

"You're freaking me out," Una said, when I glanced behind us for the hundredth time.

"I can't shake the feeling we're being followed," I confessed, my voice barely audible above the drumming rain.

"There's definitely something out there," Ember said, his usually dilated eyes sharp and focused.

I glanced over my shoulder, scanning the murky distance behind us. "We can't afford to underestimate whatever's following us."

Una halted, turned in a slow circle, wiped the dripping rain from her cheeks. "We should take shelter for a while. Babette won't be at the marina until tomorrow night at the earliest."

"We could find an abandoned house," Ember said. "Maybe build a fire and catch some z's?"

The thought of collapsing onto a soft mattress and surrendering to sleep was tantalizing. I'd only grabbed a couple of hours' sleep last night and that was after a twenty-mile hike. Every muscle in my body throbbed, blisters covered my toes, and despite the waterproof clothing I wore, rain had found its way inside. "I'm in. Next town or village we come across; we'll look for suitable shelter."

It was another two hours before we reached Cleator Moor, a sizable village with a main road leading through the heart of it. Abandoned cars, like metallic corpses, lined the streets. Bodies lay strewn across the sidewalks, their lifeless eyes staring vacantly into the void. Trash swirled in the air, bringing with it the stench of decay.

We continued along the deserted roads, our footsteps muffled by the layer of wet leaves and debris. Unease settled in the pit of my stomach like a heavy stone, and I couldn't shake the feeling we were walking straight into a nightmare.

As we approached a row of houses, Una peered through a grimy window, her breath fogging the glass. Wiping away a circle of dirt, she cupped her hands around her head to see better, then quickly pulled away, her cheeks tight, her lips pressed into a grim line. "Not this one."

We continued our journey down the main street, passing an elementary school which had been transformed into a nightmarish tableau. The playground was now a mass grave, tiny bodies piled upon each other in a gruesome display. Bile surged up my throat and I turned away. The image of the kids like that...I shuddered, but I knew I'd never forget.

"We should go deeper into the residential area," Ember said. "We might find something a bit...emptier...away from the shops."

Emptier. Equaled: *no dead bodies*.

We turned the corner, our senses heightened to a razor's edge, when a primal, guttural growl shredded the air. Abandoning the hiking stick, I swung my rifle toward the source of the sound, my finger tightening on the trigger.

"Gal?" Una whispered beside me. "What is it?"

"I don't know yet," I replied, narrowing my eyes as I peered into the gloom. "Find a house. Get to safety."

"What about you?" Ember asked.

"Right behind you," I replied. We were not alone in this forsaken place, and whatever hunted us was as merciless as the fog surrounding us.

Una and Ember moved away, their figures becoming mere shadows in the gloom. I took slow steps backward. Rain pounded on my head, on my shoulders, on the gun. It was all I could hear. That and my own thundering pulse.

Another growl. A different direction. I pivoted, fingers

trembling on the trigger of my gun, eyes scanning the obscured surroundings.

Shattering glass at my back. A quick glance over my shoulder revealed Una and Ember crawling through a broken window. I turned back to the street. Too late.

An indistinct form hurtled toward me, a monstrous amalgamation of fur, fangs, and fury. Was it a deranged dog, a savage wolf, or some grotesque feline aberration? It didn't matter; all that registered was the snarling, hissing beast closing in, its eyes aflame with an unnatural glint.

Inhaling sharply, I held my breath, braced myself, and pulled the trigger. The gun roared, its recoil jolting my body, mingling with the chorus of aches and bruises I'd already acquired. The creature exploded, painting the surroundings in a macabre tapestry of limbs and blood. But there was no time to celebrate. Five more creatures emerged, blocking the street's entrance, while the echo of growls behind me indicated more closing in from the rear.

"Gal!" Una shouted through the broken window.

The beasts pawed the wet ground. They advanced with calculated menace, inching closer. It was a matter of seconds before they launched a uniformed attack.

"Gal!" Una screamed.

I spun around to find another creature mere feet away, poised to pounce. I ducked under it as it sailed through the air, dashed toward the house where Una and Ember sheltered, and dove through the shattered window, one of the creatures snapping at my feet.

Three of them made it inside. I rolled to my feet, raising the gun once more, blinking the rain out of my eyes. The beasts cornered us at the foot of the staircase, their growls vibrating through the air, their breath thicker than death. Slowly, we mounted the stairs until we came to a small landing, the creatures halfway up.

Una opened a door on her left. A bedroom. Bed made. Dusty smell. No dead bodies.

"On three," Ember said.

"One," I murmured, my throat dry.

"Two," Una added, her voice a shaky whisper.

"Three," we breathed in unison.

We lunged into the room, slamming the door shut behind us as the creatures pounced, their frustrated growls rumbling beneath the door's narrow gap. The room enveloped us in darkness, broken only by the feeble light filtering through the filthy windows.

I leaned against the door, keeping it closed, while Ember and Una wrestled a chest of drawers across the moldy carpet from the other side of the room. With a final push, it wedged against the door, and I let go. The creatures continued to throw themselves at the other side of the door, cracking the frame, clawing at the wood. Ember drew the drapes across the windows, but we had nothing to barricade them with if the beasts figured out how to climb.

While I held my breath, listening to the continued attack on the door, Una laced her fingers through mine, gave me a fearful look.

Ember rejoined us, pointed at my leg. "You're bleeding."

I glanced down, realizing my trousers were torn, blood seeping from shallow wounds. Una dropped her bag, falling to her knees to examine the injury.

"Did they get you?" Una asked.

A deafening crash resounded as the creatures pounded on the door, followed by a snarl, then silence. Had they given up?

"I'm not sure," I said. "Could have been the broken glass when I leaped through the window." Either way, an infection was likely.

The next ten minutes crawled by in tense silence. Una guided me to the edge of the bed, urging me to sit. I placed the rifle on the rumpled sheets, its presence offering a thin veil of reassurance.

Una rooted through her pack, retrieving a first aid kit. After cleansing my wound, she bandaged the cut and shoved a couple of antibiotics into my mouth. "We can't afford you getting an infection."

As she tightened the straps on her bag, I put a hand on hers. "Thanks, Una."

She smiled at me, but it didn't quite reach her eyes. "Can't have you dying on us before we get the trident."

Ember peered through a crack in the curtains. "Well, this is one way to spice up a vacation. Who needs a beach when you can have mutant animals as neighbors?"

"I guess we're stuck here until morning," I said. "No way I want to face those...*things*...when it's dark."

"What were they?" Una shrugged out of her dripping jacket, hung it on the open door of a closet.

"Some kind of mutated, radioactive dog, or something," I muttered, my fingers tracing the gash on my leg. I couldn't remember if any of the creatures had gotten that close to me.

Darkness came quick, shrouding the village in an inky

blackness. With no electricity in sight, our only source of illumination was the faint glimmer of the moon struggling to penetrate the thick fog. Una lit the hurricane lantern, then veiled it with a sheer scarf from the closet, which bathed the room in a warm, orange glow.

Ember handed out food packets. We added water from our flasks and waited for the chemical reaction to take place that would heat the food. Steak pie. It didn't taste so fancy barricaded in a room with ravenous zombie dogs outside waiting to tear me to bits.

We piled our empty packets in an old trashcan half filled with gray tissues, then listened to the sounds of the night. The groan of a floorboard, the muffled hoot of an owl, the sighing of the wind as it tunneled through the street. The distant growls of *them*.

"We might as well get comfortable," Ember said. We all stared at the double bed.

"One of us should keep watch," I said, lifting my rifle from the bed and moving to the window. "In case those things decide to launch another attack, or come through the window, or something."

Ember extended his hand, waiting for me to pass him the rifle. "I'll go first. You barely got any sleep last night."

I checked the chamber, loaded fresh cartridges to replace the ones I'd used, each metallic click bringing a measure of safety. "You sure?"

"I'm sure." Ember took the rifle and stood by the window, peering through the thin gap in the frayed curtains.

Una and I approached the bed.

"Which side do you sleep on at home?"

I tilted my head. "The middle."

She laughed, playfully slapped my stomach. "Typical."

"I can sleep on the floor."

"Don't be ridiculous," Una said. "It's just a bed."

The bed, with its crumpled sheets and sagging mattress, symbolized something far different. I hesitated, glancing at the worn carpet, its colors faded into obscurity, and the patches of mold lurking in the corners like dark secrets.

I tentatively approached the right side, my fingers grazing the soft fabric of the blanket. Una mirrored my movements on the left. After turning down the blanket, I sat on the edge and took off my boots. Una did the same on her side. I tucked my legs under the blanket, fully clothed. Una mimicked my actions. As we settled in, the space in the middle seemed to narrow. I dared to steal a glance at her. Una's eyes were fixed on the same small gap.

We lay on our backs, staring at the ceiling, our elbows touching. When I turned to look at her again, her eyes were closed. Ember remained by the window. It was weird trying to sleep when someone was standing at the foot of the bed, and there was another person in that bed. A member of the opposite sex. Someone I'd known all my life.

Time passed. The village slept. Ember remained at the window. Una's hair brushed the side of my cheek. Her breaths became deep and even. She groaned in her sleep, her head tilting toward me. The pale orange light from the lantern kissed her face, highlighting the curve of her lips and the gentle slope of her nose. In the hushed darkness, she shifted closer, her head finding a resting place on my shoulder, her arm draping across my hip.

My breath caught in my throat, my body tensing as she pressed against me. Her touch was a wildfire, setting my skin ablaze with a thousand unexpected sparks.

"Una," I whispered, my voice barely audible, a plea and a warning.

I tensed, waiting to see what else she would do. Her foot pressed against mine, a soft touch.

"Una," I whispered. "Move over."

But she didn't move. Instead, she curled herself around me, murmuring in her sleep. I watched her face by the glow of the lantern, the small frown puckering her forehead, the way her eyes moved under her lids, caught in a dream. Suddenly, she yelled and thrashed out, a rogue fist catching my jaw.

I held her head against my chest, shushed her until she relaxed. Calmer, she settled against me. Her hand drifted over my waist, under my T-shirt. I lay still, trapped in the web of her presence, feeling the weight of her body against mine, my mind whirring with scattered thoughts.

CHAPTER THIRTEEN

*E*mber led the way, a rusted lead pipe swinging from one arm, his wings tucked into his back. Then it was Una, her eyes shifting left and right so quickly I thought she'd developed a nervous tic. I took the rear position, the rifle gripped in two firm hands, spinning at any sudden noise.

We'd slept well into the early afternoon. Una and I had woken to find Ember snoring on the floor, wrapped in a threadbare blanket he'd scavenged from the closet. It had taken us half an hour to ensure the creatures weren't waiting for us in one of the rooms of the house. And when we couldn't delay any longer, had crawled through the broken window and stepped into the deserted street. Fog. Mist. Gray. The same as the day before. At least it had stopped raining. But the ground was three inches of sloppy puddles and squelchy mud, which slowed our pace. Two hours later, we'd yet to see a sign of the mutated dogs. But that didn't mean they weren't out there.

No one spoke much as we walked. The feel of Una's

head laying across my chest the previous night had left an impression, a warm spot that chased the chill away. I caught her eye once or twice, but neither of us mentioned how she'd woken still draped across me.

When I caught sight of water, I heaved a sigh of relief. The fog receded as we emerged from the dilapidated buildings hugging the coast, as if spitting us back into the world. The temperature rose a couple degrees, and here the sun was having a more successful battle with the clouds.

I spotted a bright red sail coming into dock, a lone figure on deck yanking at the mainsheet.

"Over here!" Una jumped and waved both arms above her head.

The boat tacked, changing its course, heading for the concrete dock where *The Albacore* had dropped us off.

Ember chucked his lead pipe onto the ground where it clanged against a forgotten hubcap and clattered into an overflowing drain. He cupped both hands around his mouth and called behind us, "Goodbye, Mutant Mutt Manor! I'll remember you every time I hear a howl in the distance."

I chuckled and clapped him on the back. Una rummaged in her bag, removed more antibiotics, and shoved the pills into my mouth.

"Thank you, Doctor Summers." I stole the flask from the side of her bag and took a large swig, washing the pills down. "Gotta say, I'm kind of glad you two are here." I hiked a thumb over my shoulder. "That got a little hairy back there."

"See." Una twirled to face me, a hand on her hip, a haughty smile on her lips. "We can be useful."

I was about to retort when her expression shifted, her

mouth falling open and color draining from her face. Her hand trembled as she pointed behind me.

"What is it?" I whispered, the hair on the back of my neck rising.

"They're back," she replied.

The air crackled with the promise of violence. Ember threw a glance over his shoulder, gave me the same terror-stricken look Una wore. Then the growls rumbled toward us, more than I could count. Keeping my eyes on the approaching red sail, I flicked the safety off the rifle.

"We need to run," Ember said.

"Babette is still a ways out," I said.

"Then we get to another boat," Una said, her eyes fixed behind me on the nightmare I couldn't yet see.

"Ember, can you fly Una over?" I asked.

He gave me a tight nod. "I can, but with the bags, it's going to take me a while to gain altitude."

"I'll hold them off as long as I can."

Una shook her head. "There's too many."

"We don't have a choice." I pushed the words through my thick throat.

"I'm not going to leave you here," Una said.

"Una, for once in your life, please listen to me."

She chewed on her lip, a habit which made her look so vulnerable. All I wanted to do was sweep her into my arms, when I didn't feel like strangling her, that was.

"Okay," she said, hooking her hands around the straps of her bag.

Ember released his wings, one inch at a time. Una crept

to his side. The growls behind me came in staccato bursts, punctuated by eerie silence.

When Ember wrapped his arms around Una and leaped into the air, I spun to face the creatures, loosening a wild shot as I turned. Something squealed. Maybe not so wild.

They charged at me, all of them, an army of fur and teeth and glowing eyes. Muscle and power and malicious intent. I squeezed the trigger, shot again, and again and again. There were only six bullets in the chamber. At least twenty creatures. I didn't have time to reload.

When the last bullet echoed in the air, shattering a creature's skull, I turned and sprinted for the docks. Ember and Una were already landing on the boat, still a few yards away from the dock.

Pumping my arms, I ignored the searing pain in my leg and the reopening of the wound, and sprinted along the tarmac path, streaked around the corner of a dock, leaped three feet to the concrete path below. The creatures were close behind me, yapping at my heels, attempting to get under my feet.

The boat was still three yards away. Ember and Una and Babette screamed my name, told me to hurry, told me to run.

Teeth gritted, I didn't dare glance back. Something sharp bit into my shoe. I swung my rifle blindly, connecting it with something that squealed and released its grip.

Two yards.

The boat was tantalizingly close, yet agonizingly far. Babette steered frantically, her hands working the sails. With a rush of adrenaline, I pushed myself forward, my pack secured to my shoulders, the rifle dangling from my hand. I reached the end of the dock, the beasts closing in from every side. With a final burst of energy, I leaped, sailing through the air. Babette yanked the mainsheet, the sails billowed, and the boat lurched forward. Everyone was yelling.

Ember hovered in the sky, his hand brushing under my arm, keeping me airborne as I jumped. Una screamed at me, tears in her eyes.

Finally, I landed on the deck, my body rolling into the cockpit, pain flaring as my knee struck wood. My momentum carried me forward. My head thumped against a seat, and at last, I came to a stop, covering my face and neck with my hands as snarling filled my ears.

The boat shot away. Una rushed to my side, pulled my hands away from my face. "You're okay, you're okay."

I looked up. The ravenous pack of dogs lined the concrete dock. A couple floated in the water, swimming after the boat. But none had made it on board. I lay back on the deck, stared at the sky, sweating, heart pounding, grateful to be alive.

I lay sprawled on the deck for a good ten minutes, watching the turbulent gray clouds race across the sky, waiting for my heart rate to slow. Una spoke to me the entire time, whispering reassurances, telling me I was brave, but I couldn't focus on her words. A sharp sting as she cleaned and redressed my wound.

Ember waved a hand in front of my face, maybe to see if I'd floated off to another world.

"Take the wheel." Babette's voice. Shuffling noises on deck. The sails flapped. The boat lurched.

She leaned over me, hauled me to my feet, pushed me

into a chair. She was stronger than she looked. "Can't have you leaking blood all over my polished deck."

"Sorry," I muttered automatically.

She scanned my face. "You met the muttwalkers."

"The *what*?" I looked at her face, couldn't focus.

"The muttwalkers," she repeated. "At least that's what I call them." She clicked her fingers in front of my eyes. I flinched. "You're going to be okay, big guy. A little dose of shock. Una, there's chocolate below deck, can you grab some?"

Scurrying footsteps. Banging cupboards. Whispered assurances. Sweetness in my mouth.

Una sat beside me, her arm around my shoulder even though she had to stretch. "Gal? Are you okay?"

"He'll be fine." Babette's voice became more distant as she took over the helm once more.

Ember came into view. "That was some acrobatics you pulled off there."

"Thanks. I think."

"It's all that training with Ford," Una said. "Your instincts are finely tuned."

"Maybe," I said, the sweetness of the chocolate making my jaw ache. But it was bringing me around. Slowly, I became aware of my surroundings. My friends huddled around me, the brightness of the red sail, the sun peeking through the clouds, the caress of a salty wind against my cheeks. "It's good to be back on water."

Babette chuckled. "I need a heading."

"Iceland," I said, accepting another square of chocolate from Una.

Babette nodded. "I know people there."

"There are people? Alive? Not like, peoplewalkers, or something?" Una asked.

"There are more people alive than you'd think," Babette replied, jamming coordinates into her console. "Civilized too."

"Do they grow weed?" Ember asked. "I'm running low."

Babette laughed. "'Fraid not. But they have their own way of relaxing."

"As long as it's not going from sauna to ice bath..." Una muttered. "I hate the cold."

"I love the cold," I said.

"Of course you do, Mr. Snow and Ice," Una said.

"Okay, okay, Miss Spirit and Soul," I retorted.

"Mine has a much nicer ring to it."

"I actually agree with you."

We sailed out of the marina, a strong wind aiding our speed. I was thankful to leave England and the muttwalkers behind, even though I knew there would be more terrifying obstacles ahead. Slowly, I took in my surroundings, the polished decks, the gleaming chrome. Babette took pride in her boat.

"So what's the news on Atlantis?" Babette asked, her eyes on the horizon. Did she want to know about Atlantis, or was it a subtle way of inquiring about Uncle Dylan? The two of them had been together for years, but since Babette had left the island over a decade ago, relinquishing her guardianship of the Power of the Sea, they'd only seen each other a handful of times.

"Uncle D is still running the bar," I said.

"Of course he is," Babette said, a wistful smile tugging at her lips.

Ember waved a hand in front of her face. "I have a marijuana farm in the mountains."

Babette's smile widened. "Of course you do."

"He's not seeing anyone else," I added.

Babette glanced at me, her eyes perhaps searching for the words I hadn't spoken. "He should. He deserves it."

"What about you?" I asked. "Are you happy?"

Babette shrugged. "I find that question rather trite, to be honest. No offense. Happiness is something we want our children to be. Happiness is what we strive for before we grow up and know better. Happiness doesn't really come after nuclear wars. But to answer your question, I am content. And yes, there are times when I am happy. And to turn the question back on you, what about you, are you happy?"

"No, but I will be." When I kill Zale.

"Gal destroyed *The Mermaid Chronicles*," Una said.

Babette raised an eyebrow. "Bet that went down like a lead balloon. What happened?"

"I didn't stick around long enough to find out."

"But why did you do it?" she asked.

"I'm tired of living my life chained to prophecies," I replied, screwing up the chocolate wrapper. "Never knowing when the next prediction of doom is going to fall."

Babette shook her head. "I wouldn't want to be in your shoes right now."

I looked at my boots, splattered with blood and leaves and dirt and God knew what else. Puncture marks in the heel of one. "Not sure I want to be in them either."

"So why Iceland?" Babette asked.

"That's where Eudora has sent us," Ember said.

"The Lady of the Lake?" Babette asked.

"That's the one," Una said. "Have you met her?"

Babette shook her head. "I try not to venture too far inland when there are muttwalkers about."

I removed the rumpled piece of paper from my pocket, thankful it was still intact, and read the instructions to Babette.

"In Galapagos' depths where waters gleam,
Beneath the ocean's vast, cerulean dream,
A cave lies hidden, where Vorago's trident rests,
Guarded by seawolves, fierce, in ocean's crests.

To tame these beasts of the wild sea,
An ice flute you must seek, with urgency,
From Iceland's glacier, where frosty breezes sing,
Crafted by the Guardian of Snow and Ice, the winter king.

Once in your hands, the flute of icy breath,
Play the tune, weave the spell, and challenge death,
The seawolves, entranced, by melodies so deep,
Shall slumber soundly in their watery keep.

Then to the merman, trident in hand,
Gift from the ocean, a noble strand.
Vorago's power, now yours to wield,
In this enchanted, watery field."

"Cute," Babette said. "So you have to make a flute carved from ice."

"I guess," I said.

"And then travel to the Galapagos and use it to put the seawolves to sleep. You've seen that rug in your uncle's bar, right?"

"Oh shit," Ember said. "*That's* a seawolf?"

"Ugly son of a bitch," Una said.

My mind raced back to the enormous skin which lay strewn in front of the hearth in Uncle Dylan's bar. Dark matted fur, massive, clawed paws, an enormous snout lined with two rows of razor-sharp teeth, and penetrating yellow eyes. Granted, the eyes had been replaced with glass, but still. When I was little, I used to poke it with a stick, stabbing the wood into the seawolf's gaping mouth, imagining my stick was a sword and I was as powerful as Ford. Never did I think I'd have to face one in reality. Everyone said they were extinct. But then, everyone said Vorago's trident was just a myth too.

"You know their history, right?" Babette eyed us all carefully. We shook our heads. "I read about them in *The Mermaid Chronicles*. Way back when Vorago was still around, he caught wind of a coo. The Denizens of the Deep were after his weapon. So Vorago summoned a pack of ordinary wolves he'd helped in a previous battle, their loyalty eternally bound, and transformed them into formidable seawolves. They promised to guard the trident until his return, never letting another soul take it from under their watchful eye."

Ember's eyes grew wider than his wings. "Do you know how many there are?"

Babette shook her head. "The book didn't say."

"They can't be worse than the muttwalkers...can they?" Una asked.

"Oh, I'd say, five times the size at least." Babette portrayed a widening gap between her hands. "So...yeah... what's your plan?"

I gulped. "Working on it."

She patted my shoulder. "Okay, let's say you put the seawolves to sleep, then you get the trident—that's what you're after, right? Then what?"

"Then I kill Zale," I said.

Babette whistled, long and low, the sound competing with the buffeting wind.

"I *will* kill Zale," I said.

Babette gave me a once over, as if assessing my size and strength. "I guess with the trident, anything is possible."

A cold sweat broke out on my skin, and I turned my head away from her scrutinizing eyes. The closer we got to my ultimate goal, the more intense the fear became. Turning back was never an option, but I couldn't deny how terrified Zale made me feel.

I swallowed, working moisture into my throat, looked back at Babette. "You don't think I can do it?"

"I think anyone can do anything with the right tools and support."

Una smiled. "We got your back."

I could barely acknowledge her words. I was lost in morbid thoughts of Una and Ember dying at the hands of

Zale, trapped in his jaws like my mother had been. All because of me.

Ember grinned. "And your butt and your head and your arms and your legs—"

"Stop!" Una covered Ember's mouth with her hand. "I don't want to know what other parts you've got."

Laughing, Ember pivoted away from her. "But you get my point. We've got this."

I forced a smile, nodded, and caught Babette's wary eyes. "Yep, we do. We got this."

Babette yanked on the mainsheet and the boom tracked across the boat. We turned into the wind and sped across the water. "Don't you go into it half-cocked. Make sure you're prepared. And listen to your friends."

"Yes, *Mom*." The words burst out of me before I could stop them. I cringed. Una winced. Babette paled.

"Your mother was pretty special," Babette said.

"You hated my mother."

She shook her head, a faint smile touching her lips. "We were more alike than either of us cared to admit. Stubborn. Strong. Opinionated. Both of us believing we knew the right path. Both of us pushing our views onto everyone else. I miss her."

"I miss her too."

CHAPTER FOURTEEN

*A*fter breakfast the next morning, the four of us sat in the cockpit, the wind steady, the water clear, the sun shining above our heads. Babette put the helm on autopilot and slathered sunblock on her face and hands.

"How long until we get there?" I asked, scanning the horizon for a hint of land.

"Patience, Little Jackass," Babette replied.

I turned in my seat to face her. "Excuse me? What did you call me?"

"A jackass." She chuckled. "It's from a story my father used to tell me on long road trips. You know, that whole classic 'are we nearly there yet?' He never gave me a time or distance, just told me the story about Little Jackass."

"I still have no idea what you're talking about," I said.

"How does the story go?" Una asked.

Babette opened her flask of water, took a long swallow, then recapped the lid. "The story revolves around a daring journey to visit family taken by a daddy jackass and his adventurous little jackass. They cross wild rivers, climb towering mountains, and explore mysterious caves. And every time the little jackass asks, 'When will we arrive?' the father responds, 'Be patient, Little Jackass.' So when we used to go on these long car trips and I'd ask my dad if we were nearly there yet, he'd tell me this story. First time for over an hour, making a ton of obstacles for the jackasses to deal with. It was when they crossed the same river three times that I finally piped up and said, 'Dad, what's going on? Why aren't they at their destination?' and my dad turned around to me and said—"

"Be patient, Little Jackass," I muttered.

Una and Ember burst out laughing.

"Exactly," Babette said with a grin on her face. "It's a lesson in patience and perseverance, you see."

"And yet, it doesn't answer my question," I said. "How long does it take to sail to Iceland?"

"At our current speed, and if the wind conditions remain in our favor, I'd say another four days," Babette replied. "Which is just enough time for that wound on your leg to heal and to finish that course of antibiotics. You don't want to go climbing glaciers with an injury."

"Yes, ma'am." I leaned back in my seat, crossed my legs, watched the blue water meet the blue sky, but I couldn't sit still. I tapped my foot, drummed my fingers, anything to quell the urgency burning within me. I even resorted to committing Eudora's instructions to memory.

"You okay?" Una asked me.

"I just want to get on with it. Carve the flute. Get the trident. Kill Zale."

"There's no rush to face death, prince. It comes sooner than you expect," Babette said.

Restless, I stood. "I don't want to lose my nerve. I need to act while I've still got it in me."

"Relax," Babette said, lifting her face toward the sun. "Your courage will be there when you need it."

I frowned at her so hard she opened her eyes and looked at me. "Do you still see the prophecies?"

Celestial Abyss...

Vorago's Trident...

Parting the sea...

I couldn't shake the words of the prophecy, which swirled in my mind like ethereal whispers. The fragments haunted me, their meanings elusive as shadows.

"Nope," she replied. "Thank God. But if you're anything like either of your parents, cowardice is not your problem."

"Thanks. I think." With the sun shining, the water sparkling, and the muttwalkers miles behind us, it was easy to be brave. But bravery was a fragile cloak which could be torn away by the winds of doubt.

"I read some of it," Una said quietly. "The forming prophecy before you destroyed the book..."

"I still don't want to know," I said. "But thanks."

She nodded, gave me a thin-lipped smile. "If you're sure."

I sighed. "*Celestial Abyss...Vorago's Trident...Parting the sea...*Those are the words I caught before I burned the book. I have no idea what they mean."

"That's what I saw too," Una said. "It's clear you're meant to find the trident."

"No, it's not," I said. "It doesn't say anything about me. It speaks of the trident, not the one destined to wield it."

Una arched a brow, the gesture tightening the fading scar on her forehead. "We might know more if you hadn't burned the book."

Before I could retort, Ember stepped in with his own thoughts. "I reckon *Celestial Abyss* refers to your mother... what motivated you to seek revenge."

"Parting the water, eh, prince?" Babette said. "That sounds rather Moses-like."

The words had clawed at my mind in a constant loop for the better part of five weeks, and yet I hadn't spent time contemplating their meaning, only pushed them away. Ember's thoughts struck a chord, but we only had half a prophecy and there was no way we could interpret it with any accuracy, unless...unless Una, destined to be the book's oracle, already had an affinity for the language.

"The trident is your destiny," Una said. "It has to be. You're a prince. Just like King Arthur. It has to be you."

"Let's not get ahead of ourselves. You're a future oracle, Ember is the last dragon king...for now. It could refer to either of you."

"No way, dude." Ember shook his head. "The prophecies started forming before Una and I knew you were planning to leave. It's you."

"Or maybe it's me." Babette winked. "God, I hope it's not me. I'm done with all that crap."

"I thought I was too."

"So how come you can read it?" Babette asked.

"Read what?" I replied.

"*The Mermaid Chronicles*. Unless I'm mistaken, I thought only High Council members could read it."

I splayed both hands. "I've been wondering the same thing."

Ember's thick eyebrows shot over his head.

Una stood, a knowing smile on her face. "Because you were supposed to. Because it was meant for you."

I searched her eyes for hidden meaning. "Is that what you think? Or what you know?"

"I don't know what the difference is," she replied. "It's what I feel."

"Oh, boy," Babette said. "Here we go again."

My stomach churned. Burning *The Mermaid Chronicles* had been an act of defiance, an attempt to wrench control from the hands of Fate. Yet, here I stood, a pawn in some cosmic game. I had embarked on this mission willingly, yet the narrative had been penned long before my first step. But I would not succumb to the cold grip of predestination. I would forge my own path, heedless of the half-formed prophecy.

And I would kill Zale.

For two hours, I paced the deck, batting away Una's and Ember's suggestions, insisting the prophecy was not about me. I don't know why I bothered. My destiny was clearly written in that damn book, I just didn't want to face it, I didn't want to admit that no matter what decision I made, I would end up in the same place. Facing Zale, most likely. Which was what I wanted, so why did it matter what the stupid book said?

"You need to get off that leg," Una said as she shook two

more pills into my hand. "Or you're going to open the wound again."

With a reluctant sigh, I tossed back the pills and washed them down with a gulp of lukewarm water. My leg throbbed like a drumbeat. "I'm going stir crazy. When I'm on the water, I want to be on land, and when I'm on land, I'm being chased by mutated dogs..." I fisted my hands, released them, fisted them again.

"I have valium if you think that will help," Babette said.

"What's valium?" I asked.

"It'll chill you out, make you sleepy, make you not care about much for a few hours," she replied.

Ember grinned. "Cool. Maybe I can grind it and add it to the weed."

Ignoring Ember, I shook my head. "I want to keep my wits about me."

"There's nothing out here to worry about." Una placed a hand on my arm, but her gentle touch may as well have been a scalding iron. I was so wound up, I flinched.

"*Zale* is out here. Somewhere."

Babette chuckled. "You think Zale gives a shit about you? He's a megalodon. You're a waste of his time."

My ears burned, as well as my cheeks. "I don't think he'll stop until he's killed my entire family."

"It's been twelve years," Babette said. "He hasn't made a single attempt...unless I'm wrong? Has something happened?"

"No," I exhaled the word with more force than I'd intended. "That we know of."

"Perhaps you're overestimating your importance,"

Babette said as she turned the wheel. "Zale only wanted your mother. He's done."

Una shook her head. "Zale will never be done."

I was grateful for her support and some of the warmth left my cheeks.

"Maybe, maybe not." Babette pursed her lips.

"If there's one thing I know about Zale," I said. "It's how patient he is."

"The overgrown excuse for a fish is probably more interested in the trident," Ember said. It was a thought I hadn't considered before. Seeing as Zale was the size of a megalodon and had all the power he needed granted to him by the Denizens of the Deep—who the hell were they, by the way?—what would he want with Vorago's trident? "If he knows you're after him, and he knows the trident can kill him, he's not going to let you take it."

A cloud blotted out the sun and a cold wind swept in from the north.

"See? He's out there." I swirled a hand at the water.

"I guess I better get you to Iceland ASAP then." Babette worked the sails and the boat lurched in a new direction.

During the next three days, the temperature dropped, and on our final day, ice appeared in the water. The sky, a canvas of muted purples and blues, bore witness to our journey as we sailed toward the heart of the Arctic cold. The biting chill gnawed at our bones and our breath hung in the air like spectral mist. Each nautical mile we sped ushered in a deeper cold, until the essence of winter clung to our souls.

Bundled in fleeces, we huddled below deck, seeking refuge from the numbing wind. The ship creaked and groaned, mirroring the sounds of the icy expanse surrounding us. It was during these endless hours, with the haunting melody of the frozen sea as our backdrop, that I contemplated Eudora's instructions. It was clear as the guardian of the orb of Snow and Ice it was up to me to carve the ice flute, but the details of how to go about that remained frustratingly elusive. No matter how many times I scanned the words, the ambiguous instructions didn't become any clearer.

From Iceland's glacier, where frosty breezes sing,
Crafted by the Guardian of Snow and Ice, the winter king.
Once in your hands, the flute of icy breath,
Play the tune, weave the spell, and challenge death.

A flute was a flute, I assumed. I'd have to hope like hell once I found some ice, which was pretty plentiful in Iceland, that I could manage to carve it into a vague flute shape and make it produce something which resembled musical notes.

"Land ahoy!" Babette shouted.

I scrambled above deck, Ember close on my heels, to find Una yanking at the mainsheet and Babette guiding the boat toward an anchored dinghy. The shoreline loomed, a monochrome masterpiece of black sand and untouched snow, adorned with solitary houses buried beneath a blanket of white. Icy waves crested on a black beach. There wasn't a soul in sight.

"Look at that," I murmured, captivated by the desolate beauty of the land.

"No muttwalkers here, right?" Una asked as we drew alongside the dinghy.

"No muttwalkers," Babette said. "But polar bear sightings are increasing. They ride the frozen currents and icebergs from Greenland and arrive here, hungry and desperate. So keep your eyes peeled."

Ember gulped. "Noted."

"What are you worried about?" Babette asked. "You can fly away."

"Not when my wings are frozen, or wet," Ember replied.

Babette collapsed the sails, anchored the boat, threw a line into the dinghy, then jumped into the smaller vessel. "What are you waiting for?"

After collecting our belongings, we scrambled after her, clambering over the side of the boat and dropping the three feet into the dinghy.

Babette gunned the motor, and we shot toward the black and white shore. "There's a sports store nearby. You guys need winter gear. It hovers just under freezing during January. Lower at night."

The dinghy sliced through the waves. Spray clung to my cheeks, and snow drifted in the air, shrouding the sound of the motor. I couldn't help the smile forming as we sped closer to the beach. Despite the lack of color, despite the endless amount of snow, I loved everything I saw. I was the guardian of Snow and Ice, after all. I was made for this.

Babette guided the dinghy, steering us toward the obsidian beach. With a swift turn, she beached the boat, securing it to a massive granite boulder with practiced ease.

"So, this is Iceland." I raised my voice above the wind and turned in a slow circle. Every direction looked the same: black sand melded into gray rock contrasted against the pristine white of the snow. Distant yellow lights flickered from the windows of isolated houses, their glow barely penetrating the enveloping darkness. Sticking my tongue out, I caught snowflakes in my mouth. I'd never tasted anything so pure. The snow felt like my own personal Fountain of Youth. But of course, it didn't heal me. The wound in my thigh had improved remarkably, only a dull ache to remind me of the muttwalkers we had left behind.

Una stood beside me on the frozen beach. "You're up, big guy."

"I have no idea how to carve a flute," I said, kicking at the snow to reveal a layer of icy sand. "I spent years in the turret training with Ford. I can kick the shit out of someone, but I don't know how to *make* stuff."

"We'll help," Ember said. "Anything that involves rolling, I can do."

Despite his joke, I was glad of his company. And Una's. They'd made the journey more bearable, kept the fear at bay.

Babette led us up the beach, snow and sand clinging to my boots in equal measure. My boots left a trail of crisp footprints in the snow, which I found an unexpected childish glee in.

"You're like a kid at Christmas," Una laughed.

"I think that was the best Christmas I've had," I said. "On Grandpa's boat."

Una smiled. "It was pretty special. Especially when you sang Rudolph the Red-Nosed Reindeer."

"You are never to bring that up again!"

She mimed locking her lips and throwing away the key. "I

don't blame you, you really can't sing. Sounded more like a beached guppy gasping for air."

"Oi!" Laughing, I pushed her aside, then thought of the dream I'd had Christmas night. Of Una wearing nothing but a bikini and mistletoe. As if sensing my thoughts, she flushed. Was she remembering that night too? Or perhaps it was the cold bringing color to her cheeks.

Ember huffed as he walked, his fiery breaths melting the snow from his wings and turning the path to slush. "I *hate* the cold. Give me a summer meadow, a tropical island, a humid swamp even, but take me away from the freaking cold. Who wants to build a snowman? All they do is melt and lose their cute little carrot noses. And then no one wants to eat the carrots...what a waste!"

Una and I shared a look, the laughter back in her eyes. She nudged my side until her grin spread to my face.

Babette led us along a winding path, down a narrow road, and around a corner until we arrived at a clothing store. We spent half an hour kitting ourselves out with snow boots and warm waterproof clothing. Hats, gloves, balaclavas. Everything weighed a ton, and by the time we set off again I was sweating. I kept the rifle slung over my shoulder.

Una hurled a snowball at me, getting me square on the nose.

"Oh no, you don't." I ran after her, gathering snow from the top of a low fence, packing it tightly, then hurled it at her ass, scoring a direct it.

Her eyes flashed, and she rubbed her butt.

"I'm sorry!" I called.

But she wasn't hurt at all. She took advantage of my hesitation and hurled another snowball at my face.

"Oh, you little faker!" Pushing aside the dull ache in my thigh, I ran after her and poured snow down the back of her neck, ignoring her shrieks and pleas for mercy. No way was she going to win this snowball fight.

Memories flooded back. When we were little, just before the ghost pirates came. During the first snowfall Atlantis had witnessed, when the kids made an army of snowmen. She'd begged me to show her some of the moves I'd been learning with Ford. I'd helped her jump-kick a snowman, toppling its head to the ground, the carrot nose rolling away. It had been her birthday, and the smile on her face had been worth all the times she'd tried to hold my hand.

"I *hate* the snow," Ember grumbled. "And the cold. And the wind. And the rain. Did I mention I hate the snow?"

"You get used to it," Babette said.

Ember continued his long-winded complaints. "I could use a pair of those silver slippers, knock those heels together and take me back to my meadow...was that how they worked?"

"The Wizard of Oz?" Babette asked. "Not one of my favorites. And that was Kansas, not Atlantis. And there were no drugs. Unless you count the opium in the poppy fields." She slapped his back. "You may have a point."

Ember grinned with self-importance, pumped an arm in triumph, then asked, "Why couldn't it be a fire flute, or something?"

I threw a snowball at him. "Yeah...no." I turned to Babette. "At the risk of you calling me *Little Jackass* again, where are we going exactly?" I glanced at the houses we'd passed, all of them dark, but all of them welcoming.

"Twenty-minute walk. We don't stay in the village. Too many looters."

"Looters?" Una asked. "In Iceland?"

"A lot of people took to the sea to escape the aftermath of the war," Babette said. "They pop up here occasionally, looking for a place that had a low population to start with where they might find what they need. Some of them aren't so nice."

I followed her gaze, my eyes flicking over the spread of snow which stretched endlessly before us. It was a world of frozen silence broken only by the occasional howl of the wind, a mournful cry which echoed the desolation of the land.

Babette led us along a snow-cleared road, the crunch of our footsteps breaking the stillness. We arrived at a cul-de-sac of five houses, their darkened windows staring like empty eye sockets. The first thing I noticed were the skidoos parked in a line under a corrugated roof, their metal bodies gleaming dully in the muted light. Next were the dogs—twenty or so huskies fenced into a large snowy field, their breath forming clouds in the freezing air. Some of them nipped at each other, wrestling playfully, while others huddled together, seeking solace in the cold.

"No cars?" I asked.

Babette shook her head. "Roads are unreliable."

Atlantis had no cars, and I had harbored a secret hope I might get a chance to ride in one during this journey. Yet, all the cars I had seen so far were nothing but rusted skeletons.

As we neared one of the homes, the front door opened and a tall man wearing nothing but plaid stepped onto the small porch. He was a weathered man with eyes that held the wisdom of centuries. He nodded at Babette before his eyes flicked over the rest of us, his gaze sharp and assessing. Babette took a few minutes to explain our presence. Ember's wings were nowhere to be seen. Babette introduced him as Kristín.

"The Lady of the Lake?" Kristín raised his eyebrows, his tone laced with skepticism. "Thought that was just a legend."

"So did I," I said.

"You thought mermaids were mythical too," Babette reminded him.

"So I did." Kristín leaned against the door frame, clearly not ready to invite us in. "What are the instructions?"

I closed my eyes to remember the words. *"From Iceland's glacier, where frosty breezes sing. Crafted by the Guardian of Snow and Ice, the winter king. Once in your hands, the flute of icy breath. Play the tune, weave the spell, and challenge death."*

"You'll need to go to Mýrdalsjökull," he said.

I frowned. "What's that?"

"A glacier. It's where the wind whistles over the ice and plays its own song. Beautiful. And a little creepy." He gestured toward the steep hills where snow and ice glistened like a frozen kingdom under the winter sun. "She's talking about Mýrdalsjökull."

Una gave me a wary look.

My frown deepened. "I thought I could pluck an icicle from the roof and be done with it." I pointed at the porch overhang, the twenty or so icicles I'd have to duck under every time I went in and out. If Kristín ever invited us in.

Kristín placed both his hands over his stomach and laughed so hard he cried.

"Thanks a lot," I muttered.

Once Kristín had sobered, he addressed me once more. "It's twenty miles to the glacier. You're going to need a dog team. And keep in mind Mýrdalsjökull covers an active volcano, which hasn't erupted in fifteen years. It's overdue."

CHAPTER FIFTEEN

areful not to disturb Ember, I slipped out from
beneath my cocoon of blankets. The night had
grown chillier, the air biting as it snaked its way through the
cracks in the walls. I stuffed my feet into the thick slippers
Babette had insisted we grab from the store, glad of the insulation. Tiptoeing downstairs in the middle of the night, I
inched past the room Kristín shared with his wife, past where
Babette slept with her door ajar, a hand over her face, snoring
softly. She was bunking with Una, but I couldn't spot my
friend from my vantage point.

I winced as the stairs creaked, filling me with an inexplicable unease. I was only after a glass of water. No one would
mind that. At least, that was what I would say if anyone
caught me.

The staircase emerged into the central room in the house,
the living area. The wooden floor was strewn with thick rugs
and a heap of blankets lay piled on one of the comfortable
armchairs. The fire was still breathing, as if recently rebuilt. I

watched the flames for a minute or two, marveling at their primal beauty, wondering what it felt like to wield them as a power.

"Are you coming in, or are you just going to stand there?"

I nearly jumped out of my skin. I bent over, a hand over my heart. "Damn it, Una, you scared the crap out of me."

She gave me one of her impish grins and patted the couch beside her. I hadn't noticed her sitting in the dark, her hand wrapped around a mug of cooling coffee.

"Couldn't sleep?" she asked as I settled beside her.

I shook my head.

"Me neither."

We both watched the flames, their flickering shadows casting eerie shapes on the chimney breast.

Una drowned the rest of her coffee, grimaced. It was probably stone cold. "Gal?"

"Yeah?"

"I'm scared."

"Me too."

She nodded, a short sharp movement as if she were confirming a troubling suspicion. She reached for my hand, laced her fingers through mine, squeezed gently. "We've come so far."

"And we still have so far to go."

"How are we going to get to the Galapagos?"

"I don't know yet."

Another silence. She didn't let go of my hand. I didn't remove it. I didn't know what that meant.

"I'm glad you came," I said.

She looked at me, a question in her selachii eyes. "You are?"

I raked my free hand through my hair, teasing out the tangles. "I feel less alone."

"Is that all?"

"What do you mean?"

She searched my face. "Nothing. Don't worry about it."

"Una? What is it?"

A faint smile ghosted her lips. "A journey isn't only about distance."

I frowned, unsure what she was getting at. "Have I done something wrong?"

"No, of course not." She raised our joined hands, planted a friendly kiss on my knuckle. Companionable, like comrades in arms. Wasn't it?

I moved closer to her, put my arm around her shoulders. The action felt strange, but right somehow. We were in this together, we might as well draw strength from each other. "I won't let anything happen to you."

That smile again, as if she knew something she wasn't yet willing to share. "You can't promise that."

"Maybe not, but I will always protect you, Una. Always."

"I know." She curled into me, her head resting on my shoulder. It reminded me of the night we spent in England nestled against each other, her head on my chest. "You can talk to me, you know. About anything."

"Talking isn't really my thing."

"Considering the conversation we just had, I have to disagree."

I chuckled, brushing a stray lock of her spiky hair from

my face, traced the faint line of the scar on her forehead with my thumb. A squeeze of guilt. "Yeah, well, you bring it out in me."

"Gal?"

"Yeah?"

"Don't do anything stupid."

My uncle had said the same thing. "Define stupid."

She poked my thigh and we both laughed.

Una fell asleep with her head resting on my shoulder. Although I hadn't come down in the middle of the night to sit in the dark and watch the fire with her, I found myself unable to move. I no longer craved water, but something else I couldn't put my finger on.

While Una slept, I breathed in her scent. I'd never taken the time to notice how she smelled before. A mixture of snow and sunblock and whatever she used in her hair. Coconut, maybe. Whatever it was, it smelled kind of nice. I sat with her for an hour, delaying what I had come downstairs to do. As the fire dwindled to a mere flicker of embers, I slipped out from under her, tucking her in with a warm blanket. After rebuilding the fire so she wouldn't get cold without my presence, I searched the house for a flashlight, then went into the kitchen where I'd left my outdoor gear and suited up.

I spent a full five minutes analyzing a map Kristín had pinned to the kitchen wall. It detailed Iceland's five primary glaciers. Mýrdalsjökull, the nearest one, was still a daunting twenty miles away. The thought of trekking that distance on foot was less than appealing.

I braced myself as I crept out the back door into the biting cold. Dawn was a distant dream, and a persistent wind whipped through the snow-laden landscape. I considered the shed where the dogs were housed, pondering the possibilities of a sled, but I had no idea how to guide them, so quickly dismissed that idea. Instead, I trudged through the snow to the small hut housing the snowmobiles. I breathed a sigh of relief when I saw the keys were in the ignition. With a leap of faith, I swung my leg over the nearest snowmobile, confident the controls wouldn't be too different from the electric carts I'd used on Atlantis.

Gritting my teeth, I turned the key and the engine roared to life, cutting through the silent night. I kept my eyes trained on the house as I sped out of the hut, praying I hadn't woken anyone. Glaciers, polar bears, active volcanoes...there was no way I was putting my friends through that. I had just told Una I would protect her. This was my way of doing that. She was much safer in the house, away from all the dangers. It was up to me, and only me, to carve the flute.

I switched the headlights on and sliced a path through the fresh snow, tucking my chin into my balaclava and squinting against the swirling snowflakes. Visibility was limited. What with the dark and the snow shooting at me like spectral bullets. I tried to remember the route I'd devised when studying the map, but everything looked so different at night, with my heart pounding loud enough to attract a polar bear.

Turning the speed to max, I sped through the snow, the skis leaving a wild and uncharted trail behind. An exuberant grin stretched across my face, despite the solemn purpose of my journey. It had been years since I'd felt such unadulterated joy.

After ten thrilling minutes of maneuvering through a dense forest of aspens, the terrain became more treacherous, and the engine groaned in protest. I urged the skidoo on, whispering sweet nothings, coaxing her up the increasingly steep incline. Hill became mountain. Snow became ice. Cold became freezing. My teeth slammed together, and my eyebrow and nostril hair froze. Moisture from my breath stiffened on my balaclava, leaving my chin raw and chafed.

The skidoo careened across the icy expanse, clipping the side of a massive boulder, metal parts spiraling down the mountain. The engine complained.

A bruise of dawn streaked across the distance, casting a cerulean hue on the ice. I swerved around a menacing crevasse, glancing briefly at its unfathomable depth. I'd have to look out for those.

As the sun erupted over the horizon, casting a mythical radiance on the glimmering ice, I brought the skidoo to a shuddering halt. The machine was more battered and missing more parts than I'd initially noticed. Regret lodged in my throat. These snowmobiles might be all Kristín and his friends had to get around. I'd offer to repair it before I left.

I stood atop the ice-covered volcano, my senses attuned to any signs of movement in the rocks or the imminent eruption of molten fury or for a blizzard to attack my exposed position. But I saw nothing, sensed nothing, felt nothing but the thrill of adventure...and the cold. I loved snow and ice, but I was fucking freezing. Despite the gloves, my fingers stiffened into useless stumps.

From Iceland's glacier, where frosty breezes sing,

Crafted by the Guardian of Snow and Ice, the winter king.
Once in your hands, the flute of icy breath,
Play the tune, weave the spell, and challenge death.

The frigid wind howled past me, its icy fingers reaching for my woolen hat, slipping down my neck. But it did not sing, did not create music. It screamed and moaned, a brutal cacophony. The glacier sprawled over six hundred square miles. How the hell was I going to find the right patch of ice? While an active volcano bubbled beneath my feet? It could take years.

I sat in the snow, rested my elbows on my knees, and cradled my head. Why had I imagined I could disappear in the dead of night, journey to a remote glacier, and find the elusive ice without anyone noticing my absence? I cursed myself for not seeking Kristín's advice before setting off.

I scooped a handful of snow, fashioned a snowball, and hurled it toward the horizon. The sudden crack of ice behind me sent me leaping to my feet. Whirling around, I saw a gaping crevasse forming, threatening to split the land in two. A giant crack streaked down the mountain. With tension tingling in my limbs, I braced myself for an eternal drop, or a geyser of lava. But neither happened. The ice settled once more, revealing a deep gorge I had no intention of approaching.

Admitting defeat, I gathered some clumps of ice, hoping I'd somehow stumbled on the right area, and threw it into the saddle of the skidoo. I slipped a leg over the seat, started the engine, and sped back down the mountain. Halfway to civilization, the engine coughed and sputtered, eventually giving out. I cursed myself for not checking the gas tank.

I spent five minutes yelling at the snow and kicking the skidoo before I finally accepted I was going to have to walk down the mountain. With gritted teeth, I cradled the precious ice in my arms, its cold seeping through my gloves, making my fingers ache. The descent was treacherous, the path obscured by huge drifts of snow. My boots sank into the deep drifts, and every step was a battle against the elements. The wind howled like a vengeful spirit, whipping against my face, blurring my vision with a veil of white. I stumbled over unseen boulders, my muscles burning with effort, enduring the grueling temperatures.

When I finally staggered into view of the cabin, smoke curling lazily from its chimney, relief flooded through me. The warmth of the hearth beckoned like a siren's call. But my triumph was short-lived.

Babette stood in the doorway, a hand on her hip, a scowl on her face. "What the hell do you think you're doing?"

I took a deep breath, steeling myself for her wrath. "Looking for the ice."

She crossed her arms. "You know how big the glacier is, right?"

"Yeah."

Her voice lowered to a dangerous whisper. "You know it's filled with crevasses that mean certain death?"

"I do now."

"The volcano could erupt any day," she continued, her words hanging in the air like an ominous prophecy.

"Yeah..."

"You know there is a limited gas supply to fill those skidoos?"

I gulped.

"And where is that skidoo you stole, by the way?"

"Ran out of gas," I admitted, dropping the ice at her feet, my arms finally giving in to exhaustion.

"You found the ice?" she asked, her tone softening.

I shrugged, my frustration bubbling to the surface. "I didn't hear any frosty breezes singing, so I'm thinking *no*. But I didn't want to come back empty-handed."

"You're an idiot." Babette grabbed me by my collar and yanked me inside the house. "You have a lot of apologizing to do."

Inside, Una and Ember waited, their expressions a mix of concern and disappointment. Ember, clad in a thick wool sweater, and Una, wrapped in a blanket, stood silently, their eyes fixed on me.

Una shook her head at me, turned and went upstairs.

"We were really worried, dude." Ember said. "Not cool."

"I'm sorry." I hung my head.

Kristín came out of the kitchen, gave me what I now realized was his standard once over, making my skin crawl. "You'll need to work off the gas you used. You can start by feeding the dogs."

And so before I'd even shrugged out of my frozen clothes, I found myself back outside, trudging through the darkening day toward the dog shed. When I entered, they yapped and yipped and nuzzled me, their warm breaths a stark contrast to the biting cold. Eager for pats, they almost pushed me over, but I wasn't in the mood for canine affection, especially with the experience of the muttwalkers not far enough behind me.

When I returned to the house, Babette placed a steaming bowl of soup in front of me, along with a thick slice of buttery bread.

"Thanks," I murmured as I sat at the kitchen table on my own.

"You still need to go back for that skidoo," she said, sitting opposite me.

"I will."

"What were you thinking?"

I met the challenge in her eyes. "I was thinking I'm the one who has to carve the flute, so I should be the one to find the damn ice. I don't want volcanoes erupting and killing my friends. I don't want my friends being attacked by polar bears. And I don't want them falling into a damn crevasse. That's what I was thinking."

"Your mother's death is not your fault."

I glared at her, dabbed a piece of bread into my soup and swallowed it whole. "What would you know?"

"I was there."

"If I hadn't run toward Zale—" I cut myself off. This wasn't a conversation I wanted to have. With anyone. Let alone Babette.

"You can't do this alone."

"Why not?"

Babette placed her palms on the table. I continued to eat, jamming bits of soup covered bread in my mouth, swallowing it down, scratching the hell out of my throat with the sharp crusts.

"All the missions and journeys and voyages and quests your parents were part of...they were together. And it wasn't just them, but their friends too. Family. Me. They never did it alone. And you shouldn't either."

"I couldn't live with myself if anything happened to Ember and Una."

"That's not your choice to make," Una said from the doorway, a banket still wrapped around her shoulders.

"Have you ever stopped to consider why your friends are here?" Babette asked.

I didn't have an answer for that, so I just stared at them, finished my soup.

"Zale and Caol turned my father into a selachii, without his consent," Una said. "And they kept him prisoner in the ocean."

"Ember's grandmother was a sea witch," Babette added. "A sea witch in league with the Denizens of the Deep. They are the dark water gods who granted Zale his megalodon size. Ember wants to make sure the Denizens can't create any more powerful beings which might threaten Atlantis. Because he can't breathe fire, and he feels he can't protect his friends."

"Is that true?" I asked.

Una nodded.

Babette tapped the back of my hand. "Maybe if you talked to your friends, asked them about their motivations, you'd realize this journey isn't all about you."

I sat back in my chair, the truth of Babette's words hitting hard.

"We also want to support you," Una said. "We want you to trust us. To let us in. Let us help, Gal. Please."

Chewing on my lip, I considered their words, my hands tracing patterns on the table's surface. "I don't know how to do that."

Babette stood, patted my shoulder. "I suggest you give it a long, hard think."

I thought all night long, staring at the ceiling, kicking off the covers, picturing Una's and Ember's faces in my mind. How I'd let them down. How I still wouldn't have done anything differently. I tossed and turned, the weight of my indecision pressing down on me like a suffocating blanket. Eventually, exhaustion claimed me, but even in sleep, there was no respite. I found myself in a nightmare, my mother's face contorted in terror as she swam in a lake of molten lava, monstrous jaws lurking beneath the fiery surface.

The next morning, Kristín showed us how to check the gas on the skidoos, told us it would be the fastest way to the glacier, and that he was happy to lend them to us as long as we asked first. Then he showed us the dogs, the sled, how to attach them, what their commands were. We practiced mushing across the frozen meadows, the dogs' paws crunching on the snow, their eager barks mingling with the wind's mournful song. During lunch, Kristín shared the legends of his people, tales of winds which sang and ice so blue it mirrored the boundless ocean. That's where we needed to go. Kristín pointed to the area on the map, the very center of the glacier.

"I'll go get that skidoo," I announced, while Kristín's wife handed out a second round of hot cocoa. "Before it gets dark again."

Una and Ember stood at the same time. "We'll come with you," Una said.

I shook my head. "There's no need. I know where it is."

They both gave me a sharp look. Babette too. Then Kristín.

"He has much to learn still, he does," Babette said, not without humor.

"That was one of my favorite movies," Kristín said with a chuckle, then turned to me. "I could take you on one of the doubles. It would be much faster. Then we can come back together."

"I appreciate that," I said. "But I'm the one who left it there, I'd feel better if I was the one to retrieve it. Alone. And I'll have time to think about my...actions."

Una half stood, her selachii eyes flashing black.

"It's really not far," I said. "I'll grab a jerry can, be back before it gets dark. Honestly. I'm not trying to be a dick about it. I'm not trying to lose you in the snow. I'm not going to do anything stupid. I promise. You guys don't need to go out again. Tomorrow. Together. I promise."

Una walked around me in a slow circle, her eyes never leaving mine. "Okay, fine. But if you're not back in two hours, I'm sending the dogs after you."

I grinned at her, planted a kiss on her head, then flew out the back door with no intention of retrieving the skidoo. I left the safety of the cabin and plunged headlong into the unknown.

CHAPTER SIXTEEN

*G*uilt clung to me like a sinister shadow as I made my way to the dog shed, but I would not turn back. I stood by my decision to keep Ember and Una out of harm's way. With Kristín's knowledge, I knew where to go, and there was no way I was going to risk my friends to a volcano. Or frostbite. Or anything else Iceland chose to throw in my direction. I was the guardian of Snow and Ice. I had an affinity for the colder climates. I had this.

I crept through the snow, my rifle hanging by a strap from my shoulder, relieved the hushed landscape hid my steps. After vaulting over the fence, I made my way to the dog shed. Soft yips greeted me as the dogs nuzzled my hands, their warm breaths forming misty clouds. Kristín's instructions echoed in my mind, guiding my hands as I fastened their tug lines to the central tow line, ensuring their leads were free of tangles. The lead dogs went first, Sif and Runa, beautiful huskies with big blue eyes. The rest fell into line, instinctively knowing their positions. With each dog I clipped to the tow line, their yips and barks grew in volume, until I had to shout at them to keep quiet.

When I was ready to leave, I threw the shed doors open and climbed onto the sled. "Hike!" I yelled.

The dogs surged forward, their muscles rippling beneath their fur. I gripped the handrails, leaning to the side as they curved around a corner and out of the snowy meadow. I worried I'd be spotted from the house, but by the time we exited the other side of the meadow, the house was but a speck in the gloomy landscape.

We ran on, the directions clear in my mind. Once again, my eyebrows froze, my fingers grew numb, and an icy ached formed at the base of my skull. But this time I knew where I was going. This time I would succeed.

Our speed slowed as the dogs met the incline. They leaped over huge snowdrifts, their bodies straining with effort.

"Hike!" I yelled into the wind, encouraging them to run faster, but they were already doing their best to battle the elements.

We passed the marooned skidoo, the guilt a passing thought as I considered how proud everyone would be when I returned with the ice. The magical blue ice which I would carve into a flute and play a melodious tune with. My lips were already tingling with anticipation. Or was that frostbite?

"Geel!" I shouted, directing the dogs to the right, their powerful legs propelling us forward. "Hawl!" I commanded for a left turn, determined to maintain our course. "Easy!" I called, though my heart urged them to run faster, to outpace the encroaching night. Time blurred, the endless dusk stretching before us like a treacherous labyrinth. We pressed on, the dogs' pants mingling with the sound of the sled slicing through the snow.

A couple hours later, the muted sun disappeared behind a bank of low white clouds. The moon sailed into the sky, bright and full and smiling at me. It was the sign I needed. Finally, I was doing the right thing. I was almost there. Soon, I would have that ice. I could feel it calling to me.

"Hike!" I encouraged the dogs, even though they were panting hard. The dogs strained against their harnesses, eyes alight with primal determination. We couldn't stop now. We were so close.

The moon flew high, its soft beams stroking the frozen mountain. The earth beneath my boots quivered, a whisper of the immense power that lay dormant beneath the surface. I paid it no mind. I'd be in and out before the volcano could even think about catching me.

As the ice transitioned into a mesmerizing shade of blue, I knew I had reached the fabled destination. It stretched before me, resembling an endless, frozen ocean, its pristine immensity inviting, beckoning me closer.

"Whoa!" I called to the dogs, bringing them to a stop. They mewed, chuffed, pawed at the ground.

The earth shivered, a minor shockwave reminding me of the tunnels beneath Atlantis. But we were above ground. Nothing could collapse on us. The dogs barked, pulling at the towline, but I yelled at them to be calm.

With one hand on my rifle, I stepped off the sled, surveying the blue ice, careful to avoid any hidden crevasses. A glowing green light appeared in the distance, rising in the sky with each passing second. I stood on the snow-covered volcano, my eyes fixed on the darkening heavens, feeling the pulse of magic in the surrounding air. Slowly, the sky awakened with a subtle hum, as if the universe were tuning an otherworldly instrument. The first tendrils of the Northern Lights emerged, delicate wisps of emerald and violet weaving through the obsidian expanse. Ribbons of color swirled and twirled like celestial dancers, painting the night with hues so vivid they seemed borrowed from dreams. I stood there, utterly captivated, as the auroras decorated the inky canvas of the Arctic night.

The dogs settled into the snow as I watched. The howling wind morphed into something else. I'd expected a gentle sighing, a mournful moaning, a seductive whispering, but as I stood and listened to the wind, I heard words.

"Gather the ice, as the northern lights aglow,
Shape it with care, let the music flow.
Guardian of Ice, in your frozen domain,
Craft an ice flute, let it sing through the glacial rain.

Guardian of Snow and Ice, heed this plea so true,
In your realm of crystal frost, where dreams of winter brew.
With fingers cold as starlight, craft an ice flute bright,
From glacial magic spun, beneath the Northern Light."

Words. Instructions. A presence. The tangled song

surrounded me, seeping into my skin, burrowing deep into my bones, filling me with its essence. I relaxed my hand on the rifle. I couldn't describe the physical or emotional sensations I was experiencing, but I was filled with an overwhelming sense of wonder. The possibility of answers. The awareness of ancient wisdom. And I felt...humbled.

Sinking to my knees, I dug my hands into the hard blue ice, watching the Northern Lights dance in the sky and listening to the song surround me. I barely noticed the tremors beneath me, not until the dogs started barking again. Not until they'd already sped a few hundred yards down the mountain, leaving me stranded.

I yelled at them, but they paid no attention. After pushing myself to my feet, I lurched left and right, struggling to keep my balance on the shifting ground. The song fell silent, and above the thundering earth, all I heard was the howl of an unforgiving wind.

"Shit," I muttered.

With more curses hanging on my lips, I forced myself to move, stumbling through the snow. I ran after the dogs, but I could no longer see them, and I only made it a few yards before I was buried waist deep in a drift.

I pulled my foot free, only for the earth to shake once more. A crevasse yawned open beneath my feet, and I fell, my body twisting in mid-air as I clung desperately to the edge. But I couldn't hold on, and I dropped into the mouth of the glacier.

A sudden rush of movement yanked me sideways, and I plunged down an ice chute, my limbs flailing in the freezing air, the hard steel of the rifle digging into my side. The world became a blur of white and blue as I hurtled downward.

Finally, I crashed into a small cavern, colliding with a solid mass of unforgiving ice, every nerve in my body screaming in agony. My breath left my lungs. Pain seared through my right ankle. Even though the wound in my thigh had healed, my leg throbbed with a new insistence. But I had come to a stop.

With a thunderous boom, my rifle discharged, blasting a hunk of ice from a stalagmite and sending a deadly shower of shards raining down. I held my breath, waiting for it to end, recalling the last time I'd been buried alive. With my mother in the tunnels beneath Atlantis. *Mom.*

I was so like her, wanting to protect everyone, running off on my own without a care for my personal safety. I sensed her smiling down at me, shaking her head as I made the same mistakes she did.

"I'll do better," I whispered. The icy walls seemed to suck in my words.

When the last ice shard settled, I rolled onto my back. I lay there, gasping for air, my eyes fixed on the hole above me. It wasn't as far as I had feared; there were potential hand-holds, a chance to climb back to the surface. If only I had the energy. Or the will.

I clutched the rifle, firing a shot at the hole above, triggering another shower of snow and ice. But I didn't care. I wanted to feel the ruthless shards attacking my exposed skin. I wanted to feel the frozen snow worming its way under my clothes. I wanted to feel pain.

Lying on the hard-packed ice, rifle pressed against my

chest, I stared at the hole above, the Northern Lights dancing in flickers of purple and green. I took inventory of my body: a twisted right ankle, possibly a broken rib, a multitude of cuts and scrapes. I was lucky. Yet, I couldn't muster the strength to move. And so I closed my eyes and waited.

The night passed in a blur of colors and stars, sleep eluding me. Every time my eyes slid shut, a whispering wind swept over my face, stirring unwanted thoughts and a deep chill. My teeth chattered. I pulled the hood of my jacket high, tucked my chin into the collar, and curled into a ball around the jagged blue stalagmite. I stared at it as I waited for dawn to arrive. The blue of the ice was deeper than that on the surface. Sapphire colored. The most intense blue I'd ever seen. Apart from Una's eyes, maybe.

I continued to cradle the rifle, the only object that bridged the gap between where I was now and the world above. The only item which offered a semblance of security. But I couldn't shoot myself out of an ice cave. I'd more likely bury myself whole.

I shot into a sitting position, memories of the ice demons my parents had fought during their quest to find Atlantis flooding my mind. That cave had been a million miles from here, but still...

The glowing ice gave good visibility, and I scoured the cavern for any signs of lurking danger, but all I found were shadows and blue ice, silent and unyielding.

"Gal!"

My eyes snapped open at the sound of my name. The cave appeared brighter now, the blue ice shimmering with an otherworldly glow.

"Gal!"

I looked up at the hole. Daylight filtered down. I had fallen asleep after all.

"Gal!" Ember's voice

"Down here!" I called, my voice echoing back at me. Relief flooded through me when Ember's face appeared in the hole above. "Thank God."

Ember's grin was laced with both relief and exasperation. "You know you're a giant-sized idiot, right?"

"I do."

"You seem to have a talent for making people absolutely furious with you."

I noted the lightness in his eyes. "But not you?"

Ember laughed, causing snow to fall through the hole. "I get where you're coming from. But you're still an idiot."

"You don't need to tell me twice," I muttered.

"But apparently, we do." Ember's face disappeared and I heard him talking to someone else. The gentle tones of Una's voice filtered down and my heart began to race. She was going to be furious.

"How did you find me?" I called.

Ember stuck his head back into the hole. "Dogs came back. Kristín said it was too dangerous to go out at night, so we waited until morning and the dogs led the way back. Una didn't sleep a wink."

Ember disappeared again, but a rope dangled down in his place. I got to my feet and tested my ankle. Sore, and I couldn't put much weight on it, but I figured I could make it the twenty or so feet to the hole. I heaved a sigh of relief and tied the rope around my waist. Thinking I could use the rifle as an ice pick, I removed the bullets from the chamber and stashed them in a pocket. Catching sight of the blue ice, I held the rifle in both hands and used it as a club. I swung at the thin stalagmite, on the third blow snapping off a spear of dark blue ice. Rifle in one hand, ice spear in the other.

"Ready!" I called.

Ember tugged the rope, signaling me to climb. Each step sent a jolt of pain through my right ankle, but I pushed through it, refusing to give in. I dug the spikes of my snow boots into the ice, using the rifle to carve secure footholds. Inch by inch, I ascended, the ice spear clutched tightly in my hand.

"Almost there!" Ember called.

Before I could respond, Una's scream ripped through the air, thundered down the chute. A cold sweat flashed over me.

"Una!" I yelled.

Ember's shout mingled with mine, but the rope slackened suddenly, and I plummeted down the chute, grappling with the icy walls. Grasping for the sides, I dug my boots in, then the rifle. I held my position like a frozen monkey halfway up the chute, dread thick in my throat. "What's going on?"

Una's scream came again.

I didn't wait for an answer. Propelling myself upward, I scaled the wall with the spikes of my boots and the rifle as my ax. I poked my head through the hole, hurling the rifle and spear onto the snow, my eyes locking onto a terrible scene. Ember soared through the sky, and Una, terror etched on her face, sprinted toward me, a polar bear on her heels.

I scrambled out of the hole, glanced at the rifle, felt the

weight of the bullets in my pocket. The gun would take too long to load now.

"Gal!" Una screamed, her face pure terror, the polar bear only feet behind her.

I tried to run, but my ankle buckled, and I fell to one knee. I grabbed the ice spear, closed one eye, breathed out.

"Gal!"

Ember huffed, breath mingling with sparks and steam, but it did nothing to deter the massive white bear.

The bear leaped, and Una dodged. I threw the spear as the bear's claw descended. The spear pierced the bear through its heart. It fell, its paw knocking Una to the ground, her body skidding across the ice. As the bear tumbled after her, time slowed and blood poured. I limped toward her, pain shooting up my ankle with every step.

The bear landed on top of Una, its paw clawing the side of her head, and settled on the snow. Blood pooled around them. I didn't know whose it was.

Ember landed beside them, yanked at the polar bear's paw, managing to free Una. The sound of engines. Skidoos on the horizon. Babette and Kristín. Too late.

I halted by Una's side. She lay there, face buried in the snow, blood staining her blonde hair and the icy ground beneath her. Trembling, I knelt beside her, noted the rise and fall of weak breaths.

"She's alive," I said to Ember.

Ember kneeled with me, helped me to turn her over. One glance at her ravaged face and he recoiled, stumbling backward in the snow, overcome with nausea.

Blood covered Una's face, mattered her blonde hair.

Three deep scratch marks ran from her right temple to her left jaw. Her eye dangled from the socket. My heart squeezed painfully. I couldn't breathe. I couldn't think. My limbs turned to mush.

"Una?" I whispered. "Una?"

CHAPTER SEVENTEEN

I cradled Una in my arms, her blood leaking over both of us, staining the snow the color of dread.

"Una," I whispered in her ear. "Una, please! I'm sorry. I'm sorry I wasn't there to protect you. I'm sorry you're hurt. I'm so damn sorry." There were so many more things I wanted to say to her, so many things I wanted her to hear, my feelings crystallizing in that moment.

Ember sat in the snow, his bronzed skin unusually pale, staring at the blood. The polar bear lay in a bloody heap, the ice spear stuck in its chest, melting away.

"Move!" Babette's voice cut through my anguish as she shoved me aside, her hands moving with practiced urgency as she kneeled by Una, staunching the flow of blood. I could only watch, helpless, as Babette worked tirelessly to save Una's life. Regret clawed at my throat; I had entrusted the Power of the Sea to Eudora, leaving us defenseless.

The bleeding slowed. Babette repositioned Una's dislodged eye, then packed the wound.

"I've got a stretcher on my skidoo," Babette said, darting off to her snowmobile.

I held Una's gloved hand, willing her back to consciousness. But then maybe it was better she remained unconscious. I couldn't imagine what the pain of a wound like that would cause.

Babette returned with a stretcher attached to her skidoo. After plucking Una's petite body from the ground, I laid her across the stretcher, then climbed in beside her.

"There isn't enough room for you," Babette said.

"I'm not leaving her."

Babette sighed, her lips pressed into a thin line, then mounted the skidoo, revving the engine to life. Ember hurried to the dog sled and anchored himself to the frame. We followed Kristín down the mountain, away from the blood, the bear, and the rumbling volcano.

I cradled Una protectively as we raced across the ice, her head nestled against my chest to minimize the jolting ride, apologizing to her in a constant stream.

Within an hour, we had descended the mountain, the icy landscape blurring past us. Babette steered us past Kristín's house, bringing us to a halt in front of a brightly lit building—a clinic. She killed the engine and ran around to the stretcher. Ignoring the fierce pain in my ankle, I helped her carry Una into the building, into what looked like an operating theater. The hum of a generator sounded in the background and occasionally, the lights flickered.

"Is there a doctor?" I asked.

Babette, her back to me, rummaged through metal drawers filled with gleaming instruments. "I *am* a doctor."

During the aftermath of the nuclear war, Babette had become a combat medic, and later, she had established a hospital on Atlantis, training medical professionals for the humans who couldn't benefit from the Fountain of Youth. And me—she had tended to my injuries more times than I could count.

"Get out. I need to think. And send Kristín in," Babette ordered, her words clipped and focused.

I looked back at Una, her fragile form sprawled across a cold metal table, her bandaged head tilted to one side, blood staining the pristine white cloth. "Is she going to be okay?"

Babette slammed a drawer shut. "Just get out, Gal!"

I backed away, my guilt heavier than ice, out of the clinic, into the muted day. The sun was above the horizon, its weak rays barely penetrating the gloom, reflecting the darkness gripping my heart.

Kristín parked his skidoo next to Babette's.

"She wants you inside," I said.

He met my gaze with a silent nod before darting into the clinic, leaving me alone with my thoughts. I paced a line outside the building, wearing away the snow, turning it into dirty slush. The subsequent pain in my ankle wasn't enough of a punishment. Ember arrived on foot a few minutes later, having put the dogs back in the shed.

"How is she?" Ember asked.

"I don't fucking know! Babette kicked me out."

"And you listened to her?"

I gaped at him. "Of course I listened to her."

Ember didn't offer a comment.

"I *always* listen."

Ember shoved his hands in his thick coat. "And then you do the opposite."

"Why are *you* mad at me?"

"Dude, I'm not mad at you—"

"I told you guys not to come!" My voice rose, stirring the drifting snow. Digging my fingernails into my palm, I fisted both hands. "I told you I wanted to go alone! I told you it was dangerous. And did you listen to me? No. You came anyway. Stowed away on my boat. Both of you. Even when I told you I didn't want you. Why did you come? Why, Ember? Why?"

Ember didn't answer, just shook his head and walked away.

"Why did you come?" I screamed after him.

He didn't look back but disappeared around a distant corner.

I leaned against the clinic's cold wall listening to the hopeful hum of the generator. My body gave way, and I slid into the snow. I kicked at the ice, sending shards flying. Kick after kick, until a searing pain shot through my injured ankle. I kicked once more, hot tears streaming down my face, freezing on my cheeks. I couldn't remember the last time I'd cried. Maybe when Mom died. But I couldn't stop the tears now. It was Una. Una, who'd always looked up to me. Who'd always tried to hold my hand. Who'd always been there, even when I'd treated her like shit. She defended my actions, didn't bite my head off about destroying *The Mermaid Chronicles*, came on a dangerous journey with me because...because...because she loved me. And I loved her.

The realization struck harder than a crashing avalanche. I loved Una. Her irritating optimism. Her refusal to let me get away with any shit. The inner strength inside her was second to none. And her sapphire blue eyes, the slope of her button nose, the curve of her graceful neck, even the sharp spikes of her blonde hair. I loved her lopsided smile, the way she would never walk, but skip, the way her head rested against my chest when we fell asleep together, leaving a warm impression which lasted for days, and the way she forgave me every time I fucked up. Even when I didn't deserve it. And I didn't. Deserve her. She was too good for me. I knew that.

My heart cracked in two. I could never confess my feelings to her. I refused to be so heartless, to bind her to a love destined for sorrow. Not only was I the Prince of Atlantis and most likely doomed to a premature death, but my honor was lacking, my worth found wanting, my love...not good enough. I didn't know *how* to love.

The anger which had consumed me upon finding her aboard my boat stemmed from fear. I couldn't bear the thought of anything happening to her, not only because of the guilt I would carry, but because I loved her beyond all else. I always had. Even when I didn't want to. Even when I pushed love away. Even when I sought solitude, her image was always with me. Her laughter resonated through the courtyards, her jokes painted perpetual smiles on my lips, a constant reminder of the love I dared not reveal.

But I could tell her while she was asleep.

I pushed myself to my feet, limped through the doors of the clinic, and hobbled into the operating room.

"I'm sorry," I stammered, my voice barely above a whisper, but the weight of those words hung in the air, echoing the regret that gripped my soul.

Una was attached to an IV line. A monitor beeped softly in a corner. Babette and Kristín were finishing. A clean white bandage surrounded Una's head, exposing her one good eye, which was still closed.

"She's strong." Babette threw instruments into the sink. "And it's not me you need to apologize to."

I glanced at Una, at the steady rise and fall of her chest, and inched across the tiled floor, wincing at the pain in my ankle.

Kristín put a hand on my shoulder. "Inga's got a stew bubbling on the stove. It's ready when you are."

I nodded and mumbled my thanks. I stepped closer to the operating table, my eyes fixed on Una's pale face. The machines beeped in a rhythmic pattern as they monitored her vitals. I reached out, my fingers trembling as I brushed a strand of hair away from her marred forehead, then wiped the remnants of the frozen tears from my cheeks.

"I love you," I said, my voice breaking. "I love you, Una, more than anything in this world. I should have told you sooner, should have shown you how much you mean to me."

Babette raised an eyebrow but didn't comment. Instead, she glided around the room, checking Una's vitals. I was too afraid to ask the question burning my lips.

"She's going to be fine," Babette said, catching my look. "She's lost an eye, and there will be scars, but she's going to be fine."

Una's fingers twitched, a small, involuntary movement that sent a surge of hope through me. Time stretched into eternity. The world outside faded away, leaving the two of us in the quiet sanctuary of the operating room. I leaned closer, my lips brushing against Una's forehead in a gentle, desperate kiss.

An ache in my chest, so tight it hurt to breathe. I faced Babette. "She'll be healed when she goes back to Atlantis. You'll take her, right?"

Babette locked her eyes on me. "You really think you can carry on, on your own? After everything? After what Una just went through? You think she's going to let you go that easy? You just told her you love her. Why don't you trust her?"

"I do trust her!"

Babette crossed her arms.

"I don't want her to get hurt. Again. Because of me. She deserves so much more than that."

"You know that's her choice, right? When she wakes, you two can have a conversation. And God dammit, Gal, do whatever she says. And do it with a smile on your face."

I sighed. "You're right. Of course you are."

"Old habits die hard. But it's time to bury your loner tendencies under the snow. Got it?"

"Got it."

She glanced at my boots. "Take off the boot and let me look at that ankle of yours."

I sat in a chair in the corner and pulled off my boot, wincing as the sharp tug sent a new flash of pain tearing through my ankle. Babette held my heel in her hand, turning it one way, then the other. A deep, black bruise circled my ankle, spread under my foot, and halfway up my shin. The outside of it was swollen too.

"A nasty sprain," she said, and wrapped it in a tight

bandage. "You'll need to stay off it for a couple of days. No trekking in the snow. No going to the glacier. It's time to sit by the fire and drink cocoa. Got it?"

I nodded.

"Gal?"

"Okay. I got it. I'll sit still."

"I never know with you." She poked my knee.

"I'm a changed man," I said.

She didn't laugh, didn't even crack a smile. "Way too soon," she replied. "And I'm not used to you cracking jokes."

"Yeah, that didn't feel quite right. That's more Ember's style. Speaking of which, I owe him an apology. Can you stay with Una until I get back?"

Babette helped me put my boot back on, and I limped out of the clinic. Before I left, I turned back with another question. "Babette? All that rumbling on the glacier...are we safe?"

Babette's eyes clouded. "The volcano is long overdue for an eruption. Kristín says there's been more activity during the last couple of weeks than there has been in the last decade. So to answer your question, no, I don't think so. Kristín is talking about an evacuation."

"I need that ice."

"I know."

I drummed my fingers on the door frame, then left. There was nothing more I could say to change the situation. When I arrived at Kristín's house, Ember was sitting on the porch smoking a spliff.

"She okay?" He exhaled toward the darkening sky.

My lips quivered as I pushed the words out. "She lost the eye. But yeah, she's okay."

"That bear came out of nowhere."

I sat beside him, took a drag of the offered joint. "I'm sorry I was such a dick."

"You do have your moments."

"Why are you even friends with me?"

"Someone's got to be." He elbowed my ribs.

A laugh erupted from me, draining away some of the tension of the day. "But seriously?"

Ember gave me a side-eye. "You struggle with the prophecies. I struggle with my fire...or lack of it. I get what it's like to feel...less. Like you're on the wrong path. That you don't belong."

I stared at him.

"What?"

"I'm waiting for the joke."

He shrugged. "I can be serious sometimes, you know."

"I don't know what to say to serious Ember,"

He laughed, punched my shoulder.

"But on a *serious* note, I didn't know you felt that way."

"Maybe ask once in a while." Ember took a drag, the cherry flaring in the darkness.

I brushed my shoulder against his. "I will. And I'm sorry I haven't."

"Appreciated. But don't turn to mush on me now."

"I'll do my best."

He cracked a grin. "Besides, I've been thinking about my other talents. I might not be able to set things ablaze, but there's always my scorching wit."

"Who needs to breathe fire when you can charm the scales off a sea serpent?"

We both laughed.

"Gal! You made a joke." Ember thrust his hand out for me to shake. "I'm so proud."

"I'm learning from the best," I replied. "And speaking of things to learn. Una is—"

"Your destiny."

Surprised, I flinched, but my heart split wide open. "What makes you say that? Was there a prophecy or something?"

"No prophecy. None that I'm aware of, anyway. But it's obvious. The way you two look at each other." For once his expression was devoid of humor.

"It is?" I searched his face for lies, but found none. "We do?"

Ember flicked my head. "Earth to Gal."

I leaned my head against the house, inhaled the crisp air, massaged my swollen ankle. "She's going to wake up and hate me."

"She'll never hate you." Ember blew a smoke ring. "What you have is too strong. Stronger than a puff of my finest weed." He waggled his eyebrows. "You just don't realize it yet."

A surge of anger rushed through me. "I'm going to skin that damn polar bear and take its hide back to Uncle D's bar where it can stare at the seawolf."

"Gross." Ember shuddered. "And please don't remind me of the seawolves, we have yet to face them."

I stood, limped toward the door. "I'm going to grab some food and go back to the clinic. Sit with Una."

"Good idea. But make sure you avoid the kæstur hákarl."

"The what now?"

Ember tilted his head. "It's in the larder. At the back. A jar of fermented shark."

"Fermented *shark*?" I gaped at him. "That's like eating Una."

Ember grinned, offered a sly smile. "Is that what's on your mind?"

Heat swarmed my cheeks. "That's not what I meant."

"Uh-huh."

"Seriously."

"You tell yourself that."

There was no point digging the hole any deeper, but I had one more question before I went inside. "Ember?"

"Yeah?"

"Is there anything I can do to help? With your fire?"

He shook his head. "Nope. But thanks for asking."

I drummed my fingers on the door frame, watching my friend as he puffed from his spliff, exhaling perfect smoke rings toward the sky. Being my cousin, he'd always been in my life. Forced together on family occasions, attending the same school, his parents looking after me when mine were busy with royal duties. We never fought. He never complained, even when I teased him about his lack of fire. They said blood was thicker than water. But Ember was so much more to me than family. He carried half my soul.

"Ember? Do you have an Una?"

He chuckled, glanced my way. "No. But I'm actively interviewing."

"I hope you find her, or him, real soon," I said, then went inside the house.

Avoiding the jar of fermented shark in the larder, I devoured a bowl of steaming stew, then thanked Inga and retraced my steps to the clinic. Una had been moved to a recovery bed. Sheets, blankets, pillows. The monitors continued to beep. The IV line dripped into her arm. I stared at her pristine bandage, wondering what lay beneath, wondering if she would blame me.

I spent the night offering prayers to Vorago, his brother, Tempest, and his sister, Cascadia. I didn't know what I was praying for exactly, but I knew I needed courage. Not for the journey ahead, not for facing Zale, but for when Una finally woke.

CHAPTER EIGHTEEN

The tremors rocked me awake, the house pulsating with each quake, the bed frame skidding across the floor. My heart raced as I glanced over to see Ember tumbling out of bed, his blankets twisted like a serpent around him.

"What's going on?" he yelled.

A carved reindeer ornament fell, striking my head. I winced, massaging the sore spot, then forced myself up despite the sharp pain shooting through my ankle.

"Kristín mentioned volcanic activity is spiking," I said.

Ember lunged toward the window, his eyes scanning the horizon. "No fire in the sky."

The house settled, the chaos reducing to a low rumble. I could hear Kristín and Inga calling, their voices laced with concern. Ornaments settled back into their places, some dangling precariously from the shelves.

I looked at my cousin, weighed my decision. "Ember, I need your help."

He looked at me, his eyes wide. "Dude, we can't stop a volcano."

I chuckled. "No, but I need that ice. The ice spear I used to kill the bear."

"Back on the glacier." He swallowed. "Where the volcano is."

"Yeah...you don't have to come..." I searched the dim room for where I'd left my clothes. "I thought with your affinity for fire...I don't know..."

"I'm coming." He untwisted himself from the blankets and threw them onto his bed. "Glacier trips are all the rage, and I could use a souvenir, something to impress the ladies, maybe a frozen lava lamp, and—"

"Ember?" I pushed my arms through the sleeves of a thick fleece.

"Yeah?"

"Thank you."

He gave me a tight nod. "Don't mention it."

We dressed quickly, dawn melting the darkness in the sky, ignoring breakfast and Kristín's warnings.

"We have to go, Kristín," I said. "I need that ice."

He stared at the weather outside, then assessed the winter gear I wore. "Take the skiddoos. Take two, in case one of them breaks down. And hurry. There's talk of an evacuation."

Ember and I sprinted across the frozen road to the shed where the skidoos were stored. The engines roared to life simultaneously. We gave each other a grim nod of acknowledgement, then shot across the snowy landscape. I pushed the throttle to max, urging the skidoo to go faster, ignoring the whine the engine made when we hit the incline.

Ember maintained pace beside me, his wild hair trailing in the vindictive wind, his hot breath coming in heated gusts of sparks. How I wished there was something I could do to help my friend. Maybe when this was all over.

We reached the carcass of the polar bear in under an hour. It lay sprawled on the ice, a grotesque tableau, its body frozen and scavenged, birds pecking at its remains. The volcano remained oddly silent. I couldn't decide if that was a blessing or a curse.

Snow fluttered in the air and the haunting melody enveloped me once more. I disembarked from the skidoo and limped toward the polar bear, my eyes fixated on the broken spear of ice next to its hulking form. Still frozen. Still an otherworldly blue. The bear stared at me with dead black eyes.

A surge of emotions gripped me. Here was the thing that had stolen Una's eye. Here was the thing that had almost taken her from me. I wanted to kick it and punch it and stab it a thousand times. The anger swelled within me, mirroring the fury of the volcano beneath my feet. But as I stood there and stared at the lifeless animal, the song surrounded me in a comforting shroud, and my anger drained away. It was just an animal. Merely trying to survive. Like the rest of us. And it couldn't hurt us anymore.

Ember put a hand on my shoulder. "Let's get out of here."

I grabbed the ice spear, felt the weight of it in my gloved hand. Three feet of solid ice. Enough for three flutes. I had three tries to make this work.

"I have no idea how to carve this into a flute," I admitted.

"We'll figure it out together," Ember replied. "And if it doesn't work, we'll find another way. I can offer my fiery beat boxing skills, that'll scare the seawolves away for centuries."

After grabbing my rifle from where I'd dropped it, I secured the spear to the handles of the skidoo, as far from the warm engine as I could get it, hoping the subzero temperatures would keep it frozen as we traveled. Leaving the mystical wind and the eerily silent volcano behind, we traveled down the mountain.

We parked the skidoos, and after burying the spear under layers of ice to maintain its frozen state, hurried to Una. Ember and I entered the clinic to find her still asleep, so we sat with her for a while, each of us holding a hand, reminding her of stories from when we were young.

When the lights flickered and the ground rumbled, Kristín burst into the room. "Got data from the seismologist in the north. Volcano is due to erupt in five days. Evacuation is starting tomorrow. Some folks have already left for the west."

"But I haven't carved the flute yet," I said.

"Best get to it, son," Kristín said.

I glanced at Una, desperate for her to wake, desperate to hold her.

"I'll stay and watch her," Ember said. "I once fixed a paper cut with a band-aid. This is just a giant-sized version of that, right?"

"We both will," Babette said. "You get on with the flute, prince."

With my heart heavy in my stomach, I left the clinic and

retrieved the ice spear. I couldn't risk it melting inside, so I settled near the dog shed, the Northern Lights flickering in the sky, wondering how to begin.

I stared at the blue ice for five minutes, hoping it would impart its secrets. When it was clear nothing was going to happen, I took a quick breath and broke it into three uneven chunks. A few shards fell loose, but I had three sections to work with.

My breath puffed, my eyebrows froze, and my ankle ached. I took off my gloves to manipulate the ice and my fingers quickly turned into useless stumps.

"Fuck!" I thumped the ground.

Taking a deep breath, I turned my attention back to the ice, desperately hoping it would offer guidance. I half-expected it to speak, like the wind whispering on top of the glacier, but it remained stubbornly silent.

Carefully, I picked up one of the sections, my fingers immediately freezing to the surface. I kissed it, whispered words of encouragement, and then, using a glove, attempted to smooth its rough edges. The phallic symbolism wasn't lost on me and I wondered if I had issues Freud would have a field day with. The thought brought a smile to my lips and a surge of new confidence. While Una lay in the clinic recovering from her injuries, I would make her accident mean something and figure out how to carve the damn flute.

I blew on it experimentally, hoping for a sound, but there was nothing—only the silent void of unfulfilled expectations. Clearly, I needed to do something more than stare at it. Determined to make progress, I scavenged through the kitchen drawers of Kristín and Inga's house, my eyes falling upon the pile of belongings stacked by the door, a tangible reminder of the volcano situation. Armed with a knife, a fork, some wire, and a handful of other makeshift tools, I went back outside.

As I settled back into the snow, I noted the rush of activity from the five houses in the cul-de-sac. I hadn't met Kristín's neighbors, but they were all outside, hastily packing belongings onto sleds and skidoos. I didn't know where they planned to go, how far was far enough, how Ember, Una and I would get away. I couldn't think about that right now. I could only focus on the flute.

I gripped the ice spear in one hand, a knife in the other. Gently, I tapped the end of the spear, hoping to hollow it out, to coax music from its frozen core. It shattered with the first touch, splintering in my hand, raining icy blue shards which disappeared beneath the snow.

"Fuck!"

I slumped against the shed, uttered a few more curse words, then wiped the frozen hair out of my face and tried to re-focus. Two attempts left. But I couldn't do this alone.

I returned to the clinic intending to ask Ember for help, to find Una awake, her one good eye focused on Babette, who was checking her wound. Hovering in the doorway, I watched Una respond to Babette's questions, listen to the news about her eye, see her body slump as she accepted her fate.

"I can feel you hovering out there, Gal Waters, get your ass in here," Una said.

I approached her bed, my frozen fingers trembling with a

mix of fear and guilt. I wanted to hold her hand...but couldn't.

"I'll give you a minute. Don't upset her." Babette left the room, the warning flashing in her eyes.

"This is all my fault," I said.

Una looked up at me, her good eye sharp and piercing. "Did I miss the part when you made a decision to drag me up a glacier and entice a polar bear into an attack?"

How could she make jokes after what had happened? "You wouldn't have been in that position if it weren't for me."

She glared at me with that piercing blue eye. "I made the decision to come on this quest. To board your boat. I knew it would be dangerous. Come on, *Vorago's trident?* It's the most powerful object in our world. I knew there would be risks. I knew I could get hurt. Or you. Or Ember. But I came anyway. Because I chose to be here. I was not going to let you do this alone. And I am not going to let Zale win. I want him dead as much as you."

I slumped into the chair beside her bed, my heart pounding with unspoken words.

"Please tell me you at least got the ice?"

"I got the ice." I raked both hands through my hair. "You lost an eye."

"I have another one."

I shook my head. "How can you be so blase about your eye? It's your fucking *eye*, Una."

"If my eye is the only thing I lose in a fight to take down Zale, then I'm good with that."

Speechless, I stared at her.

"Or am I not pretty enough for you?"

"That's not...no...yes...of course you are...I'd never...*fuck!*"
Una smiled. "Why are you smiling at me?"

"Because you're adorable."

I stood. "I'm not a fucking puppy."

"You are so easy to wind up." She grabbed my hand,
pulling me closer. "You are also strong and brave."

I wanted to yell at her. I wanted to take her back to
Atlantis so the fountain could fix her eye. I wanted to kiss
her. I wanted to tell her I loved her.

"What is it?" she asked.

I buried my feelings. "I need to carve the flute. We have
to leave before the volcano erupts. I do not want you here
when that happens."

"Go," she said, releasing my hand. "Go forth and carve
the magical flute."

I backed away from her, staring at her bandage, her blue
eye, her beauty, the pureness of her heart...I would never be
the same again.

CHAPTER NINETEEN

*E*mber and I found ourselves perched on the snow-covered ground while the Northern Lights danced mockingly above our heads. How could a scene of such beauty be the backdrop of so much angst?

"Is this going to take long?" Ember huffed, his warm breath defrosting the icy air. "My balls have already retreated. Way up in there somewhere."

I threw a snowball at him. "It only took me five minutes to shatter the last one, so I'm going to hazard a guess and say, no."

"Sorry, buddy. I know you're trying. But I'm freezing my ass off out here."

"I thank you from the bottom of my twisted heart for being here with me."

We sat opposite each other in the middle of the meadow with a view of Kristín's house, the two remaining shafts of blue ice half buried in the snow.

"What do you need me to do?" Ember asked, his gloved hands tucked under his armpits.

"See that metal wire?"

"Yep."

"I need you to heat it gently with your breath, just enough to warm it. Then I'm going to use it to melt the central shaft of ice, hoping like hell the entire thing doesn't melt or break."

Ember clapped his gloved hands. "This is the perfect job for a dragon king who can't breathe fire."

I slapped his knee. "See? Who needs fire?"

Chuckling, Ember plucked the piece of wire from the ground, held it aside, and gave it a gentle blow. Sparks emerged from his heated breath and the wire began to glow.

"Yes!" This was going to work.

I extracted one of the ice shafts from the snow and held it firmly in one hand. Ember passed me the wire and I brought it to meet the end of the shaft. But I was too slow, the wire already cool in the night air, only a drip melting from the spear.

Ember nudged me with his foot. "I think you're going to need to get your big balls out and go a little faster."

"I've only got two sections. I can't afford to make a mistake."

"Still need to go faster. Or we're going to age slower than a fine wine."

I sighed.

"Ready to try again?"

I passed him back the wire, watched him heat it, the end of it glowing once more. With quicker actions than I was comfortable with, I snatched the wire, pressed the tip to the end of the spear, and shouted 'Hallelujah' when water dripped onto the snow, instantaneously freezing. The end of the shaft now had a slight indentation.

"We're making progress!"

"Can we make progress quicker?" Ember asked. "This is taking longer than it takes a penguin to select the perfect pebble for its nest."

I ignored his joke and chucked the wire at him. "Go again!"

We sat together for an hour. Ember heating the wire and me carefully melting the inner shaft until we had a hollow tube. Ember went into the house a couple of times, returning once with lukewarm mugs of hot cocoa and another time with a freshly rolled joint. He'd brought enough weed with him to last a few lifetimes. But then if shit went to hell and we were all going to die...why not?

"Give me some of that," I said, reaching for the joint.

Ember shook his head, holding the joint out of reach. "Nope. No way, dude. You need to focus."

I sighed, placed the shaft in the snow, contemplating my next move.

"You need to make holes in the top, you know, like notes." Ember puffed a perfect smoke ring toward the sky, the smoke turning green and purple under the effects of the Northern Lights. I barely noticed them anymore.

"Give me the wire," I said, keeping my eyes fixed on the emerging flute.

I spent two hours meticulously crafting five holes along the icy surface. Finally, it resembled a flute. Crudely crafted, but a flute nonetheless. I wasn't sure how many keys a genuine flute boasted, but I figured five might suffice for an ice version. Now I had to find a way to play it without peeling a layer of skin off my lips.

I lifted the flute, my fingers freezing to the shaft once more, and held the mouthpiece an inch from my lips.

"Go on," Ember said.

I attempted to produce a note without letting my lips touch the freezing surface. I blew a breath down the shaft, covering one of the holes with my trembling forefinger. Nothing. No sound. Not even that creepy noise you get when you run a finger around the rim of a glass.

In the distance, the ground rumbled, the dogs barked, and the wind picked up, coating us in snow. A warning, perhaps. If *The Mermaid Chronicles* still existed, I'd wager a large amount its pages would be turning.

My hand ached with cold, but I couldn't give up. I tried to play it again, this time using two fingers to cover the holes. I placed my lips around the ice, hoping the warmth of my mouth wouldn't melt it.

"You got this," Ember said. "I'll let you have a drag when you produce a note."

I laughed, then blew through the flute once more. The fragile ice cracked in my hands, splitting right down the middle, rendering my efforts utterly useless. Ember and I stared at the shattered remains of the blue flute.

"Guess the ice flute didn't appreciate your musical talents."

"It's not funny, Ember."

"Sorry. I don't know what to say, dude...we've only got one more..."

"I know." I gritted my teeth, got to my feet, kicked at the snow.

Ember stood with me, passed me the joint. "One puff, then back to work."

I shook my head. "I can't. Not tonight. I need a break."

"Tomorrow then?"

"Tomorrow."

The biting wind cut through my layers, stinging my cheeks as I stowed the last sample of ice in a bucket, shrouding it with snow before hiding it behind the dog shed. One more go, or I'd have to go back up the glacier and risk the eruption. Leaving Iceland without the flute was not an option. Ember's suggestion of an alternative route echoed in my mind, but it was too uncertain. We had no room for chance, no luxury for risks.

Ember and I returned to Kristín's house to find Una settled in a room downstairs, Babette bustling about, clearing away a tray of stew. The room was warm, the flames in the hearth crackling softly and casting a flickering light on Una's face. Wind thumped against the window.

I stood in the doorway. "Are you feeling better?"

"My head hurts like hell, but Babette's got some great pain killers." She winked. Or maybe it was a blink. Hard to tell with one eye.

"We closed the clinic," Babette said. "With everyone evacuating, we thought we'd bring everything we needed here. We're the last house left. Kristín and Inga want to leave tomorrow. I have a pilot waiting at an airfield in the west waiting to take you further—"

I took a step into the room. "You didn't need to do that—"

"How else are you going to get to the Galapagos?" Babette balanced the tray on one arm, thrust her free hand at me. "It would take you months to sail there. And the plane isn't big enough either, but it can get you across the ocean. To Greenland."

"Thank you, Babette," Una said, pointing at me.

"Thank you, Babette," I echoed.

"It'll take you a day or two to travel there," Babette said. "The pilot will wait as long as he can."

"What about you?" I asked her.

"I'll help evacuate Kristín and Inga. There's a snowstorm heading our way too, so I want to get on the water before it hits."

I glanced out the window once more, at the swirling snow, at the icicles hanging from the roof, most of them jagged and broken. It reminded me of my dismal efforts with the flute. "Does that happen often?"

"Every few years there's a storm bad enough to put the fear in the locals. Add that to the rumbling volcano, well, then you've got a bunch of real uneasy folk." Babette shifted the tray, patted my shoulder as she headed to the door. "I'll leave you two to talk."

Babette shut the door behind her. It felt like a kick up the backside.

Una patted the bed. "Sit."

I perched on the edge, fidgeting with my gloves. Una took

them from my hands and set them aside. "How did you get on with the flute?"

"Shouldn't you be asleep? It's really late."

Una laughed, then winced, holding her bandaged head. "Ouch. Don't make me laugh. It hurts."

"Sorry."

"The flute?"

"No joy."

She covered my hand with her own, her touch warm and welcoming.

"Una—"

"Gal—"

We smiled at each other.

"You go first," she said.

"Una, I'm scared." My voice came out in a trembling shudder, revealing the depths of my fear. I hadn't wanted to appear afraid in front of her. I had wanted to portray an inner strength; one she could rely on. But inside, I was fracturing, falling apart like the pieces of that damn flute. "We only have one sample left."

"You can do it."

I shook my head. "Una, please, I've tried. It's not working. I'm scared. I'm scared I can't carve the flute. I shouldn't be the guardian of Snow and Ice. If I can't control my own elements, how can I possibly find a trident in the middle of the Galapagos? I'm not worthy of that kind of power. I don't deserve it. And knowing all that, why did I think I could kill Zale?"

"Slow down, Gal—"

But I carried on. "What if something happens to you? I

left Atlantis because I couldn't bear to witness any more death. I was weak, too weak to face my fears. Too scared to admit how much I love you, Una." And there it was.

I stared at her beautiful blue eye, the only one she had left, the one I would cherish forever if she let me, even if I didn't quite know how.

Una inhaled sharply. She sat up, then clutched her head, a grimace tightening her lips.

"Careful." I moved closer, eased her back onto the mountain of pillows.

"What did you just say?"

I chewed on my lip, couldn't find the courage to push the words out a second time.

Una smiled up at me, took my hand in hers. "You can do it."

"I love you." I repeated, the words tasting unfamiliar on my tongue, but I savored every syllable.

A tear leaked out of her eye.

"I'm sorry."

"Oh, my God!" Una wrung her hands at me. "Do not apologize for telling me you love me. I've been waiting to hear those words for like...my entire life. I'd kind of given up, to be honest."

"You had?"

"Duh!"

"I'm a little slow on the uptake."

"No shit."

"I'm sorry."

"Stop apologizing and get down here and kiss me."

"I don't want to hurt you."

She laced her hands behind my neck and tugged me back onto the pillows with her. Una. Touching my neck, her warmth leaking into my cold skin. Soft. Gentle. And so full of a love I'd never experienced. All in that one touch.

Una pulled me closer until our lips met. But I was afraid to move, afraid to do anything.

"That's not a kiss, Gal Waters," she mumbled into my mouth. "I've been dreaming of this for years and you're kind of letting me down."

I couldn't help but laugh. I kissed her again, this time with more certainty. It was a kiss woven from years of unspoken emotions. She had always been the constant flame, illuminating my darkest corners, even when I had been too blind to see it.

The world outside, the biting cold, the violent wind, all of it faded away, leaving the two of us in the warm cocoon of the cabin. The chill of the snow clinging to my skin melted away in the heat of her touch.

Her lips were soft, a tender contrast to the roughness of my own. In that simple, intimate connection, an avalanche of emotions crashed through me—regret for the time lost, gratitude for her patience, and a burgeoning hope for the future. Could I, Gal Waters, Prince of Atlantis, be rewarded with a love as great as my parents? My heart, once frozen in self-doubt, began to thaw beneath the warmth of her kiss.

I pulled back, just enough to look into her eye, that lone blue gem set in a face which bore the scars of her battle. It was a gaze that held the depth of oceans, a gaze which spoke of resilience and unwavering love. Her missing eye didn't define her; it was another testament to her strength, her ability to endure the harshest of trials and emerge, not broken, but forged anew. In that gaze, I found my purpose.

"I love you," I whispered, my voice a raw whisper, as if speaking the words aloud solidified their truth.

She smiled, a smile which held a lifetime of understanding. "I love you too."

I leaned into her warmth, careful to avoid her wounds and bruises. I left a chain of kisses along her neck, the edge of her jaw, the curve of her cheekbone, and around the ragged claw marks marring her skin. Her hands roamed under my fleece, tracing the contours of my back, pulling me tight against her. She pressed her hips against mine and yanked at my clothes with a fierceness that would not be subdued.

"I don't want to hurt you," I whispered as she pulled the fleece over my head.

"You won't."

I locked the door, helped her to remove her clothes, then snuggled under the blankets with her. I pulled her close, my hands finding the small of her back, fingers brushing the gentle curve where her body met mine.

"Who would have thought I would be naked in a bed with Gal Waters?" Una smiled. "Wait until I tell the girls back home."

I blushed. "We don't have to..."

"Uh-uh. You're not getting away that easily." She kissed me, her lips tugging at mine, her tongue sweeping into my mouth. It was the most glorious sensation I'd ever experienced.

"Gal?"

"Yeah?" I replied, still lost in the whirlwind of her kiss.

"Have you ever...done this before?"

Ears burning, I shook my head. "You?"

"Once."

I raised my eyebrows.

"It didn't live up to expectations."

"Great. Way to put pressure on a guy."

She laughed. "Because it wasn't you."

"I have no idea what I'm doing."

"It takes two, you know."

I smiled at her, losing my self-doubt in an instant, and kissed her deeply. Una rolled over, rummaged in the bedside drawer, removed a foil packet.

"Where did you get that?"

"Babette."

"Babette gave you condoms?"

Una giggled, the most delicate sound. "She told me there was something in the drawer I might need."

"How did she...I'll have to thank her later...before I die of embarrassment."

"Sex is nothing to be embarrassed by." She tore the wrapper open with her teeth, took out the condom, and rolled it onto me. I groaned under the lightness of her touch, wanting more, needing to be inside her.

Her arms encircled my waist, pulling me back to the bed, our bodies shifting until I was on top of her. She took me in her hand and guided me to her entrance. I hovered there, doubts swirling in my head, guilt thickening my throat.

"Una..."

She cupped my face. "It's you and me."

I pushed inside her, her warmth surrounding me, and

sighed into the shell of her ear. She gripped my hips, pulled me tight against her, urging me deeper. I thrust gently inside her, savoring the sweet sounds of pleasure escaping her lips as she nipped at my ear.

"Wait," she said.

I stopped. "What's the matter?"

"It's the scratches. They're rubbing."

"I'm sorry." I pulled out of her. "We should stop."

Shaking her head, she smiled a twinkling smile. "Lie on your back."

I obeyed immediately, finding a position in the center of the bed. Una straddled me, taking me inside her once more, sliding down my length with a sensual moan. I gripped her thighs, watching her face as it contorted with pleasure. Cupping one of her perfect breasts in my hand, I leaned forward to take her nipple into my mouth.

She arched her back, her pace increasing, drawing pleasure from me in pulsating waves. I collapsed back on the bed, pressed my fingers into her hips, pulling her down as I thrust into her. Her eye closed as she bucked against me, her muscles contracting around me, her moans growing more frequent, until she dug her fingers into my chest and whispered my name through clenched teeth. It was enough to send me over the edge.

"Una," I yelled, as the orgasm ripped through me.

"Shh." She laughed and covered my mouth with her hand. "Shh, they'll hear."

"I don't care," I said as she collapsed on top of me. "I don't fucking care."

She rolled off me, and we lay together in the aftermath, nestled against each other, our bodies cooling.

"Are you okay?" I asked. "Did I hurt you?"

"Only in all the right ways." She grinned, the smile pulling at her scratches.

"There are right ways to hurt?"

She ran her fingers across my chest. "I can't wait to show them all to you."

"I thought you said it was just once?"

Una laughed. "I read a lot of books. And I have a very active imagination."

I pulled her close, kissed the top of her head. We lay there for a while, watching the flames in the hearth, and the moonlight spilling through the window, neither of us interested in sleeping.

"Una?"

"Yeah?"

"I've only got one more try to make this ice flute work."

"Grab my bag, will you, please?" She pointed to the dim corner where her backpack lay propped against the wall.

Naked, I crossed the room, the chill seeping into my skin, and retrieved her bag. Once we had both nestled back under the covers, she unzipped it, revealing a small box.

My pulse quickened. "I know after what we've just done...but I think it's a little soon for—"

Una slapped my chest. "Open it, you idiot."

I hesitated, searched her face for signs of a joke, then lifted the lid from the box. A small white orb drifted from its cushion of black velvet and hovered in front of my face.

I gaped at it. "It's the orb of Snow and Ice."

CHAPTER TWENTY

T marveled at the magical beauty of the white orb as it floated in front of me. When I extended my hand, it nestled into my palm as gently as a whisper, cooling my skin.

"I brought mine too," Una said.

"You've had this the whole time?"

She nodded. "Thought it might come in useful."

"But how did you get it to go with you? The orbs only respond to their guardians."

"After Ember told me you were planning on leaving, I went in the great hall, told all the orbs how stupid you were being and asked for their help. Your orb decided to come along for the ride."

I stared at the tiny sphere nestled in my hand, its size belying the immense power it held. If it possessed even a fraction of its rumored magic, it could be the key to crafting the flute we so desperately needed.

"Do you think it will work?" I asked.

She put a hand on mine. "Yes."

I cupped her face. "Thank you, Una. Thank you for having the foresight to bring it with you."

She kissed my cheek. "That's me. The sensible sidekick."

"You are so much more than a sidekick." I brushed my thumb across her lips. "You are the reason for everything."

"Oh, Gal." She cradled my hand against her cheek, kissed the pad of my thumb. "If I'd known you were capable of saying such sweet things, I'd have forced myself on you ages ago."

I had a strong temptation to throw her onto the bed, ravage her one more time, but I didn't want to hurt her more than she already was.

"And besides," she said, with a twinkle in her eye. "The sidekick job belongs to Ember. He's the pot-wielding dragon king desperate to breathe fire."

I laughed, genuine amusement bursting out of me. "Maybe if he wasn't so stoned all the time, he could breathe fire. We need to help him when this is all over."

She stuck two thumbs in the air. "Operation Ember is a go."

Our amusement faded abruptly as the window imploded, shards of glass scattering across us, the bed, and the floor. Snow and ice followed, and a howling wind colder than I'd ever felt.

Una and I sprung out of bed, our bodies moving as one, as Babette burst into the room.

"Time to leave," she said. "Storm came early."

"But I haven't carved the flute." I grabbed a blanket and used it to cover our modesty.

"Take it with you." Babette pushed her arms through her thick coat.

"Una's not well enough to travel," I protested.

Una touched my arm. "We have to go, Gal. I'll be fine."

I searched her face, the wounds that were still so raw. "Are you sure?"

Babette pointed to Una's bedside table. "Take the pills. They'll keep the pain at bay. And keep the physical activity to a minimum." Her eyes flickered to the blanket wrapped around us. "Ember is outside getting the skidoos ready. The three of you will leave together."

"What about you?"

"I'm going to get Kristín and Inga off this forsaken island and into the boat, as well as a few others who returned after the road was blocked."

"It is safe to sail?" Una asked.

"There aren't enough skidoos for everyone," Babette said. "And you need them more." Her eyes settled on me. "You're going to take down Zale. And you're going to take him down big."

Unexpected emotion clogged my throat. Babette was about to sail off into a storm, and I was one step closer on my journey to confronting Zale. I might never see her again.

"I left the skidoo on the glacier."

"It doesn't matter now." Babette pointed at my hovering orb. "That'll help."

"Is there anything we can do?" Una asked.

Babette shook her head. "Get dressed. Get on your way."

After Babette left the room, Una and I threw our clothes on, pulled on boots and gloves. I wore my mother's cap under my beanie, praying it would bring us luck. I positioned Una's woolen hat over her bandage, and she moved a few strands of hair to hide her injury. Then we darted outside, my orb sticking close to my side. The ground shook and sparks of fire appeared on the horizon. Looked like the volcano had decided to wage a war with the storm.

We wrestled against the raging wind, my grip firm around Una's gloved hand, shielding her from the worst of the onslaught. Snow swirled around us, furious and frenzied, reducing the world to a blur of white. The cold cut through my clothing, seeped into my bones. As the guardian of Snow and Ice, I thought I knew cold, but this was an entirely different beast.

When we reached the shed, Ember was hunched against the wind, filling the skidoos' gas tanks, and piling a heap of jerry cans into a couple of small trailers.

"Thanks, buddy!" I called, but the violent weather stole my voice.

Ember responded with a thumbs up, then leaped onto one of the skidoos.

Kristín and Inga emerged from the house, pushed a back-pack full of food and a couple bottles of water into my arms. I tied it into the trailer, then gave them both a hug goodbye.

Babette appeared, wrapped Una in a fierce hug, whispered something into her ear I couldn't hear. Then she came to me, slapped my shoulder. "Good luck, prince," she shouted over the roaring storm.

I hugged her back, then urged her to leave.

I trudged to the empty dog shed—Kristín had released them all. After tugging the bucket containing the last sample of blue ice out of the deepening snow, I fought my way back across the meadow, each step painfully slow as the weather impeded my progress.

I caught sight of Babette leading Kristín and Inga toward the coastal trail. A small tornado formed in their path, carrying rocks and pebbles and God knew what else. Something flew through the air. A large dark object caught in the wind. A sheet of corrugated metal dislodged from a shed roof, heading straight for the small group.

Una screamed a warning.

The object struck with brutal force, colliding with Inga's head, knocking Kristín to the ground, slicing into Babette's waist. All three of them went down.

I charged through the snow, desperate to reach the fallen group. Inga and Kristín were moving, but Babette lay motionless. Una's figure blurred in the darkness as she sprinted toward them.

After dropping the bucket by the skidoo, I gestured to Ember to follow, who'd been unaware of the accident. We stumbled forward, the wind driving us back with each step. Even my orb struggled to make progress. Visibility was nearly nonexistent amid the swirling snow and debris. It felt like a cruel dance, two steps forward, one step back.

Finally, we reached the fallen group. Kristín and Inga were struggling to rise, while Una knelt beside Babette's broken form. I crashed to the ground, skidding through the snow, my ankle throbbing, my orb trailing behind me, weaving a path through the weather.

The section of metal was stuck in Babette's side. Blood seeped from a deep wound, puddling onto the frozen ground.

Too much blood. She stared at the sky, coughing, choking on her own blood.

"Babette!" I yelled, shaking her by her collar. "Babette!"

She coughed, raised a weak hand. "It's okay, prince," she gurgled.

Una and I hovered at her side while Kristín put pressure on Inga's head wound. Ember sent heated air in our direction, dispelling some of the snow and raising the temperature a couple of degrees. Una cried, tears freezing on her cheeks. Snow surrounded us, hiding us inside an icy veil of despair.

"You have to go," Babette murmured, trying to push me away. "You have to go."

I shook my head, glanced at my pulsating orb. "I don't know if you can help, but if you can save Babette's life, that's what I want you to do."

My orb bobbed in the air, radiated a pulse of bright white light, then floated to Babette's body. It traced a loop around her, bathing her in its glowing aura from head to toe, shrinking in size as it did. My heart sank, knowing whatever remnants of magic it had possessed were now diminishing, but it was the right thing to do.

"No," Babette said, halting the orb in its path. "You need its power more than me."

"You can't die," I pleaded with her.

"Please, Babette," Una cried.

Babette coughed more blood. "I'm already dead. Cancer. Radiation poisoning. It's okay, prince. It's okay."

"You could go to the fountain," Ember said. "Hurry."

"It's too late," Babette said. "Tell Dylan I love him. I always have." Then she closed her eyes. She was gone.

I hung my head, unable to face anyone, until Kristín put a hand on my shoulder.

"You must go," he said. "It's what Babette would want."

With a heavy heart, I got to my feet, removed the metal panel from Babette's wound and threw it aside. Cold blood leaked from her stomach. "I'm so sorry."

Kristín pulled Inga to her feet, then hoisted Babette over his shoulder. He shot me a glance filled with pride before guiding his wife through the blizzard. Within seconds, they'd vanished, swallowed by the relentless snow.

"We got to move it!" Ember said, waving me back to the shed with the skidoos.

With my heart breaking, I grabbed Una's hand once more and we plodded toward the flimsy shelter, the snow tearing at us like vengeful spirits. Ducking under the tin roof, we gained a brief respite from the storm.

"I'm worried about you," I told her, gesturing to her eye.

She shook her head. "There's no time for that. We have to go."

Ember straddled his skidoo, its engine roaring to life, and I snatched the bucket containing the last sample of enchanted ice and secured it on my vehicle. I motioned for Una to climb on behind me, urging her to wrap her arms around my waist, hoping my body would block the worst of the elements. I glanced at my shrunken orb, urged it into my pocket where it would be safe, where I would feel its reassuring presence.

With a sharp twist of the throttle, the skidoo roared beneath us, headlights cutting a feeble glow into the blinding veil of snow. Ember and I erupted from the shed simultaneously, careening around the corner with no clear destination except "west" in our minds. I desperately hoped Babette had provided Ember with directions to the airfield. But in this weather, what were the odds our pilot would wait for us?

I could hardly see through the frosted goggles, relying more on instinct than sight to navigate the treacherous terrain. Snowflakes, sharp and unyielding, stung our faces like a thousand biting insects. Bitter gusts of wind cut through the blinding white haze as Una and I clung to the roaring skidoo, hurtling through the heart of the merciless storm. The acrid stench of gasoline from the strapped jerry cans surrounded us, a constant reminder of the explosive danger nestled in the trailer.

Una's pained gasps were muffled by the storm's fury. Her body pressed against mine as she winced with each jolt, but we had no choice but to press on. Each breath was a struggle, the frigid air seizing our lungs. The taste of snow and ice lingered on my lips, mingling with the metallic tang of adrenaline. Every muscle ached; my body pushed to its limits, my ankle throbbing. My heart heavy with grief.

I felt the weight of the precious ice in the trailer and checked over my shoulder every few seconds to make sure it was still attached. I tried to balance speed with caution, aware the slightest misstep could lead to disaster. With every twist and turn, I clung to the hope that the magical ice held some answers, that I wouldn't fail at the last chance we had.

CHAPTER TWENTY-ONE

The night swallowed us whole, a tempestuous fury that merged day and night into one unending blur. The blizzard surrounded us, carrying not just snow, but ice and pinecones and grit and dirt, mercilessly pummeling us every passing mile. There were no recognizable roads beneath the suffocating blanket of white, no familiar trails etched into the frozen canvas. We carved our own path through the wilderness, hoping we wouldn't drive off the ridge of an unexpected cliff.

Una clung to my waist, her head buried against my back. I whispered silent prayers to unseen deities, hoping her wounds wouldn't reopen. Because then I really would use my orb to heal her, if it could.

The ground trembled beneath us, thrusting our skidoo in erratic directions, threatening to cast us off into the chaos. Fiery sparks and gusts lit up the sky behind us, the furious volcano at our heels finally unleashing its wrath. I clenched my teeth, wishing I could push the skidoo to its limits, but with visibility so low, we couldn't risk it. We sped over frozen lakes, snaked through winding forest trails, and skirted the sides of dilapidated ghost towns, the storm chasing us the entire way. Exhausted, I gripped the handlebars, my body rigid, my ankle throbbing.

The stench of ash and fire filled the air. I trailed behind Ember, his figure a silhouette against the blizzard, his wild hair whipping behind him as he leaned into the wind, his hunched form crouched over the handlebars. Time blurred; I had no idea how long we'd been traveling or how much farther we had to go.

Be patient, Little Jackass.

A grim smile formed on my lips. Babette. Gone. Caught up in my drama. Una had lost an eye. How many more would suffer because of my choices?

We had to press on, to keep heading west, clinging to the hope the pilot awaiting us was braver than me.

As we careened around a sharp bend, a treacherous slope opened on our left. Ahead, Ember wrestled with the skidoo's handlebars, desperately trying to avoid the yawning chasm. But the movement was too sharp; the skidoo tilted onto one ski, teetered there for a few seconds.

I swerved to avoid him, thundered past him as his skidoo spun out of control. Ember was flung into the air, his skidoo careening in a different direction, jerry cans transformed into deadly projectiles.

The world exploded as Ember, skidoo, and jerry cans collided in a violent collision of metal and limbs.

"Ember!" I screamed, turning my handlebars to double

back. My voice was drowned by the deafening roars of explosions. Flames billowed, swallowing Ember whole, while the jerry cans detonated one after another, hurling shards of metal and plastic in every direction.

"Ember!" Una screamed, sliding off the skidoo, running as close to the inferno as she dared.

I slid off the saddle, my hands and body cramped from staying in the same position for so long, and tested my ankle. Painful, but I could cope. The wind wasn't as bad here, but tremors continued to shake the ground and the snow remained thick and blinding. Taking Una's hand, we took cautious steps through the swirling snow toward the fiery mess. The reek of burning metal and plastic choking the air, signposting the worst.

Then, suddenly, Ember emerged from the middle of the fire like a phoenix rising from the ashes. His clothes were scraps, his hair trailing a blaze behind him. He inhaled, drawing the fire into himself, extinguishing it with an awe-inspiring display of power.

"I didn't know dragon kings could do that," Una said.

"Me neither."

Ember approached, a cocky grin on his face. "Thought I was a goner for a minute there. Turns out I can't breathe fire because I can inhale it."

I patted his bare shoulder, then took off my coat for him to wear. "That was something else."

"That's the most extreme display of dragon king power I've ever seen," Una said.

"Ice and fire, buddy, ice and fire." Ember slipped into the

jacket, surveyed the wreckage of his skidoo, the melted jerry cans. "That ain't going to work."

I sent a quick prayer up that the ice spear, Una's bag, and our food were still safe in my trailer.

"There's not enough room for three of us on one skidoo," I said.

"We should find shelter," Una said. "Get out of the storm. We can't hike in this."

"Are we far enough away from the volcano?" I asked.

Ember tilted his head, a newfound confidence brimming in his stature. "Reckon I'll breathe in all that lava."

Una poked his chest. "Maybe we can test that under more controlled circumstances."

The three of us trudged toward the remaining skidoo, distributing clothes and bags among us. Ember took the food, and I carried the bucket of snow containing the precious ice, as well as Una's backpack.

We walked for what felt like miles, but in reality was probably not that far. At least the wind was at our backs, even if the snow hid everything from view. We struggled through snowdrifts, afraid to step off a ridge or into a crevasse. With the moon or sun—I couldn't tell what time of day it was— obliterated by the storm, I didn't know which way we were walking, could only guess.

After a couple hours, Ember dropped to his knees, shivering in the snow. "I hate the fucking cold," he muttered as I hauled him to his feet.

"We need to rest," Una said. "I'm exhausted too. I need more pain meds."

It was affecting me too. My ankle had been screaming at

me for the last hour. I turned in a slow circle, scanning all directions, but couldn't spot anything which looked like a shelter. In the distance, lava spewed from the erupted volcano. We appeared to be out of the danger zone, but ash and dirt would make breathing hard before long.

Taking a rope from Una's bag, I tied it around our waists, tethering us together so we wouldn't lose each other in the storm. But if one of us went down, all of us would. There was a measure of comfort in that.

We trudged onwards, heads bowed, stumbling frequently. I felt the presence of my orb and my mother's cap urging me on, but it was much harder for the other two who had no affinity for snow and ice. And my orb did nothing to dispel the pain in my ankle.

No one spoke. We saved our energy. Each step became a struggle, a battle against exhaustion and the biting cold. Una's injury slowed us down, Ember's unfamiliarity with the icy terrain evident in his faltering steps. My ankle screamed with every movement. The fear of not making it settled in my chest, a chilling realization that we might succumb to the elements.

After another few minutes, Una grabbed my hand and pointed ahead. A stone dwelling loomed out of the blinding whiteness. My heart lifted as hope soared through my limbs, giving me an injection of energy. We made it to the house, its windows boarded, its door frozen shut. It took all three of us to yank the door open, and before we entered, I placed the bucket with the spear beside the threshold. Then we stepped inside and slammed the door behind us, shutting out the vicious wind and snow.

The relief was immediate. No more snow. No more wind. No more cold. Although the weather continued to howl and shriek at us from outside, inside we found a temporary respite.

The house, divided into a kitchen and a living area, held an air of abandonment. And the lounge furniture was covered in dust sheets. Logs were piled near a hearth and Ember set to work, coaxing flames into life.

The three of us sat on a rug in front of the fire, shedding our coats and boots. Una eased the boot off my ankle, revealing a swelling which had doubled in size and a black bruise encasing my entire foot.

"You need to say off that," Una said, worry brimming in her beautiful blue eye.

I shrugged. I had no choice.

Una took my foot in her hand, massaged the swelling, ignoring me when I winced. She shoved a few painkillers in my mouth, then took some herself. The pain gradually dulled, and I sank into a haze of warmth, my worries dissolving in the comforting glow of the fire.

After grabbing cushions from the couches, Una lay beside me. The three of us stared at the flames, rubbing our hands together and diving into the food Inga had provided. I couldn't remember the last time I ate and devoured food without ceremony.

"Finally," Ember said. "My balls aren't the size of shriveled peas."

No one had the energy to laugh.

I turned to Una. "Your bandage looks frozen."

She showed me the first aid supplies Babette had

provided her with. I couldn't see much by the dim light of the flickering flames, but I unwound the bandage, placed a kiss on her wounded eye, then wrapped it with all the love inside me.

"You two." Ember shook his head. "Are just the cutest."

Una smiled, then her face fell. "Babette..."

"I can't go there yet." If I spoke of Babette, of everything she had done for us, I'd lose it. There was so much ahead of us, and if I succumbed to despair, I might never find the strength to leave this sheltered stone dwelling.

Una nodded, raised a hand to cup my cheek, pressed a gentle kiss to my lips. Ember rolled a spliff, and we all took part, all of us attempting to numb our grief.

"Are you going to carve your flute?" Ember asked.

I shook my head. "Not in here. It would melt by the fire. I'm going to wait for the storm to die down, then I'll give it a go."

Una patted my knee. "You'll get it this time."

I didn't reply. The unease seeped into me. It was a fifty-fifty chance. With the presence of my orb, I felt hesitantly hopeful, but it certainly wasn't a sure thing.

Ember stared at the boarded windows. "How long do you think the pilot is going to wait?"

"If the storm moves west, not long at all," Una replied. "And if the ash goes with it...no one wants to be around for that."

"We won't be able to fly if the ash cloud gets too thick," I said.

The thought of going back outside filled me with exhaustion. No way I could ask Una and Ember to continue right now. "We'll rest a bit. Then we'll carry on. If the pilot is there when we arrive, great. If not, we'll figure it out."

"How?" Ember said.

I patted the orb in my pocket, hoping it would give me guidance. "I don't know yet," I admitted, my voice a whisper.

CHAPTER TWENTY-TWO

*T*he pain shot up my leg like a lightning bolt as I struggled to my feet, the weight on my ankle making me wince. Daylight filtered through the cracks in the boarded windows. Bright light which filled me with hope. Cocking my head, I listened for signs of...I don't know what, anything that might signal danger. But the wind had died down. Peeking through the cracks in the windows, I watched snow continuing to fall, burying the landscape, mingling with a thick coat of gray ash.

Una circled her arms around my waist. "How's the ankle?"

"Sore. You?"

"Sore."

"Maybe you should stay—"

Una covered my mouth with her hand. "Don't you start with that bullshit."

I kissed her cheek. "Okay."

Ember joined us at the window. "This weather makes me

feel like I'm stuck in a snow globe that's constantly being shaken by a five-year-old kid. Spoiler alert: I'm not enjoying the view."

"We should get going," I said.

We dressed quickly, eating as we zipped jackets and pulled hats onto our heads. Una wrapped my ankle in a tight bandage and helped me ease it into my boot. I hissed as I tied the laces, worried I wouldn't make it far, worried I'd be the one lagging behind after everything I'd put them through.

When we were ready to leave, I pushed the door, but it wouldn't budge.

"Did it freeze again?" Ember asked, putting his weight behind it. But the door remained stubbornly closed. "I always dreamed of being a superhero, but I didn't expect my first mission to involve defeating the Frosty Fortress of Door-dom."

Laughing, Una tore off one of the rotten boards from the window. A whistling gust seeped into the room, stirring the dwindling ashes in the hearth. The snow came all the way to the sill. Ember knocked the broken glass from the frame, and we threw the two backpacks and the rifle into the snow. After dragging one of the dusty couches under the window, the three of us climbed through the hole, immediately sinking to our waists. The sky was heavy with ash, floating flakes mingling with the falling snow, invading my lungs, making us all cough.

I struggled against the tightening grip of packed snow. "Where's the bucket? Where's the spear?" I scanned the distance, looking for signs of movement, wondering if someone had stolen them in the night.

"It's buried under the snow," Una said, coughing into her hand.

After digging a path through the snow to the door of the house, I searched for the buried bucket. I heaved it out of the snow, then dug through it until my gloved hand closed around the jagged spear of ice.

"Thank God." I smiled, raising the spear, only to watch three inches of its length crack and fall into the snow.

My mouth dropped open. I had only nine inches of ice remaining in my hand.

I looked at Una and Ember, my shock mirrored on their faces.

Una recovered first. "Maybe it's more of a piccolo."

"It has to be a flute," I mumbled.

"It's a general term," Ember said.

"What am I going to do?" A cold dread settled at the back of my neck, making my teeth chatter and causing a prickling sensation to sweep over my scalp. "What am I going to do?"

"The first thing you're going to do, is not panic," Una said.

"How am I going to make a flute from this?"

"You've got plenty of length there." Ember winked, then suppressed his smile. "Sorry, not the right time for jokes."

Una giggled, covering her mouth.

"Honestly!" I half shouted. "What good are you two if you can't be helpful? Come on, guys, you stowed away on my boat, you stole my orb, you made me fall in love with you... and now I'm stuck in the snow with no idea which way is west and wishing on a prayer that some random pilot who I've never met is still waiting to fly us to Greenland. And then what? How do I keep the ice frozen? How do I carve the flute? How do I play it? And how do I kill Zale? This is a total fucking nightmare!"

Ember pointed. "West is that way."

I eyed him suspiciously. "How do you know?"

"It's a dragon king thing. We're like birds. Can sense the magnetic pull of the poles. We never get lost."

"One step at a time," Una said quietly. "Don't look at the end goal. One step at a time. First, we go west, find the airfield. Then we can make new decisions based on what we find. And I'd appreciate it if you didn't yell at me like that. I thought we were past that."

I dropped the spear in the bucket. "I'm sorry." Couldn't meet her eye.

"Don't do it again."

"Don't tell me what to do," I snapped.

"Guys," Ember raised both hands. "Let's chill. Come on. Can we hit pause on the melodrama? There are bigger things at stake."

Una and I locked gazes. Neither of us offered an apology. Instead, she snatched her backpack from the snow and shrugged into it, while I slung the strap of the rifle over my shoulder and dragged the bucket behind me. Ember made jokes as he used his wings to hover in the air and avoid the obstacle of snow altogether, threatening to keep the food to himself and only reward us if we promised to stop bickering.

We trudged onward, the landscape a nightmare of snow and ash, each step a battle against the icy drifts. My breaths came in ragged gasps, the air tainted by the acrid taste of fiery debris. We'd only gone half a mile when I collapsed, out of breath, no longer able to battle my way through the waist high drifts. My willpower was drained. The pain in my ankle wouldn't let me continue. Untapped anger seethed under the surface. I didn't even know what I was angry about.

"It's not far," Ember said from the sky several feet above my head.

"How do you know?" I asked.

He pointed. "I can see planes."

"Planes?" Una's face lit up. "What about people?"

Ember shook his head. "Not that I can tell."

I pulled myself out of the snow, stared into the distance, but all I could see was white snow, black boulders, and gray sky. The most depressing landscape I'd ever encountered. Anger was replaced by relief, mingled with a heavy dose of exhaustion. We may have reached our destination, but I struggled to summon the energy to fight my way through the snow.

I glanced at Una, looking for...reassurance, maybe? I wasn't sure. She tipped painkillers into her mouth, repositioned her bandage, then shrugged into her heavy backpack once more. I trudged over to her, gently slipped the straps off her shoulders.

"Let's swap." I handed her the bucket with the nine-inch ice spear.

"Thanks," she said, taking the handle. "My head is killing me. And it's so hard to breathe."

"You need to rest."

"We're almost there."

"I wish we still had the Power of the Sea."

Her hand floated between us. "I'll be okay."

"I know. You're the strongest person I know."

"I heard that," Ember called from the sky. "But you're probably right."

Una smiled, her hand meeting my shoulder. "You too."

We carried on together, me watching Una's face for signs of pain. Each grimace, each wince, each sigh, filled me with guilt. She was trudging through the aftermath of a blizzard and an erupted volcano with a horrible head injury because of me. She'd insisted she was here for her own reasons, but would she have come on her own? And so I kept circling back to how I felt responsible for both of them, even though they were grown adults and could make their own decisions. They wouldn't be here if it wasn't for me.

Sighing, I lifted my injured ankle out of the snow.

"You okay?" Una asked.

"I don't know how to answer that question anymore."

"I've got to admit, I'm looking forward to returning to Atlantis and getting out of the cold."

I gave her a side-eye. "You do look pretty hot in a bikini."

She blushed. "I didn't think you'd noticed."

"Oh, I noticed alright."

We took a couple more steps.

"Are we okay?" Una asked.

"I trusted you with my most prized possession." I gestured to the bucket in her hand. "I think that's a pretty good sign."

"Don't be mad at me...for falling in love with me." I'd never seen her smile so tentatively.

"I'll try not to hold it against you."

"We're here!" Ember called, curtailing my conversation

with Una. He waved his hands in the sky, then dropped into the snow. "I wish I could breathe all the snow in too. Without turning myself into a human icicle."

"That would be pretty helpful," I laughed.

The snow level descended. We trudged through the biting cold until we emerged onto an expanse of packed ice, a plowed road leading toward a white hangar which loomed like a fortress in the frozen wasteland. Skeletal planes sat in the forecourt, icicles hanging from their broken wings. Ash clouds blew past the hangar, coating everything in dust.

The three of us walked onto the forecourt, around a couple of small planes. I'd never seen a plane before, let alone traveled inside one. They were smaller than I expected. I marveled at how they could get into the sky.

"What now?" Una placed the bucket on the ground and turned a slow circle, eyes scanning the nooks and crannies.

"Maybe there's an office, or something," Ember said. "The pilot dude probably didn't know what time we'd arrive...could be chilling out somewhere."

"Hello?" I called, walking deeper into the hangar. "Hello?"

A distant door slammed, sending echoes reverberating through the hangar. Ember and Una stuck to my side, Una passing me the bucket. Heavy footsteps clanged down a metal staircase, and I glimpsed a figure emerging from the shadows at the far end of the hangar.

I gripped the rifle, its cold metal providing a semblance of reassurance. "Who's there?" I demanded, my finger hovering over the trigger.

"Howdy there!" an unfamiliar voice called.

It sounded friendly enough, but I kept my finger on the trigger.

A man clattered down the stairs, all blue denim and wild unkempt hair framing a weathered face, tattoos covering most of his skin, a cigarette dangling from his mouth. Maybe a distant cousin of Ember's. He pulled to a stop a few feet from us, the fake fur collar in his denim jacket turned in.

"Howdy there! You must be Babette's friends."

The mention of her name sent a stab of sadness through me.

Una extended her hand, introduced us all. We all shook hands.

"Name's Coralus, only pilot in the west. And the east. Hell, only pilot I know left in the world." He chuckled, then coughed, hacking up a ball of mucus. After stamping his cigarette out, he gestured for us to follow him. "Babette said you need to get to Greenland."

"And then some," I muttered. "It's kind of you to take us."

"Nothing is free in this world." Coralus raised an eyebrow. "Babette promised me her boat."

"She *what*?" I swallowed, glanced at Una's and Ember's concerned faces. Best not to tell Coralus about Babette's passing then.

"She didn't tell you?" Coralus asked.

I shook my head.

"As soon as the storm is over she's sailing it here." Coralus glanced at the sky. "It's pretty hairy out there, what with the ash cloud and all, we should leave now. You folks ready?"

"Super excited to ride in a plane," Una chirped, her enthusiasm a stark contrast to my growing sense of unease and the faith Babette had put in me by relinquishing her boat.

Ember eyed the tiny aircraft, suspicion written all over his face.

A well of nerves opened inside me, hollowing out my stomach. "Is there another way?"

"To Greenland?" Coralus let out a low whistle, wiped his oily hands on his jeans. "Nope. Not in this weather. And even then, we're pushing the limits." He led us to a plane which had seen better days, its once vibrant colors faded to a dull monochrome, hanging metal scraps I couldn't identify. A front propeller. A single engine. A set of metal stairs leading to the doorway. Maybe we'd be better off swimming it. Coralus rapped his knuckles against the craft, the hollow echo sounding ominously tinny. "This baby has never let me down."

"Have you flown to Greenland before?" I asked.

Coralus cocked a shoulder. "That's where I'm from."

"Didn't really answer the question," I muttered to Ember, who raised a brow, surveying the plane with skepticism.

Coralus clapped his hands together, an eager gesture, then pointed up the stairs. "We should get going. Before that ash cloud catches us."

"And what if it does?" Una asked.

Coralus whistled again. "Then I'll be wishing I was a dragon king, not an equidnid."

"Equinid?" I questioned.

"You haven't heard of us?" Coralus asked.

"Us?" I scanned the hangar once more but couldn't spot another living soul.

"Equinids." Coralus thumbed his chest. "Seahorse shapeshifters?"

I did a doubletake. "There are seahorse shapeshifters? Why aren't you on Atlantis?"

"We have our own land," Coralus said. "Although there's not many of us left. Most of us stick to the human world."

"This is so cool!" Una said. "Do you...shrink when you shift? Or do you remain human sized? Why have we never come across you before? Why haven't you ever visited Atlantis? Exactly how many of you are left?"

Coralus pumped both hands at the ground. "Slow down there, little lady. We got plenty of time to talk on the plane. We really need to get going."

I eyed the plane once more, the single engine, the double wings, the rust patches...and my throat dried out. "When was the last time you flew this thing?"

Coralus gave the craft another rap. "Just before the volcano erupted when I arrived here."

I swallowed hard, my throat dry, my mind conjuring images of disaster. Then I grabbed the bucket and mounted the metal staircase, Una following on my heels, Coralus taking the rear. As I pushed through the doorway, Ember called from the ground, unfurling his wings.

"Think I'm going to fly."

"I don't blame you, buddy," I replied.

Coralus shook his head, his mouth puckered in disappointment. "I've never had a single incident."

"All the same," Ember said, and leaped into the air.

"Plenty of room if you change your mind," I told him.

Ember gave me a curt nod. "I want to give us options."

He didn't have to say more. If shit went to hell, Ember would do his best to save us.

Una and I stepped into the plane, securing ourselves into the seats behind Coralus. He went through the motions of starting the engine, performing a safety checklist, pulling levers and pushing buttons, none of which I understood. The interior was freezing, and I was confident the spear would remain frozen on the two-hour journey to Greenland.

After placing the backpack on the seat across the aisle, and the rifle on the floor by my feet, I anchored the bucket with the ice spear between my legs. Una sat next to me. We pulled our gloves off, held hands, our fingers laced together. The single engine whirred to life, sounding far more powerful than I thought capable. Coralus clapped, rubbed his hands together, sang himself a little song, then we lurched out of the hangar, narrowly avoiding the other parked planes, and hurtled along a frozen runway. Ember hovered outside the plane's small windows.

"This doesn't feel natural," I said.

"And breathing through gills does?" Coralus asked.

"More normal than this," I muttered, as a vicious nausea coiled in my stomach.

Una squeezed my hand, a pulse of encouragement. "Flying is definitely quicker than swimming."

Not if we fall out of the sky.

The plane left the ground. My stomach remained on the tarmac as we soared into the sky. Coralus sent us into a steep climb, pushing my body into the chair, the rifle sliding down the aisle.

"This is...this is insane," I stammered, catching a glimpse of Ember's wing as he maintained the same altitude.

White clouds. Gray ash. White clouds. Gray ash. Ember's wing. The scenery never changed. Nausea continued to build, and I doubled over, gasping for air, trying to keep my rising bile at bay.

"First time, newbie?" Coralus called, his face the personification of amusement.

Scowling, I clung to the back of his seat, my fingers digging into the fraying fabric, swallowing hard to suppress the urge to vomit. I turned green. Not that I could see my face. But that's what it felt like. Coralus soared to a ridiculous height, banked a sharp turn, sending my stomach spiraling. Una handed me a paper bag just as I opened my mouth. I snatched it from her and spewed the contents of my stomach, a sour stench filling the air.

"I'm sorry," I murmured as I collapsed back in my seat, a cold sweat coating my skin.

Una gave me a sympathetic smile, then placed the paper bag on the seats behind us. "Two more hours to go."

I clutched the armrests as we climbed, biting my tongue, chewing my cheek, holding my breath. After a few minutes, we leveled out and the constant drone of white noise filled my ears. I glanced out the window. Ember maintained a pace beside us. Below a frozen sea. So far below. So, so, so far, it made my head spin.

"Why aren't you sick?" I asked Una.

"I take after my dad."

I squeezed my eyes tight. "Tell me when we get there."

She kissed my cheek, the warmth of her lips easing my discomfort.

Time passed. The white noise ebbed and flowed. My grip on the armrests remained ironclad, threatening to cramp my hands, but I refused to let go. The smell of vomit hung in the air. But I did not open my eyes. Although my orb remained nestled in my pocket, it could do nothing to reassure me so far above sea level.

I counted seconds, minutes, seconds, minutes, until I lost track and I had no idea how long we'd been flying. I clenched my teeth so tightly I was in danger of cracking a tooth. And my white-knuckle grip on the armrests was sure to leave my hands cramped for days. My parents had spoken of their youth on the mainland, trips to exotic locations via airplanes. Their journey to find Atlantis had taken them all over the world. I couldn't fathom why people willingly put themselves in a tin can and hurtled through the sky at unnatural speeds, thousands of feet above land. I would never do this again.

"You are adorable," Una said.

"Shut up."

"You should see your face."

"Shut up."

"You know there's a bathroom back there. We could go lock ourselves in and you could have your wicked way with me."

I cracked an eye open. "You have got to be kidding me."

She leaned over, her hair tickling my face. "Are you saying you don't want me, Gal Waters?"

I swallowed, tasting bile. "There's no way you'd get a rise out of me."

Una stuck her hands between my legs, and I instantly came to life. I groaned, caught between fear and desire. "You never play fair."

"All's fair in love and war."

"Good thing we're not at war."

She grinned, her hand still on me. "Not today."

"Una..."

"You can't deny I'm taking your mind off things."

I sighed. "True. Just wait until we land."

"I'll hold you to that."

"How's Ember?"

"He's...Ember? Shit. I can't see him."

I snapped the other eye open, leaned over Una to check the window, couldn't spot a single sign of my cousin. Gray clouds surrounded us. Gray ash clouds, heavy and dense and filled with the reek of fire.

"Ember?" I unbuckled my seatbelt and crept to the other side of the plane, caught sight of his wing, breathed a sigh of relief. Too soon. The plane lurched, then stalled in the air. Coralus hissed a few curse words. Una gestured me back to my seat, buckled my belt with trembling hands. The plane nosedived. A clear shot of the ocean. Snow. Ocean. Land. Iceberg. On repeat.

"What's going on?" I yelled at Coralus.

"Bird flew into the engine!" he yelled back. "We lost it!"

The bird or the engine?

"What does that mean?" I called.

"We're going down!"

I gulped, reached for Una's hand. We clung to each other as the plane spiraled out of control. The wings tilted violently, offering glimpses of land on one side and the vast ocean on the other. Smoke billowed from the engine, permeating the cabin. Ember kept pace beside us, his massive wings tucked by his side, barreling toward the ground with us.

"Brace!" Coralus called.

Una and I ducked. I kept one hand in hers, the other on the handle of the bucket. No matter what happened, I couldn't lose the ice.

CHAPTER TWENTY-THREE

There was no way we were going to survive this. We'd come all this way; battled a hurricane, fought muttwalkers, summoned the lady of the lake, dodged a volcano, parried with a polar bear, all for it to end in the frozen Labrador Sea.

Una gripped my hand, her face pale, her mouth clenched shut. She hunched her shoulders, squeezed her eye shut, too afraid to look at death rushing us in the face. I couldn't let her die. She'd been through too much already.

"I'm scared, Gal." Una's voice cut through the roar of the malfunctioning engine, the howl of the arctic wind.

"We're going to be okay." I didn't believe it, but I couldn't let her die without hope.

I kept my hand clenched in hers, the other around the handle of the bucket. Ember screamed our names, his wings tucked close to maintain our plummeting altitude. Coralus jabbed at buttons and yanked at levers, but nothing stalled our freefall.

"What do we do?" I yelled at the pilot.

"Pray!" he yelled back.

The ocean rushed at us, sizeable waves carrying jagged sheets of unforgiving ice. Closer. Faster. Closer still. Water. Ice. Rock. My heart hammered in my chest, a violent drumbeat marking the seconds until impact.

Refusing to accept my fate, I tore off my seatbelt, then unbuckled Una. I yanked her out of the seat and tugged her toward the door. "We're jumping."

One more glance at the ocean. Only a few feet below. Ember by the wing, using his body to prop the plane up, to decrease the gradient of our descent. I focused on the water's surface, mentally preparing for the bone-chilling plunge. As I anticipated the impact, Coralus pulled the control stick, and we skimmed along the surface, bouncing across the waves and ice, spinning wildly. Una and I were thrown together, the bucket torn from my grasp.

Before we came to a stop, the cabin door swung open. A torrent of water surged inside, pulling the small craft under. The bucket slipped away, carried by the tide, beyond my reach. The world outside the plane became a disorienting swirl of bubbles and icy currents as we were submerged into the heart of a merciless sea.

I clung to my last gasp of air as the icy tendrils gripped my ankles and readied myself for the transition.

"Go," Una said, releasing my hand. "Get the ice."

The bucket was swallowed by the depths. I caught the barest hints of its bright orange as it sunk beneath the surface. I dove into the frozen sea, pushing my tail into existence. Although I could withstand colder temperatures in my merman form, the water was below freezing, cold enough to cause hypothermia in even the strongest of ocean shifters.

With a desperate kick of my tail, I reached for the elusive bucket, only for it to swirl away, as if the ice had forsaken me.

I released the orb from my pocket, where it kept a silent and hopeful vigil, then shrugged out of my thick jacket. It was an anchor, dragging me down. I resumed my pursuit of the ice spear. At least it wouldn't melt down here.

Visibility dwindled to a mere pinprick as the light was extinguished by the ocean's depths. A shadow to my right— Una coming to help? I dismissed the thought, focusing on the vanishing bucket, kicking my tail with all my might. Finally, my fingers closed around the plastic handle. I abandoned the idea of hauling the bucket up, instead clutching the ice spear, and turned to face the surface.

Another shadow. This time to my right. A flicker caught in my peripheral vision. I prayed it wasn't Una foolish enough to venture this deep.

My orb hovered by my shoulders, casting a feeble glow in the frigid darkness, highlighting me to any creature in the vicinity, to whatever shadow lurked nearby.

Another flash of movement. Quick and menacing. My heart knocked against my ribs. My gills stuttered, battling against the chill and fear threatening to consume me. Above, the surface was a blurry, distant beacon of light, teasingly out of reach. I caught sight of the rifle sinking into the depths.

Spear in hand, I powered my tail and propelled myself toward the surface. But before I had ascended ten feet, the shadow came again, no longer a mere silhouette, but the gaping maw of the mightiest shark I had ever encountered. Zale.

A scream echoed in my mind, a silent plea, as I sent scattered telepathic thoughts toward Una and Ember, praying they were safe. I didn't know how far from land we were.

Zale glided past, his massive pectoral fin slashing my gills, winding me and leaving me spinning helplessly. I hadn't yet crafted the flute, hadn't secured the trident, and yet here I was, facing Zale, unprepared and vulnerable.

Clenching my teeth as well as the delicate shaft of ice, I scanned the water for an escape. Zale could have easily killed me already. Why hadn't he?

A dark roving eye. A flash of white teeth. The swish of a fin. He turned the surrounding water into a deadly whirlpool, the freezing cold numbing my fingers and tail, making it almost impossible to grip the ice I held.

Una.

I had promised I would never embark in a relationship because of the pain it could bring. The pain of loss and death. I couldn't allow her to mourn me.

Avoiding the next menacing bump, I kicked for the surface. I ignored the presence of Zale in the water, propelling myself to safety, hoping against hope that I would make it. Ember met me halfway, his dragon king wings spread wide, far more powerful than my merman tail.

Zale's shadow loomed once more. This time, his jaws were wide. This time, they intended to kill. But Ember tugged me out of Zale's path, higher, higher, higher, until we breached the surface.

I spotted Una and Coralus dragging themselves from the

water and onto an icy beach. Only a few yards away. Not daring to look for Zale, Ember and I swam after them. Terror kept my limbs locked. The temperature kept my hands numb.

"Gal!" Una screamed, her gaze locked behind me.

Ember gripped me under both arms, yanked me toward the air, and we flew out of the water together, Zale's jaws snapping closed on nothing but ice.

We made it to the desolate beach, collapsed upon the rocky land, panting and shivering, teetering on the brink of hypothermia.

I sat on the frozen ground, barely able to keep myself upright, my eyes fixed on the spot where Zale's dorsal fin had disappeared under the water. He did not return. An uneasy atmosphere filled the void of his sudden disappearance.

It wasn't until my chattering teeth broke off the corner of a tooth that I came back to reality, the reality of freezing to death. Due to the nature of our shifting abilities, the four of us wore only our underwear in a temperature of under minus twenty degrees. My orb buzzed around me, animated with frantic activity, but being a magical sphere of snow and ice, it could do little to prevent hypothermia.

Miraculously, Una had recovered her waterproof backpack. She dug through it now, hurling dry clothes at us. Fleeces and sweaters and socks that would never fit, but they were better than nothing. She chucked me my mother's cap, the sight of it bringing me a measure of hope, and I tugged it down tight on my head.

Once we'd draped the dry clothes around us, we staggered away from the isolated beach and followed an inland path out of the bitter wind. I was desperate to be free of the frigid shaft of ice, but without it I had no hope of defeating Zale.

"Is everyone okay?" I pushed the words through my blue lips.

Nods were all anyone could manage.

"My plane is gone," Coralus said. "She was all I had."

"I'm sorry," Una said.

"Maybe I'll take up sailing instead," the pilot responded.

I stopped walking, pinned him with a glare. "Babette is dead."

Coralus blanched, then his expression turned hard.

There was no more conversation as we trudged an unsteady path through piles of heaped snow and ice-encrusted boulders, slipping and falling across the slick path. After a few minutes, we reached an abandoned enclosure and fought our way inside. It was no more than a tin hut with a wood stove and a few tins of expired soup lined up on a shelf, but the rise in temperature gave us immediate relief. I didn't know who the shelter belonged to, or if I could ever repay them, but I sent them a silent prayer of thanks.

Before succumbing to the safety of the hut, I packed the ice into a pile of snow by the door, hoping it would remain untouched. While Coralus built a fire in the stove, Una, the only one of us properly dressed, poured cans of soup into a pot and started the gas hob. Ember stood in front of the fire, staring at his toes. A couple were miscolored. Frostnip. He might lose them. I glanced at my own feet to see them in a similar condition.

"Did I mention I hate the cold?" Ember grumbled as he sat heavily on the floor.

"Thank you for saving my life." I inched toward the burgeoning fire, ignoring the pain lancing through my defrosting toes.

Ember patted my knee. "You own me. Big time."

Una handed me a mug of soup, the steam defrosting my eyebrows and hair. The aroma of food surrounded me. I'd never smelled anything so delicious. Una dried out her bandage by the stove, then rewound it around her head.

"That was Zale, right?" Una asked, as she propped herself against the rickety countertop.

"Yep," I replied.

"Why didn't he..."

"Kill me?" I asked.

Una nodded.

"I don't know."

"Well, I, for one, am glad he didn't." Coralus took a noisy slurp of his soup. "You guys owe me a plane. And a boat."

Ember opened his mouth and a balloon of fiery sparks gusted toward the pilot. "You almost killed us!"

"Yeah, but I didn't." Coralus winked. Did he take anything seriously?

"How are we going to get to the Galapagos now?" Una asked.

"You're going to drive," Coralus said. "That is, if you want to keep that ice in its current state."

"And I suppose you know where to find a car?" I asked. Not that any of us knew how to drive.

"Yep," the pilot replied.

Una crossed one ankle over the other. "And I suppose that's going to cost us too?"

Coralus smirked. "Yep."

We were trapped in a frozen wilderness, our lives hanging in the balance, and the only way forward was through a dangerous alliance with a man whose motives remained as murky as the depths of the ocean we had just escaped.

CHAPTER TWENTY-FOUR

*T*wenty-four hours passed within the confines of the small hut, each minute marked by the savage wail of the Arctic winds. When our log supply ran out, we were forced to venture outside once more. Thankfully, Una had spent the time scavenging the nearby village and came back with clothes and shoes to fit us all. My orb was once again secure in my pocket. While Ember grumbled about his toes and Una eked out the last dregs of soup, I spent the time drifting in and out of an uneasy sleep, worried Zale would return on foot for his final reckoning. That would be almost preferable. In his human shape, he was just a man. And a man I could kill.

Coralus led us the few miles along a discarded road toward the hangar where he'd intended to land his plane, both Ember and I limping with our frostnipped toes. The crunching of our boots and the bellowing wind dogged every step, muting my ragged breathing. Worried the sounds might disguise a stealthy ambusher, I kept my eyes peeled in all directions, and my frozen fingers wrapped around a rusted tin container I'd uncovered where the ice spear now rested amidst a bed of snow. Although I doubted I needed the snow considering the temperature hovered at a ball-freezing minus twenty degrees.

The trail weaved around ramshackle huts and over small drifts of compacted snow. Trash skittered across the street and a dog barked in the distance. I hoped it wasn't a muttwalker. No way did I want a repeat experience with mutated zombie dogs. The four of us huddled in a tight group, as much for safety as shelter.

When I didn't think my frozen toes could take more walking, a large hangar appeared, although its vastness was swallowed by the endless stretch of snow and sky. It mirrored the one we left behind in Iceland, a haunting sense of déjà vu creeping over me, but we had no intention of flying this time. Countless planes stood frozen on the tarmac, ghostly relics of a world which had once thrived.

"Plenty of planes for you to choose from." I gestured to the glistening array.

Coralus nodded. "Bertha was my favorite."

"Babette was one of my favorites too," I said, unable to suppress my resentment.

He shot me a swift glance, his eyes assessing. "She was a fine woman. I know she'd want you to take down Zale. So I'll give you what you need."

"What's it going to cost us?" Una asked.

"Your promise," Coralus said, his voice as cold and unyielding as the winter winds. "That you'll kill him. I never want to see a shark that size again."

"I can't make that promise," I said. "But I'm damn well going to try."

We spent the night on dusty pullouts in the back office of the hangar. Before we went to sleep, Coralus tipped a cache of rations into Una's bag. Granola bars and trail mixes. I didn't inspect the expiration dates. It hardly mattered anymore.

While Una and Ember slept, Coralus handed me a battered cooler once used to transport organs to medical facilities. Together, we packed it with snow, ensuring the ice spear remained frozen. "You'll need to refresh the snow every day," he said. "Keep it as cold as possible."

Suspicious of his sudden altruistic turn, I watched him sleep, wondering if he'd spill his secrets in his mumbled dreams. But he slept soundly, hardly moved, and snored louder than a waterfall.

I settled into an armchair and watched over the others. Not because I feared an ambush, but because I couldn't banish the image of Zale's jaws from my mind. The previous night, shock and frost had numbed my senses, but tonight, the reality of our situation gripped me. Zale was tracking us, preparing for the final showdown just as I was. And yet he had spared my life. The only reason I could think Zale wanted me alive was his desire for the trident, and he didn't know where it was. Once I reached the Galapagos and seized the trident from the guarded caves, I wouldn't have to search for Zale, he'd be right on my tail.

I had embarked on this journey with the sole purpose of bringing Zale to justice. But deep down, I knew I might never find him. Or that he might kill me instead. Although I'd imagined us in combat more times than I could count, the reality of it stole my breath. In the water yesterday, his fin slicing ragged wounds across my gills, the sheer size of his jaws, the immense power in his muscled form...how could I beat a thing like that? How had I underestimated the magnitude of his strength and size? The night stretched on, a silent battle-field where my fears waged war against my resolve.

I tried to visualize the trident in my hands, to feel its weight and balance, seeking comfort in the belief that it held the key to my victory.

My gaze shifted to Una's face. I couldn't let her die. I couldn't let her succumb to another injury. Zale was too powerful for her. For all of us. A force of nature that threat-ened to crush us. I vowed to keep her away from the final confrontation. I would be distracted if I had to worry about her safety. She could kill me after.

"Hey." Una's voice pulled me from my thoughts. I hadn't realized she was awake. "You look serious. What are you thinking about?"

I mustered a smile. "How I'm going to kill Zale."

Una sat up, swung her legs to the floor, and tiptoed over to my chair. She sat on my lap, straddling me, and laid a gentle kiss on my lips. "How *we're* going to kill Zale."

"Of course." I couldn't look her in the eye.

She held my chin in her hand, lifted my face to look at her, stared into my eyes for eternal seconds, then kissed me once more, this one deep and hungry, leaving an impression, leaving her mark. I knew what she was doing, but I still refused to put her in danger. I could be equally stubborn.

"Gal Waters, don't think I don't know what you're up to."

I didn't bother to lie, but instead wound my arm around her, cupping the back of her neck, and brought her face close once more, crushing her lips to mine. My other hand cupped her ass, my thumb circling the bare skin beneath her shirt. Her sweet moans filled the air as I invaded her mouth with my tongue. Kissing was far better than arguing.

"Oh. My. God!" Ember's voice jolted me out of the moment. He sat up, one arm covering both eyes. "Is this the latest trend in wake-up calls? Because I usually prefer a strong cup of coffee, not a front-row seat to a kissing marathon."

Una crawled out of my lap, socked his shoulder. "Good morning to you too."

Grinning at my cousin, I covered my arousal with a tattered cushion. "You could have given us another five minutes."

Una spun to face me. "Five minutes?"

"Ten?"

Ember stood, both arms covering his face now. "I hate to think!"

Coralus chuckled from his couch, then sat up and slapped his thigh. "Young people." He wagged both eyebrows. "Reminds me of the love dens in Equinia."

"Equinia?"

"Love dens?"

Coralus waved a hand, his eyes clouded with memories. "Long time ago." He stood, stretched, let out a mighty belch. "Best get you on your way."

After a measly breakfast of stale porridge, Coralus handed us the keys to a battered pickup with four snow tires that had seen better days. The truck bed brimmed with jerry cans, like soldiers readying for battle.

"It's two thousand and five hundred miles to Cordova Harbor," Coralus warned. "You're going to need to fill up a couple times. Gas stations are unreliable."

"And then it's over three thousand miles to the Galapagos." Ember scratched the back of his head and yanked his hair into a messy topknot.

"We'll be sailing right past Atlantis." I could drop them both off. "We will have done a complete circle. And then some."

"Hey, if that old guy can make it around the world in eighty days in a hot-air balloon, we can get to the Galapagos," Una said. "Have a little faith, guys."

She squeezed us into a group huddle and made us chant a cheesy inspirational jingle.

"I could drop by the fountain on our way past Atlantis," Ember said. "Heal these toes of mine." He looked at me. "Shit, sorry man, I forgot the fountain doesn't work for you."

"It's fine," I said. "I'm used to it." It would be a great excuse to drop them off and sneak away once more.

After securing the ice spear in its cooler amidst the jerry cans, the three of us clambered into the pickup's cab.

"Who's driving?" Coralus said as she shut the door after us. Ember rolled the window down.

Una and I exchanged a look. Neither of us had a clue about driving. We'd been hoping Coralus would say his good-byes, disappear, and leave us in peace to figure it out.

"You do know how to drive, right?" Coralus asked.

Una and I shook our heads. Ember raised a tentative

hand. "I drove the patients from the hospital around in the electric carts?"

"Electric *carts*?" Coralus goggled at us. "You don't have cars on Atlantis?"

This time all three of us shook our heads.

Coralus let out an exaggerated sigh, rubbed his face. Leaning in through the window, he pointed at instruments and dials, fired off rapid fire instructions on how to drive a car. "It took kids six months to pass their test. You don't need to be a perfect driver, but try to keep it on the road."

"On the road," Ember echoed as he put both hands on the wheel. "Where's the respawn button?"

Ignoring his joke, Coralus corrected his grip. "Ten to two. Like a clock."

Ember turned the key in the ignition like Coralus had shown us and the engine rattled to life. Although the truck shook and rumbled, it wasn't half as scary as the airplane. Until Ember plonked his heavy boot on the gas pedal and the truck fishtailed away from the hangar.

In the rearview mirror, I caught a fleeting glimpse of Coralus, his figure shrinking in the distance, hand held in a wave. At least there hadn't been time for meaningful goodbyes.

Ember shot across the tarmac, narrowly avoiding a few planes, over the bank of a small hill, and onto the frozen road. Una clutched my arm while Ember turned to us with a grin. "I'm going to be a racing driver when I grow up!"

"Watch the road!" I shouted at him, yanking the steering wheel to avoid careening into a ditch.

Una made the sign of the cross and muttered a prayer under her breath. "I do not want to lose another eye!"

"I got this," Ember said as we fishtailed along the icy road. "Give a guy some credit."

The engine's roar echoed through the frozen wilderness as Ember floored the gas pedal, leaving a trail of churned snow and ice in our wake. No one spoke. I sat in the middle, which offered the perfect view of potential obstructions in our path. Una clutched the door handle, bracing herself against the jerky movements of the truck. The jerry cans and the cooler slammed around in the bed behind us. But the grin never left Ember's face. At least he embraced danger with a smile.

Once I insisted Ember ease his foot off the gas pedal, he got control of the car and settled into a less terrifying rhythm.

"The faster we go, the sooner we get there," Ember complained.

"We won't get there at all if you keep driving like that," I retorted.

"If we're going to crawl at this speed, at least pass me a spliff?"

"No!" Una and I said at the same time.

"You need to concentrate," I said.

He went through the operating instructions with us, ensuring we were prepared to take the wheel when needed. When it was my turn to drive, Una huddled close for warmth, her breath visible as she warmed her hands by the truck's feeble heaters. Ember pressed a few buttons on the central console and music blared into life. Songs I'd never heard before.

Upbeat love songs with a dance beat. Despite the freezing temperature outside, smiles spread around the pickup and the sun shone down on us during the few hours of wintry daylight. The further inland we drove, the safer I felt, knowing I was putting miles between me and my nemesis. It would be days before we reached the Galapagos. That would give me time to contemplate my next moves. Learn how to craft the flute. Figure out how to wield the trident. Decide how to kill Zale.

When the music stopped, Ember found an eject button and a cartridge popped out. It took him a few minutes to figure out that he had to flip it over and stick it back in. We listened to that same tape again and again, learning all the words as the hours and miles ran by under our feet.

There wasn't anyone out there in the frozen wilderness. This far north, in the heart of winter, where the rising sun barely broke the horizon, we might have been the only people left on earth.

We couldn't tell where the roads were. It had been several years and snowfalls since the nuclear war and the roads had hardly been used. At least, not by cars. The odd track of a dog sled was visible. So we made our own route across the ice, keeping to a flat gradient, avoiding anything which banked or jutted, and maintaining a frustratingly slow speed to avoid disappearing into a glacial crevasse. But eventually we reached the west coast of Greenland.

"Now we have to dive across...ice," Una said as she scanned the blinking white sheet sprawling as far as the eye could see. She had been driving for the last hour, and now she released the steering wheel and flexed her fingers.

"There's no other way across," I said. "Not unless Coralus flies us in another plane."

"Yeah...no thanks," Una said.

"Are we sure it's safe?" Ember said. "The ice is thick enough?"

It seemed so long ago since I'd planned the route with Babette. We'd hashed it out at Kristín's house over a mug of cocoa and a warm fire. The details were hazy. I'm sure she wouldn't have suggested driving across an ice sheet if it wasn't safe. But then she was the one who had been about to attempt sailing in a blizzard.

"I guess we'll find out," I said.

"What if Zale is under that ice?" Ember asked.

I swallowed. I hadn't considered that. "There's no way. Not even he could break through all that ice. And he'd freeze. It's too long for prolonged exposure. Even for him." I sounded like I was trying to convince myself.

Una shifted in her seat to look at us both. "We all knew this journey would be dangerous. Hell, we've been through so much already. It's not going to stop being hard just because we want it to. But we've got to keep going. Or we turn back."

"I don't want to turn back," I whispered. My pounding heart might have had other ideas, but I'd come too far to throw it all away now.

Ember grabbed Una's bag from the back seat, rifled through the contents until he removed a pre-rolled spliff. After a flick of his lighter, he took a deep inhale, the pungent aroma filling the cab. "I'm going to need some medicinal assistance for this. But hell, yeah, let's carry on. Huzzah!"

"Huzzah!" We all roared, and Una eased onto the ice.

CHAPTER TWENTY-FIVE

*M*aintaining a speed of twenty-five miles per hour, we crept across the ice. The first hour dragged by in a state of uneasy anxiety as Una slowed for every groan and crack of shifting ice. Each time it creaked, we paused and held our breath, waiting to plunge through the ice and disappear into the frozen depths. But once we'd racked up a few of those experiences, we were able to ignore the creaking ice sheet, the slight undulation of its shifting movement, and maintain a constant speed.

Although I believed the water beneath the thick ice sheet was too cold for Zale, I couldn't shake off the feeling we were being followed. The expanse of frozen nothingness stretched in every direction, the world above ground deceivingly empty. But I had no idea what lay a few meters beneath our feet. If Zale would be bold enough to swim through frozen seas.

It took four more hours to reach the east coast of Canada. We all heaved a sigh of relief when Una drove onto secure land. Ember wasn't allowed to drive until the effects of the weed wore off. He'd been babbling and giggling and singing along to the music for the entire journey. I had a headache. My toes were throbbing. But all that went away when I glanced at Una, at the bandage she still wore around her missing eye. She had lost far more than me.

Una parked in the shelter of a cluster of boulders and we clambered out of the truck. My legs were shaking from sitting still for so long, and I stretched my arms above my head and shook out my limbs. Without camping gear and with the truck far too cold to spend the night in, we were forced to find shelter. Although there were no signs of human life, evidence of recent activity showed in a plowed trail, a recent fire, and an altar with frozen flowers carved into the boulders.

Refusing to spend the night exposed to the elements, we drove inland for another hour, with me taking the wheel. When Ember spotted the dark structure of a small, abandoned building, we pulled to a stop. After heaving the cooler out of the truck bed, the three of us crept to the unlit building. Made entirely of logs and dirty glass, it looked to be an old tourist information center. Apparently, we were in the middle of Ukkusiksalik National Park. I'd never heard of it and had no idea how to pronounce the word either.

Ember broke the door open with a fierce kick, sending a few splinters flying. With no logs in sight and nowhere to build a fire, we had little choice but to huddle together in the middle of the room and hope we didn't freeze to death. Ember exhaled heated air to keep us warm.

I tapped the cooler. "I think it's time I try crafting the

flute again. If I can do it, then I know I'm one step closer to achieving my goal."

Una nodded. Ember gestured for me to slide the lid open.

We all peered inside. There was nothing but a half-frozen slush, the glint of a shaft of ice no longer than an inch.

Unable to voice my horror, I plunged both hands into the slush, frantically searching for a longer shaft of ice I might have missed. But after five minutes, when my desperate hunt was unsuccessful, I removed my numb hands and stared at my friends.

I almost cried. We were so close. And now this. Only one stubby inch of ice remained. Not enough for even a single note.

Una and Ember stared at the cooler. Neither of them offered a single word of comfort.

Celestial Abyss...

Vorago's Trident...

Parting the sea...

The words of the prophecy I'd glimpsed before I'd destroyed the book echoed in my mind. It had to mean something. Surely, I was destined to wield the trident? But if not... what exactly was in my future?

"I have an idea." Una's voice cut through my spiraling thoughts.

I sat on the floor with my head in my hands, unable to look at her.

"We melt the rest of the ice," she said. "The entire cooler. We mix it around. Then we freeze it once more. You craft a flute from that."

Ember released a low whistle, sparks dancing in his fiery breath.

"I don't know, Una." I finally raised my head. "I appreciate the thought, but it sounds like wishful thinking."

She fixed me with her one blue eye. "Do you have another idea?"

I shook my head.

"Then you might as well try it," she said.

"She's got a point," Ember added.

"What makes you so sure it will work?" I asked.

"I'm not." Una shrugged. "But I have a feeling."

I raised my eyebrows. "One of those oracle, *Mermaid Chronicles* feelings?"

She splayed her hands. "Who knows? But I'm not giving up yet."

"Me neither," Ember said. "Persistence is my middle name, right after 'Dangerously Handsome.'"

I stared at the miserable, slushy ice, the nubbin of remaining spear. Once it had been six feet long. And now only an inch remained. It had killed a polar bear, traveled across Iceland and Greenland, been lost to the depths of a frozen sea. Why not?

"Ok. Hell, let's try it. We need to melt it first, mix it, refreeze it." I turned to my cousin. "Would you do the honors?"

"That's my boy!" Ember leaned over the cooler and exhaled a heated breath, instantly melting the slush and remaining fragments of ice. The last inch of the ice spear disappeared.

"I hope this works." I crossed the fingers on both hands,

then thought to unzip my pocket and release my orb. The tiny white sphere shot from its confines and swirled a few circles around my head before coming to hover by my nose.

"If I take this cooler outside, it's going to freeze into the shape of a...cube..." I said. "Not the best shape for carving a flute from."

Ember pushed himself to his feet. "So we find a mold."

"Here?" I questioned, throwing an arm out to indicate the icy world beyond our temporary shelter. "Did you not see the miles of...snow and ice? We're in the middle of a national park. Where are we going to find a cylinder?"

Una grinned, sprang to her feet. "I know exactly where."

Unable to ignore her contagious excitement, I followed her outside. She took a couple steps away from the building, turned, and pointed. I followed her finger to the guttering and drainpipe.

I threw my arms around her and lifted her off her feet. "You're a genius."

Ember ripped a three-foot length off the drainpipe from the building. Although it was thicker than I had hoped for, I doubted I'd find a more suitable cylinder for miles. Perhaps I could carve it down to a more appropriate size.

Once inside the building again, I hauled a desk from behind the counter, its legs scraping the worn floor as I positioned it in the middle of the room next to the cooler. I yanked open the bottom drawer, which served as a filing cabinet, and emptied the contents onto the floor. With the cooler, the drawer, and the drainpipe, the three of us returned outside.

While Ember and Una steadied the drainpipe vertically

so that one of its open ends was sealed by the bottom of the drawer, I poured the contents of the cooler into the top end. Slowly. Carefully. Not daring to waste a single drop. The liquid dripped down the pipe, filling it inch by inch until it reached a height of around two feet. A small leak sprouted at the bottom, threatening our efforts. When I added pressure to Una and Ember's grip, the leakage stopped. The three of us waited. In subzero temperature, we didn't have to wait long for the water to set and the first ice crystals to appear. After half an hour, we dared to remove our hands and found the pipe was no longer in danger of leaking.

"Let's leave it out here tonight," I said. "It will be frozen solid by the morning."

Back inside, Una shared granola bars from her pack and we congratulated each other on our quick thinking. My orb hovered close, lending me a new confidence, its dim glow both mesmerizing and peaceful.

When Una and Ember had both fallen asleep curled on the floor, I put my gloves back on and ventured outside once more. Well aware I'd not slept the night before and would be a danger behind the wheel if I didn't sleep tonight, the temptation to work on the flute was too strong to ignore. The sooner I carved it and produced a musical note, the happier I'd feel. Besides, there was no way we could fit the frozen shaft back in the cooler in its current dimensions.

I removed the frozen length of drainpipe from the drawer with a crack I feared would wake my friends, or break the shaft in two. But after remaining immobile for a full minute, all remained quiet and the ice retained its shape.

Sitting in the snow, I laid the Navy cap beside me,

drawing strength from the possession which had belonged to my mother. I teased the frozen piping away from the ice, careful to collect any loose fragments within the cooler in case I needed to melt it again and start from the beginning.

Once the shaft had been removed from its encasing, I held it in both gloved hands, admiring the way reflected moonlight made its ice crystals glimmer. Somewhere in there was my magical inch of blue ice.

To reduce the diameter of the shaft, I rubbed my hands up and down its length, giggling as I imagined what suggestive comments Ember would say if he were witnessing this. After the initial burst of laughter, I calmed and found a rhythm, sliding and turning. Sliding and turning until the diameter shrank. The flute began to take shape, its diameter shrinking with every careful motion. Little nodules protruded occasionally, which I attempted to smooth away, sometimes leaving a small dent. But anything carved by hand would never be perfect. Or perhaps it was perfect in its own manmade simplicity?

When I figured the diameter was no more than an inch, and the cooler contained a couple inches of slushy water, I took a break. The emerging flute could now fit in the cooler. I figured it had been the heat of the truck's engine that had melted it as we'd traveled. Tomorrow, I would secure the cooler in a place it couldn't be touched by heat or sun. But part of me wasn't ready to call it a day.

Previously, I'd relied on Ember's heated breaths and a coil of wire to hollow the flute and craft the notes. Thinking of him seemed to conjure his shape. He emerged from the building with Una in tow.

"We thought you might be out here," Una said.

"Need a hand? I come equipped with two, plus a third for emergencies. It's detachable and great for high-fives or intimidating enemy goblins." Ember held a wire in his hands, not a spare hand.

I smiled at them both, patted the frozen ground, inviting them to join me. They sat either side of me. No more words were exchanged. As if they sensed my need for silence, they remained quiet, not wanting to disturb my concentration. My orb made frequent circles of the flute and our heads. It buzzed with excitement, which I took as a good omen.

Ember's heated breaths mingled with the sharp winter air, visible wisps disappearing into the darkness. He handed me the warmed wire. I hollowed out one millimeter at a time, catching the thawing drips into the cooler. The world outside our circle blurred as I focused on the task at hand. Heat. Thaw. Repeat. And so the night went on.

When I'd made it all the way to the end of the flute, Una clapped and Ember offered me a wide grin. My hands ached with cold and fatigue. My orb, now marginally smaller than a marble, flew through the hollow shaft, illuminating the ice from inside with a mystical glow.

"This is going to work!" Una said in a hushed voice.

"Now for the notes," I breathed. This was the pivotal moment, the part where my previous attempts had failed.

Una cupped her chin in her hands and watched me work. Ember kept the wire heated. Sometimes he puffed on the wire, other times he puffed on weed.

My gaze fixed on the wire Ember offered, fear thrashing in my chest like a vengeful shark. The wire froze before my eyes, my hesitation turning it cool in seconds. Ember reheated it, but again I froze, terrified of making a mistake.

"Even the bravest knights accidentally wore their armor backward." Ember winked. "And if all else fails, there's plenty more drainpipe to use as molds."

While what he said was true, I didn't want to go through this again. The concentration it took, the emotion trapped in my chest while I thought about what the crafting of the flute symbolized. Each time I became more convinced I would fail. And each time I carried a tentative hope that I could produce a note. Now I was afraid to find out either way.

"Do you want us to leave you alone?" Una asked.

"No," I replied, shooting them a quick glance. "No. Please don't leave. I don't want to be alone. Unless you're too cold..."

Una shook her head.

"You owe me a couple of toes," Ember said, but there was humor in his eyes.

My orb swooped through the shaft, urging me forward, its presence a silent encouragement. Ember heated the wire once more, and this time, I summoned the courage to touch it to the flute's surface, creating a small hole leading to the central shaft. I repeated the action seven times, pushing my thoughts to another place, relying on muscle memory and mechanics to take over.

My gloved hands trembled with the effort, but I didn't stop until the flute was complete. My small orb flew once more through the shaft, illuminating it from the inside, leaving a faint trail of sparkling light in its wake.

Una gasped. Ember raised both brows. When I looked

again at the flute in my hands, it was awash with an iridescent blue light, glowing with otherworldly magic.

Una nudged my arm. "Play it."

"I don't know how."

"Put it to your lips and blow," Ember deadpanned.

I shoved him with my free hand. "You'll need more than toes if you keep that up."

He raised both hands in surrender. Then, after putting my mother's cap on my head, I placed the ice-cold flute against my lips. But it wasn't as cold as I'd feared. Somehow, in the crafting and the blessing—as I thought of the action my orb had performed—the flute had become a tangible thing. An object filled with strength, a vessel brimming with ancient power.

I pursed my lips and blew delicately across the mouthpiece. A single note floated into the dark night, fragile and delicate. I blew once more, and the single note was accompanied by others, blue sparks of light escaping the flute to dance in the sky. They ebbed and flowed with each breath, creating a mesmerizing display around us.

I covered a hole with my finger, then another, then two more, experimenting with the melody. I'd never played a musical instrument, had no idea how to read its language, but what I produced was the most beautiful music I'd ever heard. Haunting and stirring. Delicate and strong. Mesmerizing and all-consuming. It created a symphony of emotions, a tapestry of sounds which stirred my soul. The notes got inside me, made me feel things I'd never let myself feel. Tears tracked down my cheeks as I watched the music play above my head. My orb danced among both my tears and the pulsing musical notes, joining their serenade in the sky.

A profound sense of pride swelled within me, drowning out the doubts and fears that had plagued my previous attempts. I felt my mother's presence, her unseen hand guiding mine as I played the flute. Finally, I had done something to make her proud.

CHAPTER TWENTY-SIX

$\mathcal{N}$ ight wrapped around us as we drove beneath the stars, hints of blue lights following the battered pickup. We fought a path through fresh snow and hidden rocks, often in danger of losing a tire or denting the axle. No one had wanted to return to the shelter. And so I sat shotgun as Ember drove, the cooler nestled between my feet, stopping every hour to repack it with fresh snow and ice. My orb chose to pass the journey inside the cooler with the flute, both of them sparkling with hidden mystical powers. I thought of them as friends. Perhaps my orb, with its limited power available, was using the last of its resources to keep the flute frozen and enchanted. Each time I glimpsed the flute, it beckoned me with a bewitching blue glow, urging me to play it once more. Playing it brought a peace to my soul I'd never experienced before. A deep-rooted calm I had only ever dreamed about.

Unable to contain our excitement for the next leg of the journey now that we had a functioning flute, we drove continuously, taking turns at the wheel. The landscape blurred into a dreamscape of white, punctuated by the occasional silhouette of trees against the sky. Occasionally, we made stops to stretch our legs and repack the cooler. With each passing mile my excitement grew. Whenever I'd envisioned my confrontation with Zale before, it had always been filled with terror and the very real possibility that I would not be the victor. But with the flute now in my possession, filling me with what I hoped was just the right amount of confidence and not brazen foolishness, I finally believed I could win.

It took us five days to reach Cordova Harbor in Alaska, and during that time we never saw another living soul. The haunting absence of humanity cast an eerie spell on us. We encountered only the echoes of life—dogs, birds, elk, a lone wolf, and thankfully no muttwalkers. There were a few signs which indicated we weren't alone. Four wheeled cars with windscreens cleared of ice, remnants of fires on the side of the road, plowed paths leading to looted convenience stores, and once smoke trailing above the trees of a dense forest. But never a person.

We found a few weapons in a camping store. Most of the goods had disappeared long ago. A mouse-eaten tent had been left behind, but none of us were keen on roughing it under the stars, not without thermal sleeping bags. Una scavenged a dusty old blanket for the backseat sleepers, and I secured a pair of small hunting knives. They didn't make up for the rifle I'd lost, but it was better than being defenseless. I doubted the humans remaining on the mainland understood the flute's importance, but I would guard it with my life. Una and Ember too.

When it was my turn to sleep in the back seat, I often dreamed of Zale. My dreams oscillated between haunting memories of the day I lost my mother and vivid visions of the looming confrontation. I envisioned myself brandishing a trident, two prongs aimed at Zale's eyes, the remaining one piercing his brain. In past dreams, such thoughts would jolt me awake, drenched in sweat, my neck hairs standing at attention, and a searing terror gripping my chest. Yet, now, a strange sense of inevitability overshadowed my fear. Once I had deposited Una and Ember back on Atlantis, I would be free to continue the journey alone without fear for their safety. Then Zale and I would have our final reckoning.

The final hours of the drive took us around a frozen lake and skirted the edge of a small mountain chain where empty chair lifts dangled in the freezing air. Although Atlantis boasted its own snow-covered mountain in the north, I'd never attempted skiing before. It was an activity my mother had disapproved of, and even though her anxious warnings had faded over the years, they echoed in my mind.

A sudden break in the monotony of the landscape caught my attention—a stretch of water adorned with a few fluttering sails. I pulled the car over and parked on a deserted road. Armed with only the cooler, my cap, and Una's backpack, we fought our way through years of untouched snowdrifts, past abandoned restaurants which promised crab and lobster and the best seafood in the west, and arrived at Cordova Harbor.

I eyed the assortment of sailboats, their decaying masts

portraying nothing but unfortunate endings. Most had their sails furled, but I feared once erected, we'd find them in a state of decay. Plus, there were only two or three substantial enough to brave the daunting four thousand-mile journey south.

"That one," Ember said, unfurling his wings for the first time in days. Perhaps they itched when unused, like my tail.

I followed his gaze past the sailboat I'd been inspecting to see a super-sized yacht casting long shadows across the water.

I laughed. "Don't be ridiculous."

Ember gave me an indignant eyebrow. "Why not?"

Una clasped her hands together, let out an adorable giggle. "Think of the silk sheets and booze fridge. The sun loungers and the soft towels. An actual toilet with proper plumbing. A crew who cooks—"

"There's no crew on board that yacht," I said.

Una clung to my elbow, her pleading gaze tugging at my resolve. "We all know how to sail. But being on a yacht? So much better. Please, Gal?" She batted her eyelashes at me. She actually batted her eyelashes at me. And it worked too.

I shook my head. "And what happens when it runs out of gas?"

Ember hiked a thumb toward the pickup we'd deserted. "Plenty of gas left in those jerry cans."

"Enough to get us all the way to the Galapagos?" Atlantis. I only needed to get to Atlantis, then I could pick up a sailboat and continue the journey.

Ember shrugged. "There are harbors and marinas all along the west coast. If we run low, we'll pull in and grab another boat."

"Aren't you worried about theft?" I asked. "Or running into an unruly mob who aren't willing to let their territory be invaded?"

"Nope." Ember stuck his thumbs in his belt loops. "We won't have to worry about sails, and wind, and tacking, and swinging booms which might knock us out. Hell, we can put it on autopilot and sleep the whole way there. And God knows, I could do with a break from the weather."

I eyed the mammoth vessel once more. Una, as if sensing I was about to give in, wiggled at my side like an eager puppy, her one blue eye wide and pleading. The yacht was insanely huge, a mansion on water with countless levels, a gleaming white thing with black windows and...solar panels? It had solar panels lining several sections of decking. That cinched it, but I made Ember and Una sweat a little more.

"I want a daily cup of tea," I declared.

"I can do that," Una replied.

I looked at Ember. "A foot rub."

He glared at me. "Only if you do me too."

I laughed and slapped his chest. "Let's do it. And I'm not going anywhere near your frostbitten toes."

"Same," Ember retorted. "Your toes are uglier than a swamp monster's butt after a week of curry."

"Thanks a lot!" I said, extending my foot as if my toes were available for all to see.

Ember slung an arm across my shoulders, nudging me in the ribs at the same time, while I wrapped my arm around Una's waist. Together, we sauntered along the dock until we reached the mammoth yacht. It took us thirty minutes to search every level to ensure no one was living or hiding inside. Satisfied it was empty, we deposited the decaying trash in the ancient dumpsters on the dock and loaded the jerry cans onto the boat.

As I scrutinized the control console, the cryptic dials stared back at me, rendering the entire system an enigma. I searched for a manual. It was another hour until I felt I'd read a sufficient amount and could figure out how to start the boat. Lights emerged throughout the vessel as it powered up, spanning control monitors, ceilings, and decks.

"Wow!" Una clapped, her face a picture of childish glee.

I scanned the monitors, noting there were no screens to indicate the gas level. It was one hundred percent solar powered and the batteries were full to the brim. Until the freezer in the galley reduced to an appropriate temperature to house the flute, I kept it in the cooler at my feet while I piloted the boat away from the harbor. Ember went below deck to catch up on sleep and Una stood with me at the helm, helping me navigate the narrow passage to the sea, and singing a song from the cassette tape we'd all memorized. There wasn't much to do. It didn't have a wheel like my sailboat, only a lever for forward and backward. All I had to do was flick a few buttons and the boat practically piloted itself. I could see why the wealthy of the time before had been so enamored by such vessels.

The hours melted away as we crossed the strait and curved around Elizabeth Island, and then we were in the open seas. I hugged the coastline, keeping a line of land visible to my port side as we sailed south. Una stood behind me, wrapped her arms around my waist, buried her head between my shoulder blades.

No longer needing to worry about shallow beds or rocky landmasses, I turned in her arms.

She looked up at me with her big blue eye. "Gal?"

"Yeah?"

"Will you help me take my bandage off?"

My breath caught. It had been over two weeks since the polar bear attack. The last time I'd changed the bandage I'd done it quickly and without looking, knowing the wound was still raw. Now, she was ready to face it.

"I'm sure there's a first aid kit below." I took her hand and led her below deck.

Rummaging through the galley, I found a first aid kit and laid it next to Una. She sat on the granite table, legs crossed, hands folded in her lap, her bottom lip quivering ever so slightly. Her beautiful face, marred by the remnants of the attack, spurred a mix of emotions within me. But I couldn't delay. She had asked this small thing of me, and I would give it to her. Gladly. Without a second thought, I kissed her nose and prepared myself for what lay beneath the bandage.

As I was about to unwind the bandage, she grabbed my wrist. "Will you tell me if...can you...what if...?"

My hands hovered either side of her head. "No matter what's under this bandage, you'll always be beautiful."

She flushed. I felt the heat flooding to her cheeks with the back of my hand.

"I know I said I didn't care, but I..." She cocked a shoulder, looked at her folded hands. "I kind of do."

Her words pierced my heart, wrapped the guilt around me once again. "It's not forever. Only until we get you to the fountain."

She gave me a quick nod, then slid to the edge of the table.

As I unwound the bandage, my hands trembled with a mix of anticipation and dread. Her breaths mirrored the rhythm of my heartbeat—short, shallow, charged with an unspoken intensity. There were so many things I wanted to say, but I didn't know how to put them into words.

Una watched my progress from behind a curtain of blonde hair. As the last of the bandage fell away, revealing the healing wound, my gaze met hers. Her remaining eye, filled with resilience and a touch of sadness, locked onto mine. I brushed the hair away from her face, forcing myself to confront the raw reality. Her eyelids were sealed together, crusted by dried blood, and the smell of it was released into the air. Yellow and green bruising swamped her forehead and cheek, but the worst of it had faded, along with the swelling.

I felt Una's rapid breaths against the back of my hand. The times when she held it completely, then let it go in a rush.

"You're beautiful," I said, and meant every word. With one gentle finger, I traced a line around her missing eye, skimming the surface of her scars. It was ugly. And it was beautiful. And I loved her so much I struggled to breathe.

"I'm not."

I lifted her chin with my finger. "Yes. You are."

She closed her eye, took a breath, then opened it again. "Thank you for lying to me."

"I would never lie to you."

I pressed my lips to her wound, feeling the rough edges of her injury. I traced a line of kisses over her missing eye, along the length of fading bruises, to the shell of her unmarred ear. I had never loved anyone more. The ferocity of my feelings for her surprised me, shocked me to the core, stuttered my lungs into breathlessness. No matter what else I achieved in this life, my primary goal was to make Una feel loved, valued, and beautiful.

I turned to the first aid kit and opened an antiseptic wipe. Gently, I passed it over her wound, removing as much of the dried blood as I could. Her eye seeped a little, and she winced as I applied an absorbent gauze to catch the rogue drops of blood.

"Do you want to see? Before I dress it again?" I asked.

Una shook her head. "Maybe next time."

I padded the wound with a dressing, and instead of using another bandage to wrap around her head, I trimmed lengths of medical tape and stuck it in place.

I stepped back to admire her. Her dirty hair stuck out in spiky tufts and the bruising escaped the new dressing, but that one beautiful blue eye fixed on me with so much trust and love I could barely breathe.

"Was it bad?" she asked.

I shook my head. "Not bad at all."

She jumped off the table. "Maybe I'll get myself an eyepatch. Call myself Captain One-Eyed Una, terrify the kids back home."

"You're too short to terrify anyone."

She whirled on me, prodded a finger into the wall of my chest, pushed me back a couple steps. "Excuse me?"

Chuckling, I grabbed her wrist, spun her around and trapped her against me. "You heard me."

With the back of her head resting on my chest, her breaths came in heavy pants. I kissed the top of her head, then pushed her head forward and moved her hair away from her nape, left a trail of delicate kisses up her spine, across her shoulders, making her gasp my name.

"Gal," she murmured, her head falling to the side, exposing a delicious stretch of skin that begged for my lips. But as I stared at her neck, thoughts of my upcoming betrayal stole my desire. I planned to take her to Atlantis where she could drink the healing water that would grant her another eye. And leave her there. Because I loved her. Because I couldn't bear for anything to happen to her. And she might hate me for the rest of our lives, but I wouldn't change my mind. It was better than her being dead. And so, as I stood there staring at her neck, wanting her in the worst possible ways, I couldn't bring myself to follow through. I couldn't betray her twice.

She turned in my arms, cupped my chin with her hands, her one eye darting between both of mine. "What is it? Are you scared?"

Unable to voice my lies, I shook my head, tightened my grip around her, then whispered, "I can't lose you."

"I'm right here."

CHAPTER TWENTY-SEVEN

O/e sped south, my conscience weighing heavier with each passing mile, the guilt amplifying alongside the brightening skies. Ember lurked below deck for four days, finally emerging from a drug-induced stupor as the temperature clawed its way past freezing and into positive realms. My ankle healed until all I felt was a dull ache, but the toes were another story.

During Ember's shift at the helm, Una and I sought time together below deck. I succumbed to her insistent kisses, but I refused to make love to her. The guilt of that act was too much. I knew she was questioning my love, how deep my feelings ran, and was confused as to why I wouldn't show her a deeper affection. But how could I explain all of that to her? How could I explain she had become my entire reason for being? That she had filled much of the void my mother had left behind? That I would never have been able to endure this journey without her? That I couldn't imagine a future without her in it? That, finally, I understood the price of love was worth everything? How could I tell her all of that?

And so I deflected her advances, cracked unnecessary jokes, concocted meals from expired cans found in the galley and fish Ember caught. I entertained with stories, and I played the flute each night, casting the boat in glorious musical notes which danced in the evening sky. Sometimes I would catch her watching me, suspicion lingering in her gaze, yet I swatted away her questions. My flimsy answers would only deepen her confusion.

When we were a day or two away from Atlantis, I maintained a vigil in the cockpit intending to commandeer the helm at the right moment. Una fell quiet, brought me cups of stale coffee, and sat with me in the silence.

"We're almost there," I said.

"I know." She blew across the top of her mug.

"I'm preparing to meet Zale. Mentally."

"You've become quite skilled with the flute."

Our conversations remained superficial, my anxiety palpable in Una's presence, fearing she might discover my deception.

The night before my anticipated arrival at Atlantis, Una brought me a cup of steaming tea. "You need to sleep. Coffee will keep you up," she said as she pressed the mug into my hand.

"We've still got a couple of days until we reach the Galapagos."

"All the same."

I drank the tea, giving into a rare surge of emotion, kissed her deeply, unable to resist the pull she had on my heart. I planned to dock on Atlantis during the night, leave Ember and Una sleeping in the cabin, and steal away on another boat. This might be our last night for a while. Or forever.

While I'd always known I might not survive a confrontation with Zale, thinking of it now, so close to the impending moment, with Una in my arms, was the first time I realized how much I stood to lose.

And so I allowed her to lead me to one of the luxurious bedrooms with sheets which hadn't been used in years. Breaking the internal promise I'd made that I wouldn't make love to her until after I'd killed Zale, I took her in my arms, undressed her, and cherished her until she could take no more.

After, she pressed herself against me, her head on my chest, her leg wrapped around my waist. I stroked her hair, listening to the sound of her breathing, the dull thrum of the engines beneath us, and my own irregular heartbeat. Intending to extricate myself once I was sure I wouldn't wake her, I remained in the bed with my arms around her, struggling to let her go. Unbidden, my eyelids drooped closed, and an unexpected heaviness filled my limbs. I could no more leave Una alone in the bed than I could cut off my own limb. And so I succumbed to sleep.

THE WORLD SWIRLED into focus as I woke, alone. Una's spot in the bed was empty and cold. Panic clenched my chest and

I shot up, sheets twisting around me as I scrambled for my clothes. How long had I been asleep? Judging by the daylight edging around the cracks in the blinds, it was far too long. Had I missed my opportunity to dock at Atlantis?

Fumbling with my clothes, I rushed above deck. Una and Ember stood in the cockpit, their eyes on the horizon, laughing easily at a shared joke, steaming mugs in their hands.

"Morning sleepyhead," Una said.

"What time is it?" I glanced at my wrist, forgetting I'd left my watch behind on Atlantis.

"Time?" Una asked. "Why do you suddenly care about the time?"

"Time for another cuppa, I'd say," Ember said, adopting a fake British accent.

I turned in rapid circles, scanning the horizon for signs of land in every direction. "What are our coordinates?"

Ember read our location off the console screen. I knew the coordinates to Atlantis better than I knew the back of my hand, and when Ember finished reading, I sank into a seat, my heart falling back down my throat. "Shit."

"What's the matter?" Una asked.

"We were going to stop by Atlantis, get you both to the fountain. Your eye. Your toes."

They exchanged a look.

"Should I go, or you?" Ember asked her.

"I'll go," Una said, then turned to face me. "I had—no, sorry, *we* had—no intention of being left behind on Atlantis."

"What do you mean?" I gripped the edges of the seat. "Who said anything about leaving anyone behind?"

The look she gave me pinned me to my seat. "While I'm keen to regain the use of my missing eye, and Ember would like not to lose his toes, we're not leaving you to face Zale alone. I told you from day one we would never let you do that. I told you this isn't just about you. I told you Ember and I have our own reasons for being here, irrespective of what you think or believe. And I meant every goddamm word." Her voice rose and she started jabbing the air with each angry word.

Although I was sitting, both my arms and legs trembled. I had missed my opportunity to keep them safe, and now they were in danger. Zale wanted me dead, and he would kill those I'd cared about first, to make me suffer. "You don't understand—"

Una raised her hand. "I'm not done." She gave me a piercing, one-eyed glare. "I may have been in love with you for as long as I can remember, and I've been so proud of the steps you've made during this journey, how you've let me in, how you've relied on others for help, how you didn't give up when it came to carving the flute, but I'm not foolish enough to believe you wouldn't relapse, wouldn't go back to your old ways of thinking, wouldn't be able to keep your fear at bay. Fear is a real thing. A living, breathing monster that can beat the bravest into submission. I know. I get it. I'm scared too. But that doesn't mean I'm going to desert my friends. It doesn't mean I'm going to run away. And it doesn't mean I'm not going to feel a tremendous sense of loss if anything happens to either of you. So no, Gal. You don't get to desert us. Because whether we're with you or not, it's not going to stop me from loving you. And if you're going to die, then I want to be right there with you."

Ember pointed at Una. "What she said."

I raised a hand to my cheeks to find them moist with tears. My heart beat rapidly in my chest, a painful throbbing that pounded against my ribs, threatening to break them.

"You don't understand—"

Una crossed her arms. "What is it I don't understand, Gal? Is there something I've missed? Some other excuse you want to try?"

I stood on shaking legs, faced them both. "When my mother died, it destroyed my world. The one person I looked to for support retreated. I lost my father that day too." I took a breath, clenched and unclenched my hands, tried to shake the anxiety out of my arms. "I had family, yes. I had both of you. I was lucky in a lot of ways. But I felt so empty inside. I had loved so easily, and people were taken from me." I shifted my gaze to the water, drew strength from the gentle waves. "My mother died that day trying to save me." I placed a hand over my heart. "I will always live with that guilt. Some days it's unbearable. Some days, I feel like I can't breathe. With the fountain, ocean shifters can live for two hundred years. And I stole those years from her."

"*Zale* stole those years," Ember said.

"You say you love me," I said to Una. "But I'm already destined to leave you mourning. The fountain doesn't work for me."

"I know that."

"I won't live as long as you."

"I don't care."

"*I* care."

"Don't you see, Gal?" Her hand floated between us. I was desperate to cling to her, but there was so much she failed to understand. "Love isn't about time. It doesn't have an expiration date. It doesn't go away just because you want it to. You may well die before me, but I won't regret a single second of our time together, because every second of loving you is worth it."

I felt like I'd already lost her. I knew the pain of loss too well, and it filled me now with the inevitable.

"I miss my mother every day." My gaze swept over her face. "You filled that hole. You, Una. And if anything happened to you...I'd never recover."

"Oh, Gal." She closed the gap between us, cupped my chin in her hands, delivered sweet kisses to my wet cheeks. "Don't you see? That's how I feel about you. I can't let you face Zale alone. I'd never forgive myself. I want us to face it together."

"Even if—"

"Even if," she whispered.

Something inside me broke—a dam of emotion flooding my body. A painful throbbing in my chest. A thickness at the back of my throat. The world teetered. I clung to Una, breathing her in, inhaling her scent, knowing I could never turn my back on her again. No matter what.

"Let me know when the opportune moment arises for a group hug," Ember said, managing to elicit a smile from me and a laugh from Una.

We pulled him into our hug, arms wrapped around each other. I was unsure who was clinging to who, but it felt good.

It felt right. Our conversation didn't change the situation. It didn't make Zale a less formidable opponent. But a fundamental understanding shifted in my soul. Space was made for Una and Ember. Space was made for love, and everything that might happen after.

CHAPTER TWENTY-EIGHT

The final confrontation loomed. I was no less terrified of an awful fate befalling Una or Ember, but I had finally accepted their presence. Not that I had a choice in the matter. Their fates were entwined with mine, a reality I couldn't escape, a truth I'd come to acknowledge. And to be honest, I was glad of the comradery they brought, the confidence they instilled, the love they offered.

As the days unfolded, carrying us closer to the Galapagos, we slipped into a rhythm which felt almost comfortable. Using his wings, Ember dove for fish alongside the boat, and Una and I prepared meals in the galley. We continued to take turns at the helm, keeping the yacht on course, and took advantage of the technological accessories the vessel offered. From flat screen TVs and gaming consoles to a stocked fridge of booze and soft drinks. I couldn't deny the temptation to remain on the boat forever, avoid the confrontation with Zale entirely, never return to Atlantis. The three of us could live a blissful existence sailing around the world together. If Zale wasn't following us.

Despite not seeing a sign of him since we crossed the frozen sea between Iceland and Greenland, his presence lingered like a malevolent whisper. No matter what *The Mermaid Chronicles* decreed, facing Zale was my destiny. One I couldn't avoid. One I didn't want to. And so, after I'd played the flute each night, my fingers now capable of producing rapid notes and haunting melodies, I'd sit above deck and contemplate the snatches of prophecy I'd glimpsed.

Celestial Abyss...

Vorago's Trident...

Parting the sea...

Ember had suggested 'Celestial Abyss' referred to my mother's demise, which had given me the motivation to embark on this journey. After weeks of contemplation, I concluded he was probably right. The reference to 'Vorago's Trident' was obvious enough. My grandfather had said it was the only way to defeat Zale, and Eudora had confirmed it. However, the mention of 'parting the sea' left me clueless. The only account I remembered of such an event occurring was from an old Bible my grandmother kept in her room which told a story of Moses parting the Red Sea. Centuries ago. And who knew if the account was even real? I had no idea how the idea of parting a sea played into the prophecy or my destiny. My thoughts churned night after night as I probed the hidden meanings beneath the elusive words. I doubted it would ever become clear, not until the event arrived, at any rate.

Una slid a mug of tea into my hands, snapping me out of

my thoughts. "You know there's more than one island making up the Galapagos, right?"

"I do."

She sipped her drink, her eye skimming the dashboard. "How are we going to find which caves the seawolves are hanging out at?"

I smiled. I already knew the answer. Although Eudora hadn't given us specific instructions, during my turns at the helm I had studied the maps. One of the land masses stuck out. *Isla Wolf.* I pointed it out to Una on the screen.

She smiled back at me, then gulped. "It's one of the most northern islands."

"It is."

"We'll be there tomorrow."

I glanced at the control screen, calculated our speed and the remaining distance. "We will."

"There's something I want to do before we go into the water," she said. "I want to see my eye."

I led her below deck, removed the dressing I'd applied a few days previously, and guided her to the mirror. I looked with her, held her hair away from her face so she could inspect the healing wound. Her eyelid was sealed closed, a ragged line, but the heat of the injury had dissipated, the scabs had fallen off, and the bruising had mostly disappeared.

"Okay," she said, scrutinizing her reflection, her hands clutching the sink's edge. "Okay."

"It's a lot to deal with," I said, swallowing the lingering guilt. Una didn't blame me. No one did. Not for the injury, and certainly not for my mother's death. Apart from me. I was learning to let that go, but I still had a long way to go. "Do you want a new dressing?"

Una shook her head. "It's time for the world to see me how I am. It's time for me to stop hiding from it."

I kissed the back of her head. "You're so brave."

She turned in my arms, kissed my lips. "As are you."

Ember breezed through the narrow galley on his way to the bathroom, a spliff in his hands, smoke filling the cabin.

"We're going to be there tomorrow," I said.

"Then I plan to keep a buzz on until then," Ember replied.

Una raised an eyebrow.

"Dulls the fear," Ember replied, then added, "Adrenaline is brown." He dashed into the bathroom.

Una and I burst out laughing. But Ember was right. We had less than twenty-four hours to go, and I felt a loosening in my own bowels as the muscles in my stomach knotted.

Una and I spent that night in our cabin lost in the tender grasp of each other's arms. Not talking, not sleeping, just holding each other and staring at nothing. Several times, I started to speak and then bit my tongue. We'd already said all the hard things, repeating them now would only fill us both with more dread. My orb remained with us, a silent witness, floating around the room and pulsing with its calming white light. During the previous weeks it had become an additional companion.

I laced my fingers through hers, stared at our joined hands, the smoothness of her pale skin, the fragile tips of her torn fingernails, the way her warmth soaked into my palm. Our relationship was new, the discovery of the love I held for her had taken me by surprise, but when I thought back over our shared childhood, all the memories which made me smile, it was so obvious we would end up together, that I had always loved her, even when I'd denied the possibility to myself. Whatever happened in the next twenty-four hours would define our future. And I was going to fight like hell to make sure we both had one.

When four o'clock in the morning rolled around, we both gave up on sleep, made a pot of tea, and headed above deck with my orb. On the way, I grabbed the flute from the freezer, as well as the cooler we hadn't used since setting foot on the yacht, and brought them both above deck too. I wanted the flute nearby. It was the one thing which brought me confidence as the waves of fear rolled over me. I packed it into the cooler and buried it with ice, shut the lid and held it in my lap.

Ember was at the helm, his eyes red rimmed from lack of sleep or weed, or both.

"We'll be there in an hour," he said, his face lacking his usual humor.

"Ember..." There were so many things I wanted to say, but I didn't know where to start.

He shook his head at me. "Nope. Don't start. We're not doing that. I don't want to hear false promises or vows of familial bonding or plans of what we're going to do to celebrate, or how you want your funeral to go...nope, no thanks, we're not talking about the after until we're in the after."

"Fair enough." All the same, I held Una a little closer.

Silent minutes slithered by as we monitored the console's countdown and witnessed the distant smudge of Isla Wolf evolving into a tangible entity. Images of the seawolf skin in my uncle's bar filled my mind—the massive head, the formidable jaws, the array of razor-sharp teeth. Anxiety vibrated through me, and I had to fist my hands and pace the deck to keep it at bay.

When we neared Isla Wolf, Ember released the anchor, and the three of us eyed the landscape. It was a suggestion of land, all rocks and greenery, unaffected by the nuclear war, with no signs of life in sight. That would be beneath the surface. Waves thundered against the shore, spraying into the sky, and the sun beat down on the back of my neck.

"We'll need to move quickly so the flute doesn't melt," I said.

I held my mother's cap in my hands, sent her a silent message, then placed the hat on the seating area. Clothes discarded, we stood on the deck in our undergarments, preparing to transition. I eyed the cooler, took a few deep breaths, steeling myself.

"Before we go..." Una touched my hand, then moved to the seating area and rifled through her backpack. She removed a small box and released her purple orb. She was the guardian of Spirit and Soul. The purple orb shot into the air, circled her head, pulsed with vibrant hues of purple. It was larger than my orb as none of its power had been used. "I want both the orbs to bless the flute once more."

I removed the flute from the cooler, its icy coldness immediately numbing my hand, and extended it toward the orbs. They came together, forming a halo around the flute, weaving through its inner core, and left a trail of sparkling white and purple lights.

"Thank you, Una," I said.

Ember stared at the orbs and the fading specks of light. "Feels like a good trip."

"You sure you're sober enough to dive?" I asked, avoiding the mention of seawolves and Zale.

He splayed both hands, his wings fluttering restlessly. "Why would I want to be sober to face a deadly pack of ravenous seawolves?"

"Fair enough," I said and led them toward the dive deck.

The three of us stood in a line, gave each other one more solemn look, and dove into the warm southern waters, the two orbs following our descent. As soon as I dove beneath the surface, still clutching the flute, I pushed my tail into existence. In the warm water, the diameter of the instrument shrunk, outer layers of ice melting immediately away.

"We need to hurry!" I pushed the telepathic thought toward Una and Ember.

My breathing was labored, despite the existence of my gills. I glanced at my side. My gills were still scarred from Zale's attack after the plane crash, affecting the amount of oxygen I could filter from the water. I felt lightheaded and my vision blurred.

Ember turned full dragon, his wings beating against the currents, while Una remained in her half human form, her shark tail flicking powerfully behind her.

I clutched the flute but struggled to regulate my breathing. Unwanted adrenaline coursed through my veins, increasing my heart rate, and I gasped for air.

"What's wrong?" Una asked.

"I can't breathe!"

She took my free hand, squeezed it hard, made me look at her, pressed a kiss to my lips.

"You can do this," she pushed the thought into my head.

I nodded and relied on her to lead me deeper, to pull me through the currents. As we descended, sunlight waned, the water cooled, and my precious flute began to dwindle. It wouldn't be long before the water melted it. We headed toward land in search of the caves, eyes alert to any movement. This was the first time I'd been in water since my last encounter with Zale. If he had truly been tracking us, he would be out here somewhere, waiting, watching.

Hugging the rocks, we circumnavigated the island, searching for dark crevices that might unveil the elusive cave system. Something about the experience reminded me of the tunnels on Atlantis when they had collapsed on my mother and me. The thought of her now calmed me, settled my oxygen depraved lungs. Una continued to pull me along and the flute continued to shrink. An inch of its length was lost, one of its magical notes disappearing. When a second note disappeared, I started to panic, but Ember called from ahead that he'd found something.

We caught up to Ember to find him hovering at the mouth of a black hole. None of us could see past the inky darkness, but something in my bones told me this was the right place. The rocky opening mirrored a snarling wolf, its teeth jagged and menacing.

The three of us entered at the same time, the temperature plummeting and thankfully preventing the flute from losing another note. I scanned the darkness for movement, fearful of the shifting shadows, worried a monstrous beast would suddenly attack. But all remained eerily silent, the only sounds the displacement of water as we swam. It struck me as odd that we hadn't encountered any wildlife since we'd jumped off the boat. None of the hammerheads or Galapagos sharks the area was famous for. No fish. Not even a starfish or a crab. That didn't bode well. Although I was aware the nuclear war had decimated most of the human population, sea life had remained less affected. An unsettling omen, as if the island itself repelled life. Either that, or they sensed the impending reckoning.

Lost in my thoughts, I almost didn't register Ember's warning. Something clawed by my face, leaving three painful marks that tore open my right cheek. Salt water stung the fresh wounds as red blood mingled with the sea.

I cursed, pushing oxygen through my scarred gills, and then another blow struck my opposite cheek.

"The flute!" Una yelled the thought at me.

I hadn't yet set my eyes on a vicious seawolf, but it was clear there was at least one in this cave.

I brought the flute to my lips, held the mouthpiece close, and prepared to blow. But before I could produce a single note, glowing yellow eyes materialized in the darkness. A savage beast lunged, mouth agape, a roar drowning out my thoughts. It swiped at me with one massive paw, knocking the flute from my hands. The instrument spiraled away from me, plummeting into the depths below, sacrificing a third note to the hungry abyss.

"No!" I yelled.

Before I could dive after it, another seawolf blocked my

path. A third closed in from my right, and another loomed from above. I was surrounded.

I heard Una's fearful thoughts as she prayed to Vorago. Ember remained out of view. Although his unique ability of inhaling fire was impressive, I sincerely wished he was a typical dragon king and could exhale it too.

Una and I clung to each other, our orbs hovering near our heads, their magic no use against the savage underwater beasts. I glimpsed the flute beneath me, plummeting into the depths, out of reach, melting too fast. Hope dwindled. Blood from my lacerations tainted the water. I had nothing to fight the seawolves with.

I grabbed Una, pushed her behind me, determined to protect her from the attack, but she wrestled out of my grip, a steely determination in her one blue eye, and clenched her fists. Her sweet fists that would do nothing to harm a seawolf.

The seawolves closed in, as large as elephants, a fusion of sinew, scales, fur, and those ominous yellow eyes. Their growls echoed like thunder, teeth elongated, and paws armed with claws capable of disemboweling with a single swipe.

Fear rippled through me. But there was nowhere left to go. They had blocked every conceivable route.

They swam closer, their growls a symphony of impending violence. My ribs ached, my cheeks stung, and oxygen refused to filter through my gills. My eyelids drooped. I snapped them open. They drooped once more. I was losing it. Una screamed. The seawolves pounced.

CHAPTER TWENTY-NINE

J tumbled through the water, spiraling to the depths, my stomach etched with savage claw marks which bled into the currents. Una screamed, somewhere far above my head, her agonized voice filling my head, but I was powerless to stop my descent. With the little oxygen in my system stuttering in my gills, I had no energy to control my limbs, let alone my tail.

I crashed onto the ocean floor, landing on rocks, tearing fresh wounds across my back and stealing the remaining breath from my lungs. My orb circled me, urging me to move. I lay sprawled across the jagged seabed, gasping for air, fingers fumbling to open my gill slits to allow more oxygen through. Everything hurt. Everything bled. I couldn't begin to count the number of slashes tattooing my body. But there was no time to rest. Getting my bearings, I couldn't see much in the darkness, but a glimmer of ethereal light caught my eye. There. Just a couple of feet away. My melting flute, resting among an array of coral.

Summoning the dregs of my strength, I propelled myself away from the merciless rocks, reaching for the flute buried in the sand. I grasped it and brought it to my lips. Only three notes remained, but all I needed was one. Gathering what little air I had left, I blew through the mouthpiece, and the magical notes immediately escaped the shaft, floated through the water, filled the vast expanse, bringing both light and calm to the sea.

I pushed myself off the ocean floor, leaking more blood than I thought sensible, following the guiding trail of magical notes. The current buoyed me, aiding my ascent through the water toward the seawolves. My gills rebelled with every exhale, threatening to stop working all together, but I had no choice but to play on, to save my friends. Una.

When I reached the cave, Una was pinned against the rocks, Ember holding off one of the beasts, one of his wings cut to shreds.

Afraid I would black out again before I could calm the seawolves, I covered a note, then another, playing a tune with the three remaining available notes. As the music swelled, the little specks of light became more frequent, finding a path through the water, mingling with my blood, and entering the noses of the seawolves. Their yellow eyes closed, their mouths snapped shut, and razor-sharp paws froze mid-swipe. Ensnared by the hypnotic sounds, they drifted in the currents, oblivious to our presence.

Una, trailing a ribbon of blood from a flank wound, ducked under a massive paw and swam to my side. Ember folded his injured wing and joined us.

"How long will it last?" Una said.

"I'm too afraid to stop playing," I pushed my thought at her as my fingers danced over the flute, still struggling for breath. My orb hovered by my side, inching toward my lips, lending me strength as I blew note after note. It shrunk as I played, so small now I could barely make it out. No larger than a pea, every scrap of magic evicted from its core.

"There's only two notes left," Ember said.

The flute had melted more. It now fit in the palm of my hand. I didn't have much time left to find the trident.

Leaving the seawolves in their enchanted sleep, we swam through the cave, navigating tunnels until we were spat out into a massive underwater cavern. I couldn't see all the way across, but I didn't need to. There, in the center of the cave, half buried among a pile of ancient boulders, was a dull metallic trident half wedged into a rock.

"I thought it would be bigger," Una said.

"I thought it would be shinier," Ember added. "Did we take a wrong turn and end up in the clearance section of the mystical armory?"

With one note left on my dwindling flute, I relinquished it to the ocean and watched it melt into non-existence, hoping I had done enough, that the seawolves would remain asleep.

"Go on, prince," Una said, a smile on her face despite the wound on her side. "Go get that trident."

We swam to the center of the cavern. Small fish scattered out of our path. The cave was dotted with other entrances, all leading to this central chamber. Kelp undulated to an unheard rhythm, grass swished in the currents, and plankton floated around us. The two orbs gave us enough visibility to see as we halted by the trident. A simple three-pronged fork, its shaft buried in a rock, dull and rusted with age. Unremarkable. And yet, I could sense its hidden power.

"Some time today," Ember said. "Before those seawolves wake up."

With a trembling hand, I touched the trident's shaft, wrapped my fingers around it, feeling its weight, its solidity, its magic. I remained still, attempting to still my pounding heart, sucking in oxygen through my protesting gills, and then I pulled.

Nothing happened.

I stared at where my hand met the trident. Was it *the* trident? Or was it a fake? Perhaps I was not worthy of wielding it. Perhaps I was a prince only by name. Maybe the prophecy had nothing to do with me.

Panic flowed through me. I glanced at the entrance to our tunnel, fearful the seawolves would wake and launch another attack. I no longer had the flute to pacify them, and my orb was no longer able to help me breathe.

Ember placed his hand below mine, pulled. "That's wedged in pretty tight. Shame we didn't bring dynamite."

"Oh, yeah, because that's so readily available," I retorted.

Una placed her hand over mine. "Try again."

The warmth of her hand leached into me, filling me with love and trust. She believed in me. Still.

With the two orbs hovering nearby, I wrapped both hands around the shaft, sent up a prayer, even though I wasn't entirely sure Vorago existed. But he must have, for his trident to be here.

I pulled. The trident surrendered, smoothly detaching from the boulder, and before it had cleared its rocky throne, glowed with a brilliant golden light which dwarfed the magical orbs. The light shone from each of its three prongs, brightening, and coating the ancient weapon in a glorious coat of gold. No longer was it rusty. No longer was it dull. It was the most beautiful instrument I'd ever laid eyes on.

Spears of light radiated from its prongs all the way to the roof of the cave, rebounded off each surface, filled the cavern with so much light it was like the sun had fallen to earth. A surge of power coursed through my hands, along my arms, and filled my chest with an energy and warmth I couldn't describe.

A myriad of sea life poured into the cave. Fish of all description, sharks and turtles and rays and animals which weren't even native to the area. They filled the cavern, swimming circles around me and the trident, their eyes shining with respect.

Una bowed. "King Arthur."

"I'm no king," I said.

Una touched my shoulder. "No, you're better."

"Look." Ember pointed. At each entrance to the cave, a seawolf hovered, their yellow eyes ablaze with new purpose, their paws gently lapping the water, their intent no longer malicious.

"Thank God for that," I said.

"Thank Vorago," Una said with a laugh.

"Now what?" Ember asked.

I watched the turtles float around me, the fish nibble at my fingers, the rays sweep their gentle wings over my skin, the crabs and shrimp and starfish clamber over the rocks to get closer. I'd never felt so...loved.

"Now we find Zale," I said.

"Injuries first," Una said, pointing at our still leaking wounds. "Zale after."

We swam through the tunnel, the trident aglow, the orbs trailing us, the wealth of sea life basking beside us, and emerged into the open ocean. The two orbs floated close to the trident, circling it with curiosity and bathing it in enchanting hues of white and purple.

With one hand wrapped around the hilt of the trident, and the other staunching my bleeding gills, I pushed toward the surface, but stopped abruptly when a large shadow passed overhead, followed by the pressure of disturbed currents.

Zale.

Here. Now. And I was woefully unprepared. Although I held the trident and it glowed with the power of its magic, I struggled to breathe and continued to leak blood. My strength was waning, aches and pains lancing through each limb. There was no way I would be the victor of a confrontation with him now.

The three of us hovered in the water exchanging fearful glances, the trident glowing proudly between us.

Una gripped my free hand, her orb humming with urgency. Ember shot me a grimace and extended his shredded wings.

I wanted to apologize to them both. I wanted to tell them to swim back into the cave. I wanted a million different things, but none of my wishes would change our current situation.

The shadow came again. The sea life which had

surrounded us retreated to the safety of the cave, blinking eyes and undulating fins peeking from the sanctuary of the rocks. They too sensed the aberration of nature above their heads.

The third time the shadow passed, I held tight to the trident, clenched my teeth, and prepared to die. I afforded Una one more heartfelt glance, apologized to her with my telepathic thoughts, and swam up to meet my future.

Zale met me halfway to the surface, his shark smile wide and threatening, his size incomprehensible, his power undefeatable.

He glided by me, his pectoral fin once again slicing into my gills. Fresh wounds opened, blood clouding the water as I spiraled helplessly. My lungs burned, a metallic tang of blood coating each breath.

"I see you found the trident." His voice filled my head. "Care to hand it over? I know how to put it to good use."

"Never!" I growled. "You'll have to kill me first."

"I was planning to."

I clung to the glowing weapon like a lifeline, willing it to perform, pleading with it to unleash whatever latent power it held.

Zale circled back, this time spinning me toward the ocean floor. I barreled toward the rocks once more, unable to stop my descent, until Ember and Una grabbed my arms and halted my rapid dive. Small sea creatures hid among the coral and swishing ocean grasses. Larger animals lingered by the cave entrance. Their gazes fixed on me, each one of them spurring me on. But I was half dead already. With stuttering gills and seeping wounds, I was no match for a megalodon.

Of all the outcomes I had envisaged, I'd never thought I'd die as easily as this.

"Use the trident," Ember said.

"I don't know how!" I replied.

Una pressed a kiss on my bleeding cheek. "Have faith."

Holding the trident in two hands, I inspected its shaft and prongs, as if instructions might be engraved in the glowing gold. But there was nothing.

When Zale lunged again. I ducked beneath his thrashing tail, narrowly avoiding another collision, my heart pounding with the desperate rhythm of survival.

"Time to hand it over, Gal!" he called.

"I don't know what you need to do," Ember said. "But can you figure it out before we become Zale's newest chew toys?"

I closed my eyes, listened to the currents, sensed the support of the ocean creatures hanging nervously at the edges of this makeshift arena, and felt the power surge through the trident once more.

I followed nothing but instinct as I raised the trident above my head, then slammed it into the rocky seabed. The ocean floor trembled, sending shockwaves pulsing through the water. Snapping my eyes open, all I could see were tiny bubbles. Una and Ember, although they hovered mere inches from me, were barely visible through the frenzy of activity.

Bubbles hissed and raced to the surface, each one quicker than the one before, pulling away from the sand and coral and rocks. Suddenly, my tail was dry, and I stumbled in the water. The bubbles rose, taking the currents with them, pulling the water away from the seabed, leaving me standing on two feet and mercifully breathing air through my lungs. In my human form, I was still covered in wounds and leaking blood, but I could breathe again.

Una and Ember stood beside me, wide smiles on their faces. Together, we watched as the water vanished above our heads, revealing a narrow valley enclosed by towering walls of water, held back by the unseen force of the trident in my hands.

"You parted the water," Una said. "You made the prophecy come true."

"I hate that stupid book," I muttered, but I had a smile on my face.

Despite my wounds, despite the coming fight, I already felt victorious.

Without warning, something fell out of the wall of water. Zale, still in his shark form. He writhed on the ocean floor, his gills struggling for air, and then transformed to his human shape. He was covered in burn marks. One twisted the flesh of his cheek. Another streaked the length of his side. My mother's marks. I smiled.

He pushed himself to his feet, his fist clenched, his dread-locked hair trailing down his back. He stomped toward me, murder in his eyes.

"Cute trick." Zale kicked at the corals, leaped over rocks, advancing on me. "But you're still going to give me that trident."

I stood strong, squared my shoulders, ignored the fear swimming through my veins. "As I said, you're going to have to kill me first."

Zale halted, a predatory grin twisting his lips. "Happy to."

The salty taste of the sea filled my mouth as I prepared to fight, the parted water held by the power I wielded. I narrowed my eyes at Zale. Finally, the moment I had dreamed of since my mother's murder had arrived.

"You killed my mother." I brandished the trident, swishing it between our poised forms, feeling its weight in my hands. "And for that, there is no mercy."

"Your mother denied me my legs," Zale snarled. "And for that, she had to die."

Zale lunged; his fists aimed at my face. I dodged his attack, the water towering above us as we moved in a combative dance, reminding me of the training sessions I'd taken with Ford. They had prepared me for this moment. Sparring and flipping and dodging attacks until I learned to move on instinct. The muscle memory came back to me now. I sensed Zale's moves before he swung and evaded his powerful fists.

I sliced the trident through the air, aiming for his side, and ripped a line of red along his hip, right over a burn mark. He growled, stumbled, and blocked my next attack with his forearm, taking a prong through his muscle. He tore his arm away, leaking as much blood as me now, glared at me with lethal determination.

"You've underestimated me for the last time," I said, light on my feet, ready to pounce, adrenaline lending me a new energy.

Surrounded by walls of water, our eyes locked, a silent understanding passing between us—this would be a fight to the death.

Zale charged, his fists swinging, a few blows glancing

off my sensitive wounds, but most I blocked with the trident. He was stronger, but I was faster. I twirled away from him, sometimes falling into the wall of water, other times tripping over the rocky ocean floor. But he fared no better than me.

We stood in the narrow valley, Ember and Una somewhere behind me, panting and glaring at each other, our skin turning red.

Zale stormed toward me once more, unleashing a flurry of punches, his movements fluid and precise. I blocked his blows with my trident, the clash of metal against flesh throbbing through my limbs. Zale bared his teeth in a menacing snarl. I narrowly avoided his sharp teeth as I ducked away from his lunging form. I aimed the trident at his legs, sweeping them out from under him. He fell, rocks biting into his back, but quickly regained his feet. We both knew if one of us went down, that would be the end.

Catching our breath, we eyed each other from our respective corners of the ocean floor. Una and Ember hovered near a selection of coral, their shouts of encouragement filling my mind. My orb floated nearby, a tiny glowing accomplice.

When the fight recommenced, I no longer felt Zale's fists, despite the determination evident in his black selachii eyes. Adrenaline sharpened my senses and reflexes, pushed the pain to the background. I aimed for his weak points while defending myself from his onslaught.

Zale went in low, and I spun out of his way. As I regained my balance, Ember dropped from the air, landing on Zale's shoulders, his hands clenched around Zale's neck, twisting... twisting...twisting...until Zale threw him off and Ember went flying through the air. I didn't see where he landed because Zale came for me once more.

Ducking under one of his blows, I pounded the trident into the seabed once more, released a shockwave which shook the ground and caused the watery walls to creep closer. Stumbling, Zale's eyes widened in surprise, his movements faltering.

Seizing the opportunity, I pressed my advantage. I lunged at Zale, my trident aimed for his throat. He deflected my attack with a well-timed block, but I followed with a swift kick to his abdomen, knocking the air out of his lungs. Zale grunted, but fought back, his power every bit as formidable as I had feared. The outcome was still uncertain.

Una darted into the fray, but I yelled at her to stay back. Ember was still nowhere to be seen.

We continued our fierce battle, the surrounding water pulsating with energy. Zale's punches intensified; his movements fueled by his resolve to defeat me. I felt the strain in my muscles, the exertion taking its toll on my body. But I refused to yield and drew upon the depths of my strength and the trident clenched in my grip.

I exhaled, thought of my mother, regained my focus, and aimed the trident at Zale's heart. He attempted to dodge, but I caught the wall of his chest with the three sharp prongs, sending him tumbling backward.

"You killed my mother!" I roared.

"You'll see her again," he snarled, full of bravado despite his position of weakness. "Real soon."

I threw the trident with all the power left in my muscles. It sailed through the air. Both of us watched its progress, awestruck, as it flew and released its golden light. It landed in the ground next to Zale, sending another shockwave rumbling under our feet, tipping Zale onto his ass.

He rolled, lunged for the trident, but it would not come free from the seabed. I leaped over him, released the trident, and held it over his cowering figure. Suddenly, he didn't seem so powerful anymore.

Zale stared at me, his eyes wide with shock and defeat.

"Please," he begged. He was nothing more than a coward.

My gaze skirted his scarred face, the power in his muscles, the frantic pulse in his neck. He didn't deserve to live. His reign of terror was over.

"This is for my mother." With both hands, I drove the trident through his murderous heart.

Blood spurted in glorious waves as the three prongs impaled him. It spilled from his mouth, his ears, his nose. He gurgled, raised a weak hand, gestured for me to come close. But there was nothing he could say that I wanted to hear.

Una came to my side, stared down at Zale with me. She didn't offer words, she didn't offer a touch, but stood with me as we watched the life drain from his defeated eyes.

When his eyes clouded over, the watery walls collapsed, bathing us once again in the ocean's currents. Our tails transformed automatically. I yanked the trident out of Zale's dead body and watched him float away. A shiver of Galapagos sharks descended upon his remains.

Ember approached, one of his wings broken, the other ripped to shreds. The sea creatures who'd been hiding surrounded us once more, along with the two magical orbs. The trident glowed anew, bathing the area in its golden glow, and a surge of strength filled me, despite the wounds I carried.

I glanced at the underwater world, marveling at its beauty. The sea creatures surrounded us, their majestic forms filling me with both awe and pride. The fight with Zale had tested my abilities and pushed me to my limits, and I knew more challenges awaited me in the depths of the ocean. There were more adversaries to face and victories to claim. Whether I was a prince or not, whether I resided on Atlantis or not. But in that moment, I basked in the glory of my triumph, my heart swelling with pride, and I promised the surrounding creatures that I would always look out for them.

CHAPTER THIRTY

I stood at the yacht's prow, the wind whipping through my hair as Atlantis materialized on the horizon. A jagged coastline, a golden stretch of beach that beckoned. My pulse quickened. The island stole my breath away. I never thought I'd yearn for it, not after destroying *The Mermaid Chronicles*, but my heart skipped a beat at the idea of reuniting with everyone I'd left behind. Una and Ember had led me back, had cracked my heart open, and made room for me to love again.

"It feels different from what I thought," I said.

Una stood beside me, her arm around my waist. "Coming home?"

I shook my head. "Killing Zale."

It had been a week since our battle beneath the surface. We'd taken our time returning to Atlantis, nursing injuries, delaying the inevitable confrontations, and processing everything we'd been through. But I still wasn't sure how I felt about it all.

"When I was a kid, I dreamed of joining the army," I said.

"I remember." Una smiled. "You were always jump-kicking the hedges in the courtyard."

"I didn't have a power like my mother, or an inhuman strength like my father, so I thought being a soldier would make me...worthy."

Una remained quiet, listening to me find my way through my thoughts.

"But I lacked purpose and ambition. Until my mother was killed." The words were still hard to say, even after all this time, even though her death had been avenged. "And then I could think of nothing else for twelve years. All I dreamed about was Zale's death. For twelve years. I poured all my energy into it. Because I missed my mother. Because my father retreated into himself. Because I was too afraid to love. Zale stole everything from me."

Una squeezed my waist. "Not everything."

"No, not everything." I kissed the top of her head. "But now that he's dead...it hasn't changed anything. Not that I expected my mother to return from the dead, or my father to welcome me back with open arms, or for me suddenly to not be afraid of losing...you...but I thought I'd feel...*something*."

Una placed her hand over my heart, looked up at me with her big blue eye. Both of us wore scars from the battle; wounds which were still healing and would probably always leave a mark. "You've been through a lot. We all have. It's going to take time."

I covered her hand with mine, made a circle over my heart with my thumb. "I still feel the absence of my mother."

"I think you always will."

I nodded, stared at the water, watched the dolphins play. "Was I foolish to think it would go away?"

"Not foolish," Una said. "No one wants to carry pain. But now you have me."

I wrapped both arms around her, drew her close. "I have you. But—"

She covered my mouth with her hand. "Nope. No. We're not doing that. No buts."

I smiled. "I'm still afraid of losing you." I kissed her cheek, then her ear, then trailed my lips along the fragile line of her jaw. "Sometimes I wake in the night in a cold sweat, images of you...." I shook my head. I couldn't put the terrible, invasive images which intruded my dreams into words. "I can't lose you." My voice broke.

Una held my face in both hands, rubbed a thumb across my stubble. "Don't let the fear overwhelm you. One day at a time. We'll do it together."

"I cannot wait to hang around with some people who aren't pawing at each other all the time." Ember's voice broke into our conversation. He raised his arms above his head, stretching, a glint in his eyes.

Una grabbed him and tugged him into our hug. "There's no escape from us. Mwahahahahaha."

Ember threw his head back and laughed. "Mostly I'm looking forward to checking on my product, if you know what I mean." He waggled his eyebrows and mimed smoking a spliff. He'd run out of weed three days ago.

"And there I was thinking you'd head right for the fountain to fix your toes, and your wings," I said.

"That too," Ember replied.

It was another hour before we neared the marina. I was at the helm slowing the engines, my hands trembling as I thought of all I had left behind and would now need to face. Destroying *The Mermaid Chronicles* was not an act that could go unpunished.

Ember leaped onto the dock to secure the lines. The marina and beach were deserted. It was still early, but I thought someone would have spotted us and come to greet us. I noted my grandfather's boat docked a few slips down. *The Albacore* dwarfed all the other vessels, gleaming in the morning sunshine.

Before disembarking, I went below deck to check I wasn't leaving anything behind. But really, I was delaying the inevitable. My orb trailed my movements, pulsing with its white excitement.

Above deck, I put my mother's cap on. Then I grabbed the trident, took Una's hand, and walked along the ramp with her. Before we left the marina, a lone figure appeared halfway along the dock, carrying a bundle of fishing nets. My grandfather.

He glanced from my face to the trident, offered a rare smile. "It's good to see you, son."

"You too," I said.

"Keep that trident safe now."

"Yes, sir."

"I expect you'll be needing it again before long."

Nope. No way. I'm done with all of that.

"Is everyone still furious with me?" I asked.

Grandpa laughed. "Time has a way of healing wounds."

"Still, I better go face the music."

He patted my shoulder as he walked by. The three of us strolled along the coastal path that led to the courtyard and palace. As we passed Uncle Dylan's bar, my heart lurched. I would have to tell him about Babette. A loss I wasn't sure he could take.

We walked through the marble columns, heavy with green vines and succulent grapes, and emerged into the courtyard where the fountain sat. Two figures rushed down the palace steps. Maya and Trent. Una's parents.

With tears streaming down their faces, they whisked her into their arms, muttering *Thank God*, over and over again. All three of them cried.

"Your eye," Maya said. "What happened to your eye?" She pressed her thumbs to her daughter's cheek. "Quick, drink from the fountain."

Trent brought his daughter a coconut shell filled with healing water. Una took a sip. I waited for her eye to reappear. But nothing happened.

Maya frowned. "Try again."

Una sipped the entire contents of the shell, but remained with only one functioning eye, the scratches across her cheeks, all the wounds she had amassed.

I cupped her face, brushed my thumb across her cheek. "I'm sorry. I'm *so* sorry. You lost your eye because of me."

Her remaining blue eye shone brightly and she wound her fingers around my wrist. "Don't be silly. It had nothing to do with you. Now I get to wear that eye-patch and call myself One-Eyed Una, remember?"

I knew she was trying to be brave. And I loved her for it. But the guilt pricked my heart.

Resting the trident against my shoulder, I took her face in both hands, kissed her nose, then her cheek, then the eyelid of her missing eye. "I love you."

Trent cleared his throat. "You've been gone for weeks."

"We thought you were dead...without *The Mermaid Chronicles*..." Maya's eyes fell to the trident. "What is that?"

I faced my future in-laws. At least I hoped they'd be if they ever forgave me. "Vorago's trident."

Trent and Maya gaped at me.

Una took my hand. "It's yours now, prince."

My Aunt Raina and Uncle Blaze descended the steps, ran straight to Ember, pushed him into the fountain, but again it did nothing to cure him.

Ember pointed at me. "You owe me some toes."

"I'd give you mine If I weren't in danger of losing them too," I replied.

He slapped my back. "I know, buddy, I know."

Raina and Blaze inspected the three of us, remarking on our injuries, telling us how lucky we were. My teeth chattered nervously as I waited for someone to condemn me.

Maya stared at the trident, both blue eyes wide. "What does it do?"

I presented the shaft to the small crowd of relatives, turning it in my hands. Sunlight caught its golden hue, reflecting spots across the courtyard. "It helped me kill Zale."

Maya gasped, covered her mouth with both hands.

"You killed Zale?" Uncle Blaze asked me, his wings erupting from his back.

I nodded. "And I couldn't have done it without Una and Ember."

The revelation left the adults in stunned silence, their eyes shifting between me and the trident.

"What do we do with it?" Aunt Raina whispered.

"I plan to keep it in the great hall, with the orbs and the Power of the Sea and *The Mer—*" I was about to say *The Mermaid Chronicles*, but it didn't exist anymore. "But I want to try something first."

I approached the fountain. Its mystical abilities powered our island. Placing the Power of the Sea in its waters had restored Atlantis when my parents recovered it from the dragon kings. Other orbs had been thrown in during the annuls of history. And so I wondered.

I raised the trident above my head, hesitated for a breath, then drove its three prongs into the water and through the marble of the fountain's base. My silent plea echoed through my mind, a fervent wish that the fountain would extend its blessings to all who called this mystical isle home.

A shockwave rumbled through the courtyard. Golden light erupted from the shaft, spilling into the sky, bathing the entire island in its majestic beauty. When I remembered to breathe again, I removed my hand from the hilt and faced the gathering crowd. There were many familiar faces. Guards and shop keepers and classmates from when I'd attended school. Humans, selachii, and merfolk alike.

"Try the fountain," I said to Ember and Una.

They both took sips from the water, but their injuries remained unchanged. My heart sank. I had been so sure. Perhaps now that I had defeated Zale, the trident no longer had a use for me.

I thought of Babette, what she would say to me now.

She'd tell me it wasn't all about me, that it took a village to raise an island. That I may have been the Prince of Atlantis, but I was still just a man. I'd never felt it more earnestly than in that moment.

"Is there a human here?" I asked the crowd, allowing a fragment of hope to swell in my chest.

A few hands shot up.

"Please, try drinking from the fountain," I asked.

A few wary folks stepped forward, grabbed the coconut shells from the racks and dipped them into the enchanted water. As they drank, their eyes grew wide, and smiles spread between them.

"The fountain works for us now," one woman said. "Thank you, Prince Gal."

"Please, it's just Gal," I protested.

"You try," Una said, pushing me toward the stone lip of the fountain.

I raised both hands. "It's never worked for me."

"Maybe it will this time," Una said.

I dipped a hand into the water, cupped it and brought it to my mouth. My orb followed my movements, casting its enchanting glow on the water. The cool water trickled down my throat, but I remained unchanged. As I had expected. Although the trident had done my bidding and made the fountain available for the humans on the island, Una, Ember, and I remained unaffected. I didn't question why. I had long ago given up trying to understand the mysteries of Atlantis. The island breathed with a life of its own, and I would do my best to respect all parts of it from now on.

While we gave a brief account of our journey, the two

orbs shot toward the great hall to join the others, finally home. Una and Ember gravitated toward their respective families. Siblings surrounded Una, hungering for tales of our adventures. I let them go, promising we'd meet later, and turned toward Uncle Dylan's bar.

A coil of nerves filled my stomach as I pushed the front door open. The dead eyes of the seawolf head glared back at me. It didn't look nearly so dangerous, now that I had met real ones, and I kicked its jaw as I walked by.

"What is all that commotion out there?" Dylan appeared behind his bar, caught my eye, stared at me openmouthed. "You're back."

"I'm back."

Wordlessly, he poured two drinks. I slid onto a stool opposite him. At this hour in the morning, the bar was deserted.

Dylan held out his drink for me to toast. I clinked my glass against his, and we both downed the contents in one go.

I set my glass on the table. "Zale is dead."

Dylan didn't react right away. He stared at the amber liquid in his glass, ran a finger around its rim. Then I noticed his hand was shaking. I covered it with my own. "Zale is dead."

He raised his head. "Thank you."

"It's not all good news."

He nodded, as if he knew what was coming. "I haven't heard from Babette."

"She died helping me," I said. "She is...she was..." There were no words to describe Babette's courage.

"I know," Dylan said.

"She loved you very much."

Dylan tilted his head, let out a mournful sigh.

"That was the last thing she said," I told him. "How much she loved you."

A sad smile formed on Dylan's lips. "Thank you for telling me." He poured another drink, drained that one too. "Where is she now?"

"Her friends from Iceland are sailing her back. They should be here in a couple weeks."

Dylan hung his head, gathered himself. "We'll have a funeral. An Atlantean one. She'd like that."

"She'd hate that."

"I know."

We both smiled.

"Shall I inform Rob?" Rob was head of the Atlantean army, and Babette's father.

Dylan shook his head. "I'll do it."

Before I left the bar, Dylan embraced me in a fierce hug which compressed every ache and injury. I walked back into the daylight, intending to find my father, but halfway along the path I ran into Ford.

"Welcome home, son," he said, extending his hand for me to shake.

"It's good to see you."

"Likewise."

"How is he?" We both knew who I was referring to.

"Why don't you see for yourself?" Ford pointed toward the fountain.

I said goodbye to my father's most loyal bodyguard and made my way to the fountain. He was standing there, sunlight falling on his muscular shoulders, staring at the trident still wedged in the fountain's base.

He turned as I approached. "You're home."

I nodded, not sure what to say. It had been so long since we'd had a meaningful conversation.

He shoved his hands in his pockets. "Is it true? About Zale?"

I nodded again.

His eyes swept over my face, took in the state of my bruised and battered appearance. "It wasn't easy."

"No, it wasn't."

"Are you going to stay?"

"I think so," I replied. "If Atlantis will have me."

"I'd like you to. I..." He dropped his chin, stared at the cobbled ground. "I missed you." He looked at me once more, placed a hand over his chest. "I've not been a good father to you—"

"You don't have to—"

"Yes, I do." He took a breath. "When your mother...left us...I didn't know how to live. She was everything to me. Everything. And there you were, a young boy with questions, while I was drowning in grief. I shut you out. I shut everyone out. And while you were gone...I was so worried. I worried I'd never see you again, and that would be infinitely worse. You are everything I have left. You are my son. And I'm sorry. I'm so sorry, Gal, can you ever forgive me?"

Tears tracked down my cheeks as I approached my father. I threw my arms around him and clung to him like I was a little boy. "I forgive you."

He slapped my back, apologizing when I yelped, then returned my fierce embrace.

"We have a lot to catch up on," he told me.

I smiled. "We do."

I yanked the trident out of the fountain, its shaft fitting snuggly in my hand. Then my father led the way toward the palace steps, and we climbed them together.

"Am I in trouble?" I asked. "*The Mermaid Chronicles?*"

My father sighed. "Let's not worry about that today. Everyone is relieved the three of you are home safe."

Tomorrow then, I would face the consequences.

"Vorago's trident, huh?" Dad asked, an impressed look on his face.

"Yup."

"I'd have loved to have seen that."

"It was pretty awesome."

"*You're* pretty awesome." He patted my back, leaving his hand at the top of my shoulder. "With great power comes great responsibility."

I gulped. "I'm done with all that. I've had my adventure."

My father smiled. We both knew there would be more trials ahead. Instead of voicing my fears, I rambled on about my journey. "Seawolves, ice flutes, the northern lights..."

"So you and Una?"

My smile stretched into a grin. "She's pretty special."

"That she is."

We entered the palace and made our way to the great hall, intending to home the trident with the other magical artifacts. I noted mine and Una's orbs were back in place in their orbital position around the Power of the Sea. As we walked further into the room, I realized it wasn't empty. Una sat on one of the couches, a heavy book in her lap.

When she noted my arrival, she looked up and grinned, beckoned for me to join her. "Guess what?"

I felt the blood drain from my face as I eyed the glowing pages of the book she held. "No..."

"What is it?" my father asked.

Una rose, came toward us, the book in her hands. "When you stuck the trident in the fountain, it recreated *The Mermaid Chronicles*."

I took a step back, glared at the traitorous trident in my hand. "No."

Una reached out her hand and curled her fingers around my wrist. "It's okay."

I shook my head. "I don't want to know." But the book was open, and I caught sight of words.

The Denizens of the Deep crave the power of Vorago's trident—

I tore my eyes away before I could read more. The fountain didn't work for me, but I could read *The Mermaid Chronicles*. And a new prophecy was forming.

"We should look," my father said. "We've been blind the last few weeks."

"I don't want to know." I took another step back. "I've never wanted to know."

Una cocked her head at me, squinted her one beautiful blue eye. "Seeing as you can read it, I think you're *supposed* to know."

I shook my head again. My throat went dry.

"You're not alone anymore," Una said. "You've got me."

"And me," my father added.

And so I allowed them to lead me to the couch and sit me down. After I rested the trident by my feet, Una settled the book in my lap. The pages turned, emitting a golden light which rivaled the trident's glow, and I knew once again my life was about to change. I wasn't any less afraid. But this time I had Una and my father. And while my instinct was to turn and run, I forced myself to stay and read the words on the page, to embrace the power the book offered—to seize control of my destiny.

THE END

Yep, that really is the last book in *The Mermaid Chronicles!* But it isn't all over. You can check out the companion guide; the book of prophecies and ocean shifter legends themselves. You'll discover more about all the characters from the series, their motivations and heartbreaks, as well as more prophecies and stories...

Just click this link:
Https://geni.us/TheMermaidChronicles

THANK YOU!

Thank you so much for making it all the way here. I hope you have enjoyed **Vendetta** and aren't feeling too bereft that the series has come to an end! If you enjoyed the story, leaving a review is the best possible present for an author!

You can do it here: https://geni.us/MermaidVendetta

Gal's story has been in my head since I first thought up *The Mermaid Chronicles*. I always knew he would lose his mother and that he would have his own story to tell. But perhaps it isn't over quite yet...If I decide to write Gal into another adventure, signing up to my newsletter is the best place to find out!

If you're interested in my other books, you can read the first chapter of all of them on my website at **www.marisa-noelle.com**, or buy from any bookshop. Please sign up to my mailing list to get the latest news, free stories, novellas, and chapters from all my other books. Every month I hold a competition and three lucky readers get an **e-book completely free**!

**You will also receive the first three chapters of
The Shadow Keepers FREE!!!**

ACKNOWLEDGMENTS

Well, folks, they say it takes a village to raise a child, but I'm here to tell you, it takes a whole circus to birth a book! So, grab your popcorn, because I've got some shout-outs and thank-yous that are more entertaining than a juggling act on a unicycle!

First up, my writing group, The Rebel Alliance. You guys are like the Jedi Masters of encouragement, and I couldn't have done this without you. You've had my back for so long that I'm pretty sure you have a permanent imprint of my book cover on it!

And speaking of covers, Fay, you're the Picasso of book design. Seriously, the cover is so gorgeous it's practically doing the cha-cha on its own. Bravo!

Now, let's talk about Team Swag. We navigate the treacherous waters of publishing together, and boy, do we make a splash! When it comes to sharing knowledge, we're like the Avengers of advice-giving. What a fantastic bunch of writers and friends!

Neil, my rock, my Steady Eddie. You stole my heart in a single night and have been guarding it like a precious gem ever since. I love you more than a mermaid loves the ocean (and that's saying something).

To my kids, Riley, Lucas, and Quinn, thanks for being the

wind beneath my writerly wings. You're my plot problem-solving superheroes, and you always rescue me! Just promise me you won't be embarrassed if I show up at your school fairs with a stack of books.

Mom, you're the eagle-eyed proofreader of my dreams, even if we occasionally find a typo or two. Let's just blame it on Dad when that happens, shall we?

To my early supporters, you're the MVPs of my writing journey. Sasha, Michelle, Nikki, Adrian, Darcy, Hetty, Louise, you've given me advice and feedback that's worth its weight in gold doubloons!

Twitter, oh Twitter, (and you will always be Twitter) you've been my trusty sidekick in this adventure. The writing community there has made rejections feel like mosquito bites at a barbecue—annoying but manageable. You all know who you are, and I couldn't have asked for better virtual friends. Thank you!

And then there's Booktok! What a wild and wonderful place I've stumbled into. You've made me buy so many crowns I'm starting to feel like royalty. Thanks for supporting my journey, engaging with me, and even buying my books. You're the crown jewels of my author life!

A big shout-out to my A-level English teacher, Michael Fox, who taught me to first think for myself and second defend my ideas. You're the reason I can write more than a grocery list!

Last but not least, a standing ovation for my readers. You are the true stars of this show, and I wouldn't be here without you. Stick around, because there are more books in my circus tent, and I promise they'll be worth the price of admission.

Oh, and if you fancy learning more about my books and want to be in with the chance to win exclusive giveaways, sign up to my website below!

www.marisanoelle.com

Don't forget to check out *The Mermaid Chronicles Companion Guide!*

Just click this link:
Https://geni.us/TheMermaidChronicles

ABOUT THE AUTHOR

Marisa Noelle is the author behind a treasure trove of middle-grade and young adult novels that dance through the realms of science-fiction, fantasy, horror, dystopian, and mental health. From unraveling mysteries to diving deep into the human psyche, she's your go-to wordsmith for adventures that'll tickle your imagination.

Marisa's literary exploits include "The Shadow Keepers," a spine-tingling tale to keep you up all night, and "The Unraveling of Luna Forester," a masterpiece that snagged the prestigious First Place Incipere Award, rocked the Write-Blend Finalist stage, waltzed as a BBYNA Semi-Finalist, and took its place on the Bookshelf Finalist shelf. With dystopian being one of her favorite genres, you can expect fast-paced thrills from the world of "The Unadjusteds Trilogy," a roller-coaster ride featuring "The Unadjusteds," "The Rise of the Altereds," and "The Reckoning," perfect for fans of Divergent, Maze Runner & The Hunger Games. And don't forget to dive into "The Mermaid Chronicles," a series that will plunge you into the depths of "Secrets of the Deep," lead you on a wild "Quest for Atlantis," challenge you to "Fight for Freedom," send shivers down your spine with "Ghost Pirates," and leave you craving "Vendetta." She also writes steamy romance under the penname Savannah Warner.

When Marisa's not weaving literary spells, she's helping mold the future of MG and YA authors as a mentor for the Write Mentor program.

When not writing, Marisa likes to imagine herself as a mermaid, and can often be found in the local pool...or lake... or ocean. Despite her undeniable bookworm credentials since she was knee-high to a grasshopper, the author gig took Marisa by surprise. You see, she had a secret past as a bit of a science geek during her school days. But hey, science and storytelling make a surprisingly magical concoction! Currently, Marisa calls Woking, UK, her home sweet home, where she resides with her trusty squad, including her husband, three amazing kids, and a furry four-legged friend named Copper.

Marisa loves to hear from her readers. You can find and connect with her at the links below.

Twitter & Instagram: **@MarisaNoelle77**
Tiktok: **@MarisaNoelle12**
Website: **www.MarisaNoelle.com**